MW01128314

Gene,

Hope you enjoy

the ride!

No Safe Place

Michael Hilliard

authorHOUSE®

AuthorHouse™
1663 Liberty Drive
Bloomington, IN 47403
www.authorhouse.com
Phone: 833-262-8899

Published by AuthorHouse 06/21/2022

ISBN: 978-1-6655-6241-6 (sc)
ISBN: 978-1-6655-6243-0 (hc)
ISBN: 978-1-6655-6242-3 (e)

Print information available on the last page.

Any people depicted in stock imagery provided by Getty Images are models,
and such images are being used for illustrative purposes only.
Certain stock imagery © Getty Images.

Author Photo by Heather Crowder

This book is printed on acid-free paper.

Dedicated in loving memory to
"M.L." – Mary Lou Hooper.
You weren't the typical
mother-in-law.
I loved you. I will miss you.
You will be forever missed.
I wish you could have read this,
but God took you too soon.

PROLOGUE

Tioga, West Virginia
Present Day

The President of the United States was on his knees.

He got up only to fall.

On all fours, his hands pressed into the warm mud, softened by the pockets of fire surrounding him.

His senses came back slowly—popping up as if born anew— competing against the throbbing in his skull. Thoughts rushed forward, even as delirium set in, and the ringing in his ears persisted.

He fought to think clearly.

I'm John Maclemore, President of the United States. Husband to Judy and father to Canon and Cole.

Noticing his tie was on fire, he threw himself to the ground to snuff out the small flame. The rush offered a small degree of understanding, a birth of thought and direction. He rose to a crouch and staggered, taking in the scene from a higher perspective.

It was like a war zone.

A massive piece of bent metal burned intensely, and he felt the heat, squinting through watering eyes. The president breathed in the harsh stink of burning fuel and placed his jacket sleeve over his mouth to stymie a cough.

Then he saw the American flag emblem and things became clearer. He'd been on Marine One somewhere over West Virginia and it was shot down!

He remembered looking to the Secret Service agents as the chopper suddenly swerved and alarms sounded. A blinding flare cut the craft in half, sending it spiraling out of control. There was shouting and panic, as his world erupted into chaos and time stood still.

Then everything went black.

Now breathing in short gasps, the president looked in every direction, searching one horrific detail to the next. He saw several dead men—his Secret Service detail—lying all around. One had limbs missing, another was half charred. The two pilots looked asleep, still strapped in their seats, though their broken bodies were splayed in awkward angles.

He was the only survivor.

President Maclemore spun around, seeing only trees and brush. On the distant horizon were two funnels of black smoke. Could they be the *other* choppers that had been flanking Marine One?

His thoughts were cut short by a hissing sound, as the main wreckage fell toward him, spilling the machine's innards. The thickening black smoke was gaining spirit; and a smoky cocoon swarmed him, as the raging fire stole precious oxygen from the air.

Through the madness his resolve spiked. An innate sense of survival overtook him, and he suddenly knew what to do. Whomever had taken the choppers down had to be close, and the empty seconds that passed only worked in *their* favor. Looking at a thick cropping of trees, President Maclemore threw his heavy legs in front of him in a wild dash.

A whirring sound screamed from above as a drone jetted by and banked left. This time he wasted no time. The President of the United States ran for his life.

He just didn't know where he was going.

PART ONE

THE WOLF MAN
(SIX MONTHS PRIOR)

CHAPTER 1

National Security Agency (NSA)
Fort Meade, Maryland

Pip Palmer was the best computer analyst the National Security Agency had ever recruited. Fresh out of college with a computer engineering degree, they were waiting for him.

So, when he was given only forty-eight hours to find an active serial killer, he wasn't surprised.

The FBI was coming up against a hard time deadline—one the killer had never crossed—and they'd exhausted everything in their arsenal.

That's when they called Pip.

At twenty-eight years old, Pip was just over five feet tall and physically-adoring. His brown eyes grew wide when he spoke and his easy, warm smile was naturally winsome. His thin, brown hair was medium in length and hung just over his eyebrows, accentuating his thin, pug nose and rounded face.

Pip was disciplined in everything he did; having never missed a day of work, always available to help a friend, and meticulous even with the most mundane of tasks.

He'd been called things like prodigy and genius; and unlike the other computer technicians, he was mostly self-taught. In school, he'd found the books and collegiate lectures important, and had taken them seriously, but his curiosity of circuitry and obsession with networking and cyberspace relationships was insatiable.

Pip had been that way since he was eight years old and took apart an old, broken Commodore 64 he'd found in the back room of the orphanage. He'd analyzed the components, re-wired it, and got it working; before repeating the process, and even adding more circuitry for increased storage and faster performance.

By sixth grade he was a hacker.

Nothing serious or harmful. He simply enjoyed the challenge of getting into locked systems and seeing how they were established. His first test was an auto repair shop somewhere in Philadelphia. He saw their inventory, payroll, and accounts receivable. He was only twelve, so he didn't appreciate what he was looking at but was delighted that he could spy into another life from afar.

In high school, he sailed through his computer classes with easy A's, but learned more from entering classified government mainframes, poking around, and backing out without a trace.

He was the ultimate voyeur and he reveled in it.

And through it all, he'd build on his skill set and absorb every detail. By the time he graduated from Anne Arundel Community College with a two-year degree, he could breach any system he came across. Passwords and back doors were just annoyances. He'd become a master of cyberspace and a wiz at unlocking everything within it.

If there was an algorithm or flaw to be found in any encryption software, he'd always have the answer. But it wasn't just his mastery of the craft that made him special. He thought differently than most programmers. He was creative, imaginative, and even artistic.

Pip was a true cyber-warrior and prided himself—albeit humbly—as such.

He modified his NSA workstation with his own software to make it more efficient and far-reaching. He wrote code that gained entry into the most secure places around the world, and then layered other programs to complement everything within.

Pip was talked about at every level. He sometimes heard the rumblings in the hallways and felt the stares. But all the affirmations made him feel even smaller and unworthy. He didn't like the spotlight and was content to perform without the accolades.

Though part of a larger team, he worked independently in the basement of building six, the brain of Research & Engineering, at the main NSA campus at Fort Meade.

His workstation was not glamorous. Huddled between several large monitors in the corner of a small cinderblock room, the adjacent HVAC unit would sound off at random, though he was used to the machine's drone.

But Pip enjoyed working alone, typing, clicking, and listening.

His computer system too, looked ordinary to the passing glance, though the six flanking monitors looked more like an elaborate drum set than a workstation. He called it the Key, because he could tap into and unlock satellites, computer networks, phone systems, and download data from anywhere in the world. He had layers of encryption software, most by his own invention, and could find, penetrate, unravel, and encode the most sophisticated programs.

The Key was always being modified, evolving with experience and precedent. It was a source of pride and his most cherished accomplishment. He learned something from every task and would incorporate every work-around he found.

NSA was grateful to have him. Homeland, the FBI, and the CIA had tried. He was usually working on the highest of details, so when his phone rang, he wasn't surprised to hear Jack Seargant's voice.

Or that he had two days to help catch a serial killer named the Wolf Man.

Special Agent Jack Seargant had been all over the news lately. He was the FBI's point man on an open serial killer case and led the Behavioral Science Unit. And he was also famous from the Island Hopper case.

"This is Palmer," Pip said into his headset.

Seargant rambled quickly, knowing he was on a recorded line and Pip could replay the conversation. Pip paused, securing his headphones, and speaking into his microphone slowly.

"Can you repeat that, sir?"

"You heard me," Seargant said, firmly. "Use *everything* at your disposal. I just sent you a list of parameters. Run it through everything."

"What about warrants and jurisdiction?" Pip asked, grimacing, but he felt obligated for the recorded line. He had to abide by Title 18, U.S. Code, Section 2516.

"Not a concern. Check with your supervisor, who's been briefed."

"And your name again?"

Seargant slowed, knowing what Pip wanted. Everything had to be documented.

"My name is Special Agent M. Jackson Seargant of the FBI BSU. Badge # 937052. I'm the lead investigator on Case # 1435795AB and today is May 6. I'm asking for information and analysis to catch a killer and tasking you with everything available to that end."

Pip smiled and took an instant liking to Seargant. The man's confidence was contagious. But Seargant also embraced a charge that Pip admired. Seargant took his job personally. And with domestic eavesdropping being such a hot topic, Seargant was trumpeting its validity and ordering it on record.

"Behavioral Sciences Unit? Isn't that—"

"Yes; it's where the wild things are. We track and analyze the worst of the worst. And the *thing* that I'm pursuing must be stopped ASAP."

Pip eased back in his chair, eyeing the items around him as a means of distraction. Hearing about serial killers sent a chill down his spine. He wasn't used to the intimacy that could be involved. He liked being at the Key—his tiny chamber, surrounded by his hardware and software—operating as a voyeur to the outside world.

He looked to his small Star Wars figures of Boba Fett and Yoda, and how he'd positioned them squared off in a battle, something that never happened in the movies. Then he looked to his autographed picture of Steve Jobs and finally to an old chess set missing pieces. It was the only thing he'd kept from his thirteen years at the orphanage.

"What about *your* guys, sir? Can you tell me what they've done so far?"

"Everything is in the file I just sent you."

Pip was already scanning the information, tapping, and moving his mouse. Cross-referencing the data could take days and yield countless possibilities that would take months to analyze.

"So, this is the case that's been all over the news, isn't it?"

There was a pause on the line. It was a valid question, especially because Pip was in operations on the international side, and this was a domestic issue.

Over the last five months, five young women had gone missing without a trace. All were in the mid-Atlantic region, between the ages of nineteen and twenty-five. Their bodies had been found within a few days of disappearance, but nothing was released on their condition.

"Yes, this is the case. And please call me Seargant. Also, my personal cell is in the email and I'm available 24/7."

Pip smiled, appreciating Seargant's offer. He was firm, direct, and steadfast—a natural leader—and what was needed to navigate the chains of command and bureaucracy that persisted inter-agency. He was controlling but also approachable, and Pip sensed he was a man of great respect at the FBI.

"And you can call me Pip."

Seargant softened. "I like that; how'd you get that name?"

"Well, I don't think I had much of a choice. My full name is Price Irvine Palmer, so my initials are P.I.P., and I'm about five feet tall, so I'm a confirmed pip-squeak. I've just always been called Pip."

Seargant and Pip shared a quick laugh and some of the tension lifted.

"I don't know much," Pip said. "But it looks like this guy is just the typical serial killer from the movies. Not to overgeneralize, but you think he's white, between the ages of thirty and forty-five, single, intelligent, anti-social, and sexually perverted, right?"

"Yes, but there are a few things that I *didn't* send you. This being our first interaction."

"Like what?" the young analyst stammered, swallowing hard.

"Let's just say this guy is *not* typical. He's not like any one of those eclectic monsters from the movies. And the things that I've excluded are not germane to your task. Just run the parameters and tell me where they go."

Pip had seen Seargant on television over the last several weeks. He was a tall, well-built black man; good-looking and sharp, with a shaved head and well-defined goatee. He had a commanding presence, but also an easy and engaging manner that connected him to his audience.

Pip recalled the last press conference, just two days before. Seargant was asked about the crime scenes and the man seemed to shutter. Very little had been disseminated, and even as Pip was scanning the electronic file, he could find no specifics about the remains of the victims.

"What does he do to them?" Pip asked, evenly, though he was uncertain he wanted to know.

Seargant drew a long breath and exhaled slowly.

"We've named this guy the Wolf Man because of what he does to his victims before *and* after death. And he only kills around full moons."

The words painted a visualization that left Pip cold.

He thought of the five woman who'd been taken and killed. He closed his eyes and used his photographic memory to see their faces on past news broadcasts. To think of what they'd endured at the hands of some psychopath stirred a rare anger within him.

"So, what's the latest Seargant? Why are you calling me now?"

"We've just found the fifth body this morning, in a ditch in Phoenixville, Pennsylvania. And another girl has gone missing, which goes against his MO. He hasn't taken them this close in succession before and the geography is off."

"But if that's the case, hasn't this latest girl only been missing for a few hours? How do you know they're connected?"

"She went missing within three miles of where the body was found. Phoenixville is a small community, and the preliminary investigation suggests this girl is not a runaway."

A new email hit Pip's system and a picture of Lisa Wellington lit up his screen.

Pip printed the photograph and studied it. A posed picture from a formal setting, probably a wedding or school yearbook. She was pretty, just like the other girls.

"I just got the picture of the latest girl," Pip said. "Can you give me a quick summation of who you think this guy is?"

Seargant read the young analyst easily. He knew Pip wasn't used to working with others in real-time and was probably uneasy about trying to catch a killer.

Seargant spoke slowly. "You know he's just a man, right? Not a monster that can invade your walls or find you out."

"I know," Pip sputtered. "But what about you? Aren't you a little freaked out by this guy?"

Seargant moved the inflection of his voice to be more upbeat. "You never know what's going to happen out there. But having an amazing team, and running a great offense and defense simultaneously is what's going to win."

Pip fell silent and Seargant gave him some time. Moments passed and he pressed on.

"So, are you feeling a little pissed off, Pip? Do you think you can help this girl?"

Pip tacked the photo to the wall, eyeing it. "I'll do everything I can. You have my word."

"Good Pip," Seargant said, excitedly. "Because I'm *really* looking forward to personally meeting the Wolf Man."

CHAPTER 2

Over the next hour, Pip pored over the substantial information.

He printed out the critical material and used different colored highlighters to achieve a baseline string of cohesiveness. He separated things by levels of urgency and then created a timeline.

He read the initial parameters Seargant sent over, knowing that every name was a white male between the ages of thirty and sixty who owned multiple properties, with at least one in a rural area in the mid-Atlantic region. Their normal credit card activity spanned more than a four-hour radius from their primary home and their online pornography searches were perverse. Seargant made a note to run both single and married men.

Pip's heart went out to the victims. He glanced at the photographs of the five confirmed dead, but then to the picture of Lisa Wellington, who was just taken. He could do nothing for the dead, so he concentrated on Lisa, staring at her photo, memorizing every detail.

She was stunning; a naturally beautiful girl with a broad, genuine smile, small nose, and thick, flowing blonde hair. He wondered how old the photo was, where it was taken, and what she was thinking in that flash of a moment. He found himself lost in her deep blue eyes and hoped he could help her before they closed forever.

Pip shook his head, stealing himself away from the image. A new resolve consumed him. He took a swig of Coke Zero, cracked his knuckles and craned his neck; and for the next several hours ran the programs Seargant had requested.

When it was done, he was looking at a list of over two thousand names and it was well into the evening. Definitely past normal quitting time. He shook his head, reeling at the number of outcomes, and how long it would take to investigate each one.

Time he didn't have, and time Lisa couldn't spare.

He moved his hands furiously over the keyboard, narrowing the ages by eleven years and cutting the land search in half. There were still over thirteen hundred on the list, so he filtered it further by single men and the list narrowed considerably to just over six hundred.

He rose from his chair and paced the small workspace, regarding the over-sized beach ball he kept for stress relief. He gently kicked the brightly colored inflatable against the gray wall, concentrating on the swirling colors, as it returned to him.

For a few moments he repeated the motions, kicking the ball and thinking things through. It was a simple distraction, but one he enjoyed several times each day.

Then he turned to Lisa's photograph and his eyes moved to the monitor, showing a long list of names.

Could the Wolf Man be one of them?

CHAPTER 3

At midnight Pip couldn't see straight.

He'd been staring at the computer monitors and randomly testing phone records and credit card transactions against the timeline. But so far, he'd excluded less than a hundred names, and knowing the timetable, he was growing increasingly despondent.

He'd contacted another technician to help with the caseload. They called him Frog, due to his unusually low voice, and like Pip, he was a little awkward and liked working alone.

Pip shared the parameter searches and the list narrowed.

At the same time, Pip queried the Medical Information Bureau, the group that maintains a database of medical records to aid insurance underwriting. In understanding that his target was likely a sexually perverse male, he might be taking medication to aid performance.

It was a long shot, knowing that the information was not complete and not all doctors reported to the bureau, but he ran a search for all the erectile dysfunction medications. Many other unregulated providers overseas sold generic remedies, so he ran a search there as well.

He returned to his beach ball and after a few minutes, had about eighty-three confirmed hits on his list that had purchased ED meds.

Still, there were so many names and he again wondered if the Wolf Man was among them. With every parameter he ran he could easily exclude the killer, and everything would be lost. He worried that he was just keeping busy while the Wolf Man worked unconstrained and undetected. But what could he do?

Distraught, Pip peeled himself from his chair and kicked the beach ball with unusual force, not caring where it landed. He was suddenly aware that he'd not eaten since breakfast and was famished and tired.

He sent Frog a quick email summary, knowing he'd be working the nightshift, and Pip could hopefully come in the next morning to a decreased list.

Pip shut down and left the Key, hurrying down the wide hallway and to the open air outside. He walked across the parking lot and welcomed the muggy, night air, sucking in a deep breath.

Driving home to Annapolis, he tried to detach himself from the case by working the radio and rolling down the window to fill the car with fresh air. Then he thought through the night's activities, which relieved the tension. It was Thursday night, which meant his sometimes-employed roommate, Sam would be entertaining a loose circle of friends.

Sam wasn't the most responsible person, but was well-intended; and although easily distracted, things always seemed to go his way. He was well-known at every watering hole along Ego Alley and historic Annapolis, and Pip was grateful to have a stronger personality by his side.

Pip and Sam were best friends and shared a small house half-way up Cornhill Street in historic downtown, a modest two-story yellow townhome rich in history. It was a perfect location; close to all the action Annapolis offered, but small and sequestered enough to be affordable.

Pip took a slanted right onto Church Circle and another onto School Street, before slowing on State Circle. He moved along the tightly parked cars that edged the capitol building, the oldest still-in-use state capital structure.

Minutes from home, some of the stress of the day dissipated, and Pip turned right on Cornhill Street, slowing to a crawl, looking for a parking spot. Luckily, a car was leaving at the base of Cornhill and he quickly parallel parked. He walked up the street and waved to a couple of neighbors sitting on their front stoops.

Pip heard the party before seeing it, as he swung the front door open and was greeted by about twenty friends, in different degrees of intoxication. They all turned to Pip, who was wearing his standard khakis, white button down, and lanyard, home after a stressful day and at opposite to the revelers.

Sam walked over and Pip considered him for a moment.

They'd met in kindergarten over two decades earlier and though different in almost every way, their friendship flourished. They could finish each other's sentences and knew what the other was thinking. Nothing was off-limits, and they would do anything for each other without question, thought, or consequence.

Tonight, Sam had pulled his thick lock of blonde hair into a ponytail. At six foot two, he was trim and good-looking, with striking blue eyes, high cheekbones, and an easy smile. Tonight, he wore a simple form-fitting white T-shirt and jeans. As usual his demeanor was relaxed.

"Hey man, I'm glad you finally got home," Sam said, smiling. "Erin's here and I think she likes you."

Pip looked past Sam to see Erin, a girl he'd secretly adored for several months. She was petite and pretty, with a wide flirtatious smile and short dark hair. He knew Sam was being generous with his wishful thinking, but he appreciated the effort.

He and Erin had only spoken a few times. Pip was shy around girls and usually hid behind Sam, who lived life out loud and could talk to anyone about anything. Pip lived in Sam's shadow, but he was also quite comfortable within it. Sam regaled in the spotlight and with his looks, charm, and easy way, made friendships quickly and moved with a large group of people.

"It's so late," Pip started. "Are you all still going out?"

"Of course, man," Sam replied, excitedly. "The bars are still open for almost an hour, and I found a wad of cash in some old laundry so I'm buying."

Pip smiled at his friend. "A wad of cash?"

"Yeah, like fifty bucks or so!"

It was typical of Sam. Unlike Pip, who abided by a schedule and a budget, Sam was a free spirit who lived in the moment. He always had just enough gas to get around and just enough money to make it through the next day.

"Give me a few minutes to change and I'll be ready," Pip said, bounding up the creaky wooden stairs.

CHAPTER 4

Only 144 steps away from 32 Cornhill Street, the Federal House was packed with a young, energetic crowd. The restaurant side was dormant, but the bar was hopping, and the bartenders were trying to stay one step ahead of the swelling crowd.

Three of the televisions were muted, but each was broadcasting a different sporting event from earlier in the day. The Nationals were beating the Braves, the Orioles were tied with the White Sox, and somewhere in another part of the world, there was a heated game of cricket.

Pip and Sam huddled at a pub table in the front corner and Sam shouted over the drone. "So, what's troubling you, man? I know something's wrong."

Pip didn't flinch. He knew Sam could read him, but he also couldn't talk about his job. Sam knew Pip worked for the Department of Defense and even guessed his specialty was computer engineering, but that was all. Pip had never confided in Sam about his duties, and Sam often lost interest when things got technical.

"Just a hard day cramming data into a computer. Nothing special," Pip responded, dismissively.

A beautiful twenty-something brunette walked into the bar, and it was all the distraction Sam needed. He watched her pass and climb the stairs to the bathrooms above. Pip followed his gaze, and when Sam turned to take a swig of draft bear, only Pip saw the girl turn to look at Sam.

How does he do it? Pip wondered, smiling to himself. *And to think that most of the time the guy's oblivious to everything around him!*

Then Pip looked to the crowd; the rings of people spilling out from the bar and filling the high pub tables. He took a swig of beer and closed his eyes, savoring the taste and feeling the alcohol hit him. The lights seemed to dim, the music grew louder, and he gave into the comfort that abounded. Looking around, he saw others drinking, eating, and laughing on a random Thursday night, and he drew comfort from it.

Another pull of his beer and Pip felt more of the stress dissipate

Sam turned to him. "I wasn't kidding about Erin, Pip. You're like the nicest guy in the world. You put everything and everyone ahead of yourself. I know you don't know her too well but just talk to her."

Pip frowned, setting his beer on the pub table. "I don't know. I just don't know how to act around girls."

"That's the dumbest thing you've ever said, considering you're the smartest guy I know!"

Pip looked down, refusing eye contact. He was uncomfortable with the compliments and changed the subject.

"What about you? Who are you after?"

"I might be a total slut tonight."

"Why would you drink so much, don't you have to work early tomorrow?"

"I'm not that strong a swimmer these days."

"You got fired again?"

It was the usual exchange between Sam and Pip. They had their own sub-set of speak and shared an absurd and sometimes immature sense of humor. They communicated in a language laced with double negatives and voice inflection. Sam sometimes even called Pip his Meter Man, a reference to his height, or even Meteor Man if he was proud of him.

They pulled together lines from movies, television shows, and songs that only they would understand. Almost like code, only they knew the underlying message, and it was sharpened by their vast history.

Being a slut meant being drunk. Being a strong swimmer meant you were employed. Being stupid meant you were exceptional, even the word zebra meant beer.

"I think I may just have a Shirley Temple and call it a night," Pip said.

"You're only gonna have one drink? What's the fun of that?"

"Maybe a Dolly Parton, then."

It was a reference to her cleavage which meant he'd have two.

"How about a Three Dog Night. Be my bull frog, won't you?"

The brunette was now walking down the wide stairway, slowly. Her left arm casually grasped the wooden railing, as she peered into the crowd from high above, with green searching eyes and the face of a model. Sam was still oblivious, but when he saw Pip staring, his eyes floated up to the source. He looked her over and finished the rest of his beer.

Turning to Pip, he said, "I'm so glad you're out here tonight. You've been working too hard and they're killing you."

In an instant Pip forgot the girl on the stairs as Sam's last words echoed in his head. He thought of the latest abducted girl and how she would likely be the Wolf Man's latest prize. Then he pondered what Sam had said about work ethic.

He felt shame in drinking at a bar when a girl was in distress. He looked at the rest of his beer as if it were poison, pushing it away and swiftly moving to the door.

"I've gotta go, Sam," he called out, stealing away. But then a flash of guilt hit Pip, though it didn't slow him. Sam had waited for Pip to get home and had even offered to buy drinks. And though Pip knew saving the girl's life was more important, he couldn't explain that to Sam.

But when Pip looked back at his friend, the brunette had her arms around Sam, and they were already moving in a slow dance as the throng of partiers enveloped them.

Pip exited and took a quick right up Cornhill Street, starting a light jog.

He fought the urge to drive to the NSA, but he was rational and knew he'd be more productive getting a little sleep. Besides, Frog was working diligently overnight on the list.

He just hoped Lisa Wellington was okay.

CHAPTER 5

Lisa Wellington *wasn't* okay.

She'd been stripped, beaten, and left in a small pen; suffering against the open elements and burdened by leg shackles that weighed almost as much as her.

When she moved, it took considerable effort, not that she *could* in the tight confines. She was imprisoned in a ten-foot by ten-foot square section of an old barn, with a worn wooden floor and uneven wall boards that did little to brace against the weather. Prickly straw barely covered the floor, and the stagnant air was thick with the suffocating smell of manure. The insects were unrelenting.

She'd been taken the day before when jogging. It happened quickly and she still couldn't believe the reality.

Route 202 is a simple, two-lane country road, running through Phoenixville and connecting it to busier places. On the more rural stretch, in broad daylight, a car pulled up and the driver asked for directions. He spoke well, smiled at her, and wore a suit and tie. His car was nice, and he was both charming and mollifying.

Then he got out. It only took seconds for the ill smelling rag to be forced on her, and only a few more moments for the chloroform to do its job. Then she was in the car's trunk, and in under a minute steadily heading west.

The effects of the chemicals made her nauseous and she'd vomited upon waking up in the barn. Her captor forced her to clean up the mess, providing a bucket of warm water and some paper towels. Then he stripped her down and smelled her.

He sniffed her hair—gingerly at first—before breathing hard and forcing the stray hairs to fly up around her thin neck. Grunting, he moved down and smelled her arm pits, before hastily moving to her mid-section. Arriving at her pubic area, he was pleased to find a modest covering of curly blonde hair. Then he smelled behind her kneecaps, lapping up salty sweat, before sniffing her feet.

She was positioned sideways, and his large hands easily maneuvered her small frame, as she shut her eyes tight, hoping he would stop. He finally let out a grunt and quickly moved away on all fours, like an animal.

Then she was alone in the dark night.

The chains allowed for small, erratic movements and she covered herself with a light layer of hay. And despite the spring air, prickly straw, and uncertain fate, her body gave out and she fell asleep, finding solace in better places within her mind.

CHAPTER 6

32 Cornhill Street
Annapolis, Maryland

At 5 a.m., Cornhill Street was dark and quiet.

After lying in bed with his mind racing, Pip was thankful to get a few hours of sleep, before attacking a new day. He descended the narrow wooden stairs to see at least ten sleeping bodies spilled across the floor, sharing blankets and pillows. Many were snoring loudly, and the dark room smelled of stale beer and body odor.

He shook his head in dismay, looking from person to person. They were the holdovers from the after-party that had probably ended just a couple hours earlier.

Pip's eyes settled on a young man he'd never seen before, with his arms wrapped around Erin in a couple's embrace. Feeling a twinge of hurt, Pip turned slowly and walked to the cramped kitchen to find the sink full of dirty dishes and the trash can overflowing.

He opened the refrigerator to see his yogurt and bagels gone, so he grabbed an apple and left, walking down to City Dock Coffee.

He straddled the low curb before hopping on the crumbling cobblestone from the street's historic days. He looked to the right where Thomas Jefferson had *supposedly* slept above a stable now long gone, the only remnant being the small bricks at street level. The pungent stench from the restaurant dumpsters carried through the air, but he could also pick up traces of the bleach used to clean the floor mats and trash cans.

Pip's thoughts were cut short when he accidentally kicked a beer bottle, left by someone who had probably snuck it out of a nearby bar. The bottle spun and Pip contemplated it. Whenever he came across glass or plastic, he'd pick it up and get it to a recycling bin. If in a hurry, he'd place it under his car seat until it could be disposed of properly.

His logic was simple and something he firmly believed. He thought of the future of that same item, either rotting at the bottom of some trash dump or being re-used in a matter of months, all because of a simple action he controlled.

He picked up the bottle and continued walking, before coming across another. This one was standing and half full. He emptied the beer and carried them both until he came to a third.

A jogger looked over, quizzically and Pip smiled at what he must look like. It was very early morning and he was holding three beer bottles. Pip offered the man a mock toast and chuckled as he continued walking.

Pip was thankful to see Christie, his favorite barista at City Dock Coffee, who unlocked the door for him. They weren't open for another hour, but she was always there early. He was greeted by an array of aromas from the oven and freshly-ground coffee beans, and they awoke his senses.

"You know you can't bring your own beer in here," Christie said, smiling.

Pip laughed his contagious laugh, before settling into that special smile that drew others to him. "Just some trash I picked up along the way. I'll just put them in the recycling bin over here if it's okay."

"Coffee's ready. Do you want your same ol' ham and egg sandwich?"

"That would be great," he said, already filling a large cup with fresh Sumatran brew, and taking another bite of apple.

Pip was eager to get to his favorite spot to enjoy a quick breakfast alone. He didn't have to be physically at his workstation to be productive. He had a lot on his mind, and often craved solitude to organize his thoughts.

Soon he was walking across the marketplace—passing McGarvey's and Middleton's—until he reached the brick pathway that edged Ego Alley. To his left was the Dock Street Bar, Armadillos, and Moe's Southwest Grill, along with several other closed businesses so busy the night before. To his right he peered down at the calm water of the small harbor, where several ducks moved with him.

Pip regarded the boats he passed, wondering the places they'd been, and what tales they could tell. He'd never left Maryland and often dreamed of owning a boat and setting sail to an uncertain heading.

Reaching the end of the dock, he turned left and sat with his legs dangling above the water. The sun was coming up behind him, and he unwrapped his breakfast and tested the coffee. A slight wind forced the steam to dance in a whirl, and he welcomed the warmth on this face.

Pip closed his eyes, letting the coffee warm his core. He welcomed the first effects of the caffeine and took a bite of his sandwich.

He stared at the Annapolis harbor in the near and the Chesapeake Bay beyond it. On his left, the green roof of the Naval Academy gymnasium rose proudly, and his line of sight eased to the long concrete sea wall that gave way to boulders at the shoreline.

Scores of small boats shifted at port as small white caps folded over calmer water. He looked to the far distance to see the top of the Chesapeake Bay Bridge peeking above the tree line, before settling on the three iconic radio towers at Greenbury Point, remnants from the NSS Annapolis and their efforts over a century before.

Pip loved history, and this was his favorite place to think.

Given his role at the NSA, he appreciated what others overlooked. What most saw as three large, dormant radio towers, he saw as living history. He knew all about them and could even trace his own interest in communication to those very towers.

There used to be nine in all, and they were instrumental in the Navy's early war-time efforts. Before Greenbury Point, the Navy relied on independently operated linear missions, but the radio towers introduced the electromagnetic spectrum that evolved into satellite and even GPS.

They only transmitted low-frequency signals that stayed within the atmosphere to reach around the globe; and the Greenbury Point towers were the first to provide an around-the-world signal in 1914. They had been the Navy's means of communicating with the entire Atlantic Fleet.

Smiling at the history before him, and with his breakfast done and coffee nearly empty, he turned and walked swiftly back to Cornhill Street.

He had to get to the Key to begin another grueling day.

Lisa Wellington's life probably depended on it!

CHAPTER 7

Special Agent M. Jackson Seargant wasn't a big fan of the office.

Not that his wasn't nice. It was, one of the largest on the Hoover Building's seventh floor and three down from the director. He just felt more control in the world where things happened; not monitoring them and reading reports from a leather chair.

After Seargant's first conversation with Pip, he'd sent a team to work with the Wellington family and coordinate with local police. Then he'd packed a few bags and drove into Chester County to do some on-site investigating.

The clock was ticking, and he wanted to be close to the action.

But after a day of careening across the seemingly endless one-lane roads that separated the countless farms, his optimism was fading. He checked in with Pip, who had narrowed the list to about three hundred and fifty. But that also seemed like an impossible number.

With little else to do, Seargant asked Pip for some addresses in Chester and Lancaster County, choosing to ignore Montgomery and Berks for now.

Though there were more names in Montgomery County, it was also more populated, and he wanted to concentrate on the more rural side. There were about eighty in Chester, and Seargant had been making sweeping area checks and tasking local police with the same all day.

"Talk to me Pip, what do you have?" Seargant asked, calling Pip for the third time that evening. He was leaning on the trunk of his car, wearing relaxed khakis and a red polo shirt.

He looked to the distance, seeing the same things he'd been observing all day: trees, farms, and scattered wildlife. Rolling hills expanded to the horizon and buzzing insects filled the air.

"I'm now down to under three hundred names, Seargant. But I must caution that the more specific the parameters, the more names I exclude, and the more likely the target is skipped."

Seargant checked the time and grimaced. It had been thirty-four hours since Lisa's disappearance and based on past events, they were facing a measure of time the killer had never crossed. According to the Medical Examiner, a girl never survived far into the third day.

Seargant looked to the west to see the burnt orange sky just above the tree line. The sun had dropped and the bright colors that jumped from the landscape were slowly being swallowed by a darkening sky. What should have been a beautiful sunset and the promise of a star-filled evening was now a stark reminder of a ticking clock and one girl's horrific plight.

Will Lisa live to see the sunrise? Seargant wondered to himself, as he heard Pip's working keyboard on the line.

"It's Hail Mary time, Pip," Seargant said, exasperated. "We're out of time and any activity is better than none."

"I know."

"And tonight there's a full moon," Seargant continued. "They come every twenty-nine days and all of the girls were killed at or around full moons. It's probably gonna be tonight."

Pip exhaled loudly. "Just tell me what to do," he offered in defeat.

"Get more aggressive. Do all that NSA stuff. Pick through names randomly and filter anything else you can think of. Use *everything* you have and get creative."

Pip heard Seargant loud and clear. "I'm on it; I'll give you hourly updates."

The call over, Seargant returned to his car and started the engine. He looked straight ahead to another road and in his rear-view mirror he saw more of the same. With no destination, he turned left and headed west, chasing the sunlight, and knowing he'd be up until it rose the next morning.

At the NSA, Pip stared at the picture of Lisa Wellington, transfixed by her flashing eyes and broad smile. Then he turned to the Key, hoping some crucial searches and lucky strokes could save her, though he grew more discouraged with every filter he ran.

It was 8:01 p.m.

CHAPTER 8

The idea came in an instant, without celebration.

There just wasn't time.

Pip was thinking of a cup of coffee. Not the break room brew down the hall, where no one knew how old it was or what blend. No, the real stuff at City Dock Coffee in downtown Annapolis.

He was craving a strong French Roast, which took him back to his morning ritual of sitting at the water's edge, staring out to the harbor and the radio towers at Greenbury Point.

And that's when it hit him!

The radio towers.

My God, he thought, his mind still racing. *Could it be that easy?*

The radio towers!

He was reminded that while he could monitor cell phone usage and activity while powered *on*, he could also do it when it was off. He could track what he called phantom usage. He hoped the killer would turn off his phone to avoid leaving a trace signal. And if so, Pip had a program that could use that against him.

Starting over, Pip added every name back into the filter and ran a geographical match on what cell phones were *inactive* during each victim's disappearance. Then he ran a search on credit card activity during that *same* time and created and explored ATM usage.

He estimated the search parameters would take a couple minutes, so he rose from his chair and kicked the beach ball against the wall. He became lost in the movement, watching the spinning colors.

Moments later he heard a pinging sound and he looked to the monitor to see only one name remaining. He shuddered. He just knew it was the right one.

He sat down quickly, moving his fingers frantically over the keyboard. He found the man's cell phone number and saw it was currently dormant. A few more commands allowed him to turn it on as long as the physical battery wasn't removed.

Pip typed in the go-ahead program and waited, and then researched the man's cell phone company, usage, and model. It was an old Kyocera, and the battery and SIM card were difficult to remove, without physically unscrewing the casing.

Once again, Pip looked at Lisa's picture, though he had long memorized every detail.

Another signal confirmed he had reactivated the man's cell phone. There was a passcode, but it took Pip mere seconds to gain entry. Then only moments to get the location in Chester County.

Breathing heavily, Pip worked on three immediate tasks.

He typed in the coordinates to a satellite that could reach the area, researched the vehicle the man owned and was hopefully driving, and then accessed the photos on the cell phone.

While the satellite was being positioned and the Department of Motor Vehicles system was processing the request, the man's cell phone photos started to appear on one of Pip's screens.

The first few were nothing special, but then Pip came across several that sent a chill down his spine. He immediately called Seargant, visibly shaking. He knew he was working a traffic stop with local police.

Pip couldn't take his eyes off one image that was time-stamped just a couple hours ago.

And it confirmed everything.

CHAPTER 9

Seargant looked to the heavens, amazed.

The country sky was filled with more stars than he'd ever seen; and their shining pinpoints were scattered across the earth's high dome like diamonds on black velvet cloth. He turned to see the full moon as a shining white disc against the black, and though magnificent, it was also a stark reminder of its significance to the killer.

An hour earlier, he'd been driving on yet another winding country road when he'd come across some local police at a DWI check point. After flashing a badge and a brief explanation, he became one of the team, and was leaning against one of their cruisers, looking over a map with one of the police sergeants.

It was a perfect cover, really; offering anonymity while allowing access to the vehicles driving along what could be the Wolf Man's playground. Seargant knew he was grasping at straws, but there was little else to do.

And in looking at the map and delineating the points between where the kidnappings had occurred and the bodies were found, this area—and the very road he was on—was as central as he could get. Prime territory for the killer.

Seargant's cell phone rang, breaking his train of thought.

"This is Seargant."

Pip didn't waste time with pleasantries. "I have him, Seargant. I know who and where he is."

Seargant remained stoic, as he started a slow walk away from the others. "Are you sure? What inform—"

"I have no time to tell you, but I see you through satellite imaging and—"

"Wait a second, you *see* me?"

"Seargant, I need you to respectfully *shut up*. There's a BMW M5 coming to you from the south, about two miles away. He's your Wolf Man. I know it's convenient that he's coming right at you, but we got *really* lucky here. There's only one main road in and out of that area and timing is on our side."

Seargant swung his head back to the sky. This time he didn't see the stars or marvel at the beauty of the heavens. He also didn't see Pip but had no doubt the young analyst saw him.

"I see you Seargant," Pip said. "I'm right here."

Seargant waved and Pip smiled for the first time in two days. "Yep, that's me at about 11 o'clock to your left."

"Are you sure about this, Pip?" Seargant almost shouted, now looking south to the roadway that curled away into darkness.

"100% guaranteed."

"Is he alone? Is the girl with him? Where have you tracked him *from*?"

"I just picked him up a couple minutes ago, but I'll work on the backstory. For now, though, just know he's about a mile out, so get ready. Silver BMW M5. Maryland plate 01GT59."

"Pip, I need to know—"

"Seargant!" Pip shouted. "I'm 100% sure."

And Seargant ended the call.

Dennis Martin drove the winding back road, singing along to the radio, and oblivious to everything around him. A slow ride was just what he needed to clear his mind and prepare for the important ritual of the night.

Up ahead he saw blue lights but thought nothing of it. His plan was perfect; there was nothing that could expose him. The cars ahead slowed, and he realized it was a DWI checkpoint. It was almost midnight, and he noticed a handful of police motioning drivers forward as they stopped everyone for a brief exchange.

Dennis saw a couple of cars pulled off haphazardly and a handful of young men in handcuffs, their heads hung low. A few bottles of vodka were displayed on the hood of their car and the story became clear.

He glanced at the clock on the dash and frowned. He had to be back by midnight. The car in front of him was waived on and Dennis crept to a halt, the window already down.

"Evening officer," he called out, happily.

The state trooper paused, peering into the car. Smelling, listening, and looking for anything out of the ordinary.

"Hello, sir," the officer responded. "We're conducting a random stop of traffic as part of our commitment to safety. Have you had anything to drink tonight?"

"No, sir," the driver said, without a hint of abnormality.

"May I ask where you're going?"

"My sister lives a couple towns over and I'm visiting her for the weekend."

Seargant joined the conversation and eyed the driver, before walking around the car in a wide arc. He paid close attention to the rear tires, estimating the weight in the trunk. A cursory look of the exterior revealed nothing, and Seargant moved to the back, touching the car with a smooth hand motion.

Taking the man down here would be an illegal search and seizure and Seargant didn't have time to ascertain if Pip's evidence was valid or illegally obtained.

So Seargant decided to let him go.

The officer talking to the driver withdrew and looked to Seargant, who shook his head, dismissively. Seargant was walking away as he heard the BMW take off into the night and disappear around a bend.

Then his cell phone rang. He knew it was Pip and he silenced it.

Pip's job was over for now.

And Seargant's was just beginning.

CHAPTER 10

The moon was full, and it was close to midnight.

The girl had been prepped and was ready. Everything was perfect, and the Wolf Man felt giddy with excitement. He snuck up on her with intent—watching, hearing, and smelling—his senses peaking in the moment. She stirred, but in the dark she couldn't see him. But when he sprang up next to her and unlocked the crude door to her enclosure, she shot up wide-eyed and gasping.

He shined a bright light into the small space, following the slow beam as it illuminated her slender body, perfectly frozen in fear. But the chains that bound *her* also stalled *him* and he was clumsy in unlocking them. He looked up through the crooked wooden slats of the barn to see a sliver of moon and howled loudly with excitement.

He'd grown impatient; but waiting for the moon was worth it. And now it was feeding time!

The girl curled up and moved her arms, defensively; but she was no match in her dilapidated state. She actually looked adorable, he thought. Her hair was matted down, and peppered blackness surrounded her eyes, where her eyeliner had long cracked from the crying. Even the clean tracks spidering across her plump cheeks, were almost too much to take.

She cowered and withdrew, to the extent the heavy chains allowed, then peered up through vacant eyes. Her pupils shrunk in the bright light. To her, he was a giant shadow.

"Are you ready to play some more?" he hissed, breathing erratically, hungrily looking at his prey.

He grabbed her forcefully and buried his head into her naked body in a makeshift attempt at mauling her. She produced muted screams, snaking her body away, but he held her tight. He howled again and inserted a customized mouthpiece, looking down at her with an evil she'd never seen.

Her eyes grew even larger at what her captor looked like: a hooded man with makeup and a prosthetic fanged mouthpiece that shined against the moonlight. He wore gloves on his hands, with sharp razors protruding from each finger.

But then there was a blur of activity in the periphery, as a man rushed into the barn. He was large and fast, and in a flash, he tackled her captor, who was easily immobilized. Others rushed in and flashlights lit up the barn from all angles.

"Hello, Wolf Man," Jack Seargant shouted, as he punched the man several times into submission, before cuffing him and kneeling on his back.

Then he turned to the girl, controlling his breathing. And in a soft tone that suddenly turned empathetic, he spoke to Lisa Wellington. "You're safe now and it's all over. It's so nice to finally meet you."

CHAPTER 11

Pip was mentally spent.

He'd watched helplessly from the Key as Seargant circled the Wolf Man's vehicle, only to let him go. Pip had screamed at his monitor as the car drove away and was openly cursing as Seargant avoided his phone calls.

But instead of stalling, Pip tracked the BMW and ran more filters, trying to find a viable destination. Anything that could help Seargant.

On another monitor, Pip saw Seargant was *also* on the move, and some of the uncertainty abated. Pip found comfort knowing that Seargant was a gifted and tenured profiler. Maybe the young analyst didn't know the bigger picture. So, Pip tracked the slow chase from the Key, detached physically, but connected at the highest sensory level.

What happened next was quick.

With multiple programs working simultaneously, Pip saw the BMW had stopped at a farmhouse. The satellite's eye couldn't penetrate the large trees that lined the property, but Pip saw Seargant's vehicle, and several more local police in tow, suddenly converge. Officers poured from their vehicles in full sprint, and Pip watched from above, as the tense moments passed.

Then Pip's station phone rang, and he lunged for it.

"Seargant?!" Pip yelled into the receiver. "What happened?"

"It's all over Pip and you did great," Seargant said evenly. "The girl's gonna be fine because of you. Go home and get some rest."

Pip sank into his chair as the stress of the last couple of days seemed to leave him all at once. While the adrenaline still coursed through him and his mind was reeling, his senses returned. He suddenly felt a pang of hunger, an ache in his lower back, and finally exhaustion.

"You almost gave me a heart attack when you let him go," Pip stammered, shaking his head.

"I had to think fast on that one. Didn't want to take him down there. I couldn't risk not finding the girl, so I placed a tracking device on the rear bumper."

Pip nodded. "I'm so glad this is over."

"It's over because of you, Pip. You're the real hero tonight."

"Funny, I don't feel like a hero."

Seargant laughed. "That's the beauty of being a hero. You can feel any way you want. But make no mistake, you're one of the best I've ever worked with!"

"Thanks, Seargant. I appreciate that."

"And this is something I was gonna save for the debrief, but with the special nature of these types of cases and the security clearances that we *both* share, no one will ever know the *how* behind this arrest. They'll focus on the end result. There won't be any gold stars, medals, or accolades. But you're as heroic as anyone I've met, and I hope that's enough for you."

"It is, Seargant. I'm all good. I just hope we can get back to normal, especially Lisa Wellington."

Seargant received the words and smiled for the first time in days. "Good night, Pip."

"Will we ever meet in person?" Pip asked, suddenly feeling the quick bond of friendship he and Seargant had forged.

"Yes, I'd like that. I need to go to a wedding in Alabama tomorrow, but let's catch up in a couple of weeks."

The call over, Pip sucked in a deep breath and looked around his small office, to the Star Wars figurines, the bright beach ball, and finally to the picture of Lisa Wellington.

He stood and removed it from the wall, smiling wide as he looked into her beautiful eyes. Then he placed it in one of his drawers, turned off the light, and left the Key.

Pip forgot it was Friday night, until he walked into another party at the house. Even at the late hour, scores of people Pip didn't know crowded the front walkway, passing footballs and Frisbees across the narrow street and drinking from red cups.

Inside, Garth Brooks sounded, and a few girls were watching television on the couch.

Pip saw Sam was busy at the grill in the tiny backyard, working his tongs over some hot dogs and sipping beer from a Foster's oil can.

He waved at Pip, who moved into the living room.

Pip glanced at the girls, but they didn't seem to notice him. One was Erin from the night before—which seemed like an eternity ago—and *all* were transfixed on the television.

"I'm so glad they got him!" Erin exclaimed.

Pip looked to Fox News, seeing Jack Seargant speaking to the Press about the apprehension of the suspected Wolf Man and the rescue of Lisa Wellington. The same photo that had been on Pip's wall appeared on screen, and he was again mesmerized by her angelic look, the softness of her face, and purity in her eyes.

"…And I must express thanks to the local police and others within the law enforcement community for bringing this unfortunate string of events to an end. Lisa Wellington is safe, and the Wolf Man is in custody, because of their concerted efforts."

Pip looked to the television. He saw Seargant step away from the cameras and the screen turned to a local reporter.

Pip turned to the girls on the couch. "That guy is a cop?" one of them asked, rhetorically. "He's too hot to be a cop!"

Pip smiled and headed upstairs. He closed the bedroom door and undressed. But before he knew it, he was under the sheets and didn't wake up until late morning.

CHAPTER 12

Pip awoke unrested, as his mind immediately went to work.

Any inner peace he'd enjoyed while asleep evaporated in the moment, as competing thoughts fought for consideration, and the events of the previous night flooded his mind. Moving from bed, he planted his feet on the floor and dragged his fingers through his hair.

He just couldn't get the previous day out of his mind.

It wasn't just the brutal images on the killer's cell phone or the other things he'd learned from the Wolf Man's endeavors. It was the "what if" scenarios that played out mercilessly in his head.

He'd always thought of himself as a voyeur to the outside world; a computer geek who could infiltrate and uncover things from afar. But this was so real. And while he was overwhelmed by the role he played in the investigation and felt incredibly proud, he couldn't help but think of the more likely alternatives.

What if he didn't have a fixation about the radio towers at Greenbury Point and hadn't thought of tracing a dormant signal? What if he'd slept a little longer or traffic kept him away from the Key? And what if he'd taken a job in the private sector or even left Maryland altogether?

He massaged his neck and looked around his room. It was simple, really. With no closet, a basic wooden rail hung on the far wall, and his entire wardrobe was exposed. There were a couple of posters on the wall, more an effort of hiding some uneven painting and filling space.

Upon moving in a couple years prior, he'd purchased posters of Annapolis and thrown them up. The right side of his room was more important and contained most of his net worth. Upon a simple desk sat a computer system that looked substantial, even to the untrained eye. It didn't have the capabilities of his NSA computer for sure, but it wasn't far off and contained all the technology anyone could need.

It was Saturday, which usually meant Pip and Sam would walk around Annapolis and hang out without any plans. Usually they'd make a simple breakfast, brew some coffee, and share the newspaper. Then shower and launch to Main Street and the smaller tributaries to get some exercise and grab lunch around the marketplace.

Pip walked downstairs, wondering if Sam had made breakfast. What he saw instead didn't surprise him.

On the floor there were five or six sleeping bodies buried in a random collection of blankets and pillows. A tall guy, Pip didn't know, was stretched across the entire couch. He was snoring loudly, as his large stomach hung out of a stained T-shirt.

The blinds were shut tight, but thin rays of morning sun shined through from the kitchen. Pip took in the room and frowned. The place smelled like stale beer and cigarette smoke. Beer cans and paper plates littered the floor, and the end tables were covered with empty packages of snack foods and pizza boxes.

Pip walked to the kitchen to find the microwave door open and popcorn crunching beneath his feet. He moved to the coffee pot but hesitated, choosing instead to slide into his shoes and walk outside.

The sun shined brightly, casting an optimism contrary to his mindset. He started down Cornhill Street toward City Dock Coffee, looking forward to a croissant and some caffeine.

He only hoped his mind would be eased in the simplicity of his normal routine.

CHAPTER 13

An hour later, Sam found his roommate sitting at the inlet of Ego Alley.

Pip was throwing small pieces of croissant to the ducks and staring out to the narrow pass that led to deeper waters.

"Hey, man," Sam said, energetically, joining Pip atop the concrete wall that edged the water. Their backs were to the flagpole and their legs listlessly hung over the water. Groups of people moved steadily behind them, as the locals, many with dogs, walked the red-bricked sidewalk.

Pip remained silent, so Sam continued. "So, what's up with you lately? You work all the time and then come home and sleep. You okay?"

Pip turned to Sam, indifferent. "I'm fine. Just a lot going on, but it's over for now. How's that girl from the other night?"

"What girl?" Sam asked, completely at a loss.

Pip shook his head. If a beautiful girl like that had ever spoken to Pip, he'd probably remember it for the rest of his life!

But Pip played along. "The brunette girl from Federal House two nights ago. She walked in, went to the bathroom upstairs, and then a few minutes later you were grinding on her."

Sam shrugged. "The real question is 'why did you leave?' I mean everyone was out and Erin was there."

Pip shook his head, suddenly shouting. "Erin doesn't care about me! I saw her yesterday morning asleep with some guy on the floor!"

Pip was taken back by his sudden outburst. Sam, too, was shaken, but chose another route to reach his friend.

"Whatever, man. So, what do you want to do today? Walk the docks, the Naval Academy? Grab some lunch and plan something for tonight?"

But Pip retreated inward.

It was May 8, and the temperature was in the low 70's. Everyone seemed to be out and enjoying the weather. A passing car with the windows down was playing Sara McLaughlin's "Good Enough."

Sam was thinking how perfect everything was, but when he looked at Pip, he saw a changed person. His friend's face was white, his stare transfixed, and his small frame was trembling.

"You okay, man?" Sam asked, reaching over and lightly tapping Pip's shoulder.

But Pip was unmoved, his face frozen in thought.

"Pip!" Sam yelled, waving his hands in front of his friend's face like a wiper blade. But Pip's pupils were dilated points, staring out and seeing nothing. His eyes were turning red and tears were forming.

Pip's sudden change sent a shiver through Sam. Was Pip having a seizure? Should he call 911?

Sam looked around the small harbor area for help. People moved past him without pause, the boats in Ego Alley shifted quietly, and the ducks in the water below sounded off in turn. The world was moving on unchecked, while his friend's life was in precipitous turmoil. Not knowing what to do, Sam pushed Pip, forcefully.

Pip fell sideways, recovered, and then looked to Sam, wiping away tears he didn't know were there.

"Are you okay, man? You were just freaking out."

The cars continued to crawl behind them, but Sarah McLaughlin's voice still carried.

"It's nothing, I'm fine," Pip said, quickly.

But Sam continued to study his friend. Never one to be serious and not usually selfless enough to care, Sam was in foreign territory. It was usually Pip who was Sam's rock. Pip took care of Sam, who always seemed to have the answer and was no doubt more brilliant, driven, mature, and capable.

But in the moment, Sam felt a pang of sadness. He couldn't stand to bear witness to Pip being hurt.

"Tell me about it."

"It's nothing," Pip continued, instinctively touching the scar that slid down his hair line. "You wouldn't get it."

Sam followed his hand movement and saw he was covering Frank.

Frank the Scar—named after Frankenstein—was something Pip rarely spoke of. Whenever Pip was nervous, he'd touch it and he even kept his bangs a little long so it would be covered.

Sam knew it was from his time at the orphanage, but that was it.

"Pip?" he offered, genuinely. "Please talk to me. You can tell me anything. Remember I'm a black hole. Anything you say will never leave. It always stays with me."

Pip smiled for the first time in the exchange, looking down into the water and tracking a couple of ducks.

The "black hole" thing was a time-tested code of honor. They'd been best friends since kindergarten and friends kept secrets. Another physical symbol they would use in tandem would be an okay sign, signifying the hole, and as basic as it was only the two of them knew about it. It was a code that went further than anything between them. Nothing broke the circle of secrecy, and the black hole was a safe zone.

They were "lifers," and even referred to each other as such. Sam had *thought* he knew everything about Pip but clearly, he did not. He knew Pip's complicated and unique past at the orphanage, but little about his mother's death or the early health issues that had stunted his growth. But Sam was well aware that Pip was a computer engineering genius; mature beyond his years, and the kindest soul he knew.

"Black hole," Pip repeated. "Whatever goes in never comes out no matter what, right?"

"You got it buddy," Sam said, solemnly, his right hand making a crude okay sign, which wasn't lost on Pip.

Pip took a moment to gather his thoughts, now looking to the dinghy dock to their left, more of a means of delay.

"That song," he started. "Ever listen to the lyrics?"

Sam was taken back. "You lost me already, man. What song?"

"That car way over there is blasting a Sarah McLaughlin song. It's called 'Good Enough.'"

"I thought you liked Lady Gaga?"

Pip chuckled and enjoyed the familiarity of falling into their usual banter, where Pip would talk, and Sam was pleasant but mostly oblivious.

"Hey little girl would you like some candy; your momma said that it's okay."

"So those are the lyrics?" Sam asked. "What? You're a little girl now?"

Pip continued, his voice shaking. "The door is open come on outside. No, I can't come out today."

Sam smiled, studying his friend.

"It's not the wind that cracked your shoulder and threw you to the ground."

Then he turned to Sam as he fought the tears, his voice thick with emotion.

"Who's there that makes you so afraid you're shaken to the bone."

Sam suddenly got the message and squared himself against Pip.

"Something happened at the orphanage, didn't it? Son-of-a-bitch!"

Pip fell silent and looked to the water, the gentle breeze cool on his wet cheeks.

"What happened, Pip?"

Pip swallowed hard, staring into the distance, massaging Frank.

When he spoke, it was mechanical. "There were so many kids coming in and out of that place; it seemed I was the only fixture. But the staff was also very temporary. There's not much pay in the system and people would come and go constantly.

"Some of the adults were very rough on us; but for some reason a few of them were particularly hard on me. Maybe because I was an easy target, being so small."

Sam remembered their childhood and Pip's cuts and bruises, though they were usually covered so strategically. He thought it was from the kids on the playground.

Thinking back, Sam remembered Pip being melancholy; often distracted and down, even when playing. He remembered him not wanting to go home. Pip would suffer through helping Sam with his chores and even do Sam's homework. Anything to stay away from the orphanage.

"So, they beat you there?" Sam asked. "Did you ever tell anybody?"

"It wasn't the beatings I minded, Sam. There were other things too."

The comment hung in the air and the pictures formed quickly in Sam's head. He imagined Pip as a small child, thinking about the horrors no one should ever experience, especially a naïve young boy, smaller than most.

"Oh my God," Sam whispered.

Then he looked to Pip, who was wiping the tears away, leaving his face flush.

"I'm so sorry, Pip," he said. "You know you're my Meteor Man, don't you? The strongest and smartest kid I've ever known."

"Thanks Sam, that means a lot," Pip replied almost automatically, looking back to the ducks.

But Sam was undeterred. "No man, listen. I really mean it! Look where you came from and where you are now, and you did it all by yourself! You're stronger than you know, and you inspire me and others to be better."

Pip turned to Sam and nodded. "Read the plaque at your feet."

Sam was confused but looked down and saw a series of plaques he'd never noticed.

"The one to your left. Read it."

Sam looked to Pip, quizzically, but then leaned down, straining to see the bronzed letters against the sunlight. "'We all suffer. If a man's wise, he learns from it.'"

Sam grinned, looking back at Pip. "This is exactly what I'm talking about. You're so worldly and thoughtful. You notice things that others don't and draw strength from it."

Pip matched Sam's smile, studying his friend. "It would make you a better person to see the struggles of others."

Sam nodded. Then the two friends chatted away for the next hour, paying little attention to the people walking by, or the noise from the cars merging from the traffic circle.

The conversation turned to more upbeat, happier subjects, and they laughed at the simpler things.

PART TWO

FALBY THE CHAMELEON
(SIX DAYS LATER)

CHAPTER 14

Genelle's Café
Cape Verde
(Four hundred miles
off the west coast of Africa)

Falby was the most wanted man in the world.

And he was unconscious; floating face-down in the crystal-clear sea, as utter chaos rang out around him.

Moments before, he'd been waiting for a man named Jeremy. Mutual acquaintances in the Cruz drug cartel had made the arrangements.

Falby needed money and Jeremy sought anonymity.

And it would have been a good match, too. Both could deliver *exactly* what the other needed, and they weren't in competition with each other. But Jeremy hadn't showed, and what should have been a mutually beneficial covenant had instead erupted into turmoil and death.

Genelle's Café was a perfect spot, though not accurately named. It was more of a seaside tiki bar, jutting into the ocean with a wide pier, allowing amazing water views on all sides. There was more formal seating inside the restaurant, but the outside deck was more popular, and Falby always favored a crowd.

And then there was Cape Verde; one of the most beautiful places on earth and a non-extradition country to the United States. It was perfect for a man who lived in the shadows and thrived in the spaces in between.

But moments before, as Falby picked at the remains of his salad, he'd looked up to see undercover U.S. federal agents. He even thought he'd glimpsed Steve McCallister, the director of the CIA! And with *him* present, there were certainly others, with a closing perimeter and exclusive satellite coverage.

But Falby always planned for contingencies and had *three* in place. With McCallister so close, he didn't hesitate in enacting the most aggressive action.

The one with the biggest bang.

Falby sprung up with impossible speed and reached into his pockets, throwing two well placed hand grenades and two smoke bombs to both sides. Then, unsure of the outcome or even his *own* survival, he barreled sideways into a couple at a neighboring table and over the rope that edged the dock.

The explosions quickly followed, as did the screams from the people at the wrong place at the wrong time. In midair, Falby felt the blasts, searing heat, and deadly shrapnel. With his eyes closed he went over the railing, bracing for probable death.

He was struck in the head by a flying projectile and knocked unconscious. He didn't feel himself land in the shallow water or hear the panicking screams as he floated motionless.

Several unfortunates that *weren't* able to brace for the attack were blown to bits in two circles of death. Those outside the immediate perimeter still suffered shrapnel wounds and were deafened by the blasts.

The ones coherent enough to react were blinded by the expanding white smoke that consumed everything. Incoherent at best, the crowd fled in panic; with most of the outdoor patrons jumping into the water to wade ashore.

One do-gooder saw Falby and dragged his body to land, performing CPR. A few empty moments passed before the killer coughed up water, staring blankly into a young man's face. Realization came quickly, as Falby rolled over and looked up through his delirium.

It was absolute madness.

But no one was pursuing him and there was no sign of authority. Any eyewitnesses were dead or dispersed in the chaos.

Falby seized the moment.

He managed to stand and push his rescuer in front of him, motioning with a pointed finger. People were running into each other; with scores of others wading ashore. Many more were pouring out of the restaurant's main entrance and curious onlookers were arriving from all directions to bear witness.

Falby moved with the group and found anonymity in the throng, eventually slipping into a side alley. There he saw an old bike leaning against a stone wall.

And from there the Chameleon was as good as gone.

After biking a few miles, Falby turned into a narrow side street and fell into contemplation. How had the CIA found him and was he being tracked by the invisible satellite eyes high above?

Then his thoughts turned to the melee he'd just fled and especially Steve McCallister. The last time they'd been together was in Chile when McCallister had committed Falby to be a ghost within the CIA's illegal and undocumented prison system.

But that was a few years ago.

And after biding his time and surviving the often-torturous inquisitions and constant movement, Falby had escaped and found refuge in southern Venezuela. In doing so he'd *again* lived up to his name—the Chameleon—by changing his colors and escaping into the night, though he couldn't hide the dead CIA agents he'd left in his wake.

What was most interesting about his exodus was the only thing he couldn't control. With the incessant shuffling around, and always being hooded, combined with the random cocktails of drugs forced into him, he had no idea what continent he was on, or even what time of year it was.

But he *did* have his skill set—long, deadly, and proven—and it had been enough.

So, he'd acclimated quickly, gathered resources, and disappeared into the world. Borders were invisible to him, and he moved easily and unrestrained.

Falby was a small, very physical German mercenary in his late forties, with short blonde hair and steely, gray eyes. But that was only when he wasn't in disguise, which was more often than not.

He was a master of weaponry, chemistry, electrical and mechanical engineering, and physics, with an innate sense of learning and absorption. He had a natural appreciation and curiosity of things and craved knowledge. But his most trusted skill had always been attention to detail. Inefficiencies and uncalculated outcomes were not possible. To say he was cunning and guile was an understatement.

At one time he'd been a soldier in the al Assad faction working directly for Almedi Hahn Sahn, its holy leader. The position offered Falby more money than he could spend; but the job itself lent much more than that.

He was given the opportunity to flex his skills and watch his genius play out firsthand. He'd assassinated a prominent senator, blown up much of the Golden Gate Bridge, and unleashed sarin gas into a crowd at Madison Square Garden.

It was the last strike in New York he was most proud of, simply because of the technicality and *patience* that led to the action. He'd worked tirelessly creating the sarin mix, which he'd estimated at being over 93% pure.

A thought suddenly occurred to him, and he smiled for the first time.

With the CIA following him in such a clandestine manner, and with Cape Verde being a non-extradition country, their mission was probably undocumented and not known to the local authorities.

And although the CIA was certainly *trying* to track him, there was probably only a small team doing so.

It was all the advantage Falby needed to disappear.

He thought back on how things went so awry; when now *former* President Harold Bowman ordered missile strikes that eventually unraveled Falby's life. A newfound sense of rage welled up within him. Falby became incensed; fueled by years of isolation and containment.

"Harold Bowman," he whispered to himself. "I'm coming for you."

The smile erupted into a grin as his mind worked. It was time to take the war to the United States Presidency, itself.

There would be blood and he knew exactly what to do.

The Chameleon was back.

CHAPTER 15

Southwest of Diana
Webster County, West Virginia

Weeks after his escape, Falby still walked with a limp. But he didn't mind. Reminders of his past only motivated his future.

And it was bustling all around him.

The tiny cabin wasn't much, but it served its purpose well. Totally isolated within three hundred acres of booby-trapped and perfectly monitored forestation, it allowed the killer the space and anonymity to work uninterrupted.

There were five separate workplaces—one for each of his presidential targets—and as he regarded each one, even *he* smiled at the wonder of it all.

The perfect, intricate design of each station was like artwork to him, and no less magnificent. They were labeled accordingly—Preston, Bowman, Montgomery, Gilmore, and Maclemore—each with its own timer counting down to a hard deadline.

Falby's gray eyes settled on the small jar at station one. He couldn't see the fine misty white ricin powder due to the small quantity, but he beamed at its lethality. Adjacent to it was the oil press, raw castor beans, and the precious oil cake he'd used to make the most highly purified ricin he'd ever tested.

He'd manufactured and used ricin before, but only for ingestion and much more was required. This time it would be inhaled and twenty-two micrograms—about three grains of crushed rice—would most definitely be enough.

Falby thought about his victim and how the poison worked in the body. Ricin is a carbohydrate-binding protein that acts as a toxin by inhibiting the most basic level of cell metabolism, which is essential to life. Because the symptoms are caused by *failure* to make protein, they emerge only after several hours of exposure.

The best part was the timing!

It would take about fifteen hours to emit symptoms and mirror the flu, with imminent death in about five days.

Former President James Preston's days were numbered.

And there was nothing anyone could do about it.

Falby finally took a break from station five at midnight.

He'd just finished work on the Garrett TPE331 engine, cleaning the two-stage centrifugal compressor and assembling the reverse annular combustor. It was the latter that had taken the last several hours; simply due to the condition of the axial turbine and the combustion chamber itself.

He knew it was probably overkill, but Falby left nothing to chance. He'd soldered and molded the chamber to guarantee stable combustion, even though the MQ-9 Reaper drone wouldn't be testing its top speeds or upper altitude limits.

The two drones still had to be assembled, but that wouldn't take long. They were hiding in the woods nearby, in a narrow ditch almost seventy feet long and covered by dense brush.

Falby stood and stretched his legs, before walking to the eight laser-guided Hellfire II missiles lying dormant in the corner. Bending at his small waist, he moved his right hand over the smooth copper liner—all sixty-four inches of it—smiling at his messengers of death.

Perfectly lethal; perfectly his.

They were fourth generation radar frequency seekers. And when employed in tandem with the EMP device he'd finished the day before, there was little standing in his way.

Falby walked to the bank of video monitors, covering the south wall. In sum they covered every bit of the land around him, and he took his time scanning each one. The thermal images were silent and still, just as they should be.

Satisfied, he moved to station four, his favorite. Tomorrow it would consume most of the day but prove the most fulfilling. He'd be replicating a large armoire that was currently in the Presidential Suite at the Waldorf Astoria. Everything was ready on site; he just had to mentally prepare and acclimate his body.

Despite the excitement, Falby moved to his cot and laid down.

His last thoughts of the day amused him. He would kill four American presidents over the next several days.

And no one could possibly see it coming!

CHAPTER 16

Chartwell Golf & Country Club
Severna Park, Maryland

On the day of his assassination, former president Harold Bowman had a dream.

He was drifting through the halls of a nondescript place, until he stopped and peered into a room without edges; a vast whiteness extending into nothing. He stumbled into the parlor, focusing on a casket, his eyes getting wider as he approached. There were others, but he could distinguish nothing pertinent, and no one regarded him. He was drawn farther into the room, almost like a magnet, only to peer down at his own dead body in a casket.

The vision was cutting in its reality, and it shook him awake.

But Bowman didn't tell anybody or overthink it, even though he knew it was similar to the dream Abraham Lincoln had a few days before *his* death.

The details became lost in his morning routine. A quick shower and shave offered the small degree of separation needed, and his morning eggs, bacon, and coffee wiped the thoughts away completely.

The seventy-year-old Democrat had been a popular president. He'd also been one of the more mobile ones; jetting around the country delivering charged speeches to his energized constituents. He never missed an opportunity to shake a hand or promote an agenda; and his stamina was the talk of the news media.

He'd been a favorite on the late-night talk shows and had been on *Saturday Night Live* more than once. He was grounded in the old-line democratic base; but had also connected with the younger liberals and their progressive ideas.

His two terms had been some of the best years in recent history. The economy boomed, terrorism was limited to the Middle East, and the people were in good spirits. The American dream played out in backyards all over the country and his approval ratings had soared.

But that was when he was president eighteen months ago; and now he was riding in a limousine, part of a reduced motorcade, carrying him, his chief of staff, three Secret Service agents, and two junior aids.

"So, what's today look like?" he asked to nobody in particular, looking out the window and watching the traffic.

Minnie Porter, new to his staff and eager for the opportunity, cleared her throat. She'd been tasked with the golf event weeks ago and was excited to discuss the details.

"Mr. President. It's a charity golf tournament. Steve Bisciotti, owner of the Baltimore Ravens will be in your foursome, along with Dudley Dixon, a real estate developer, and Rob Agresti, the golf course pro. Mr. Bisciotti and Mr. Dixon have donated generously to your foundation to bring you out, and those details are in your folder."

Bowman glanced at his leather binder and cracked it open, eyeing the itinerary, the location, weather conditions, and more importantly the details of the donations.

"That's mighty nice of them," Bowman said, smiling. "I guess a quick round of golf won't be so bad."

"Yes, sir," Minnie added. "You'll be playing the back nine because it's flatter and has more of an interior. Later, you'll have lunch at the governor's house in Annapolis and be done by late afternoon."

Bowman continued a blank stare out the window. He had heard very little. It was just another day to smile and wave.

Arriving in Severna Park, they rode up and down Saint Ives Drive, and took a quick right into Chartwell Golf & Country Club. The Secret Service emptied the vehicles and spanned out, their eyes looking in all directions, as they joined the agents already on-site.

But there was nothing dangerous here. Not for a former president.

Several hundred spectators gathered on the manicured front lawn, where the American flag flapped in the moderate wind. The activity on the practice range stalled, as everyone looked expectantly to the guest of honor.

Keeping his thoughts to himself, Harold Bowman was all smiles as he walked past the people and waved. He was whisked into the pro shop and presented with his score card and photos were taken.

Suddenly he remembered the dream he'd awoken from, where he was looking at himself dead.

But he shrugged off the images once more.

Because who would ever want to kill a former president?

CHAPTER 17

Ocean Beach Park
New London, Connecticut

The assassin woke without the slightest movement or sound.

Decades of training, conditioning, and concentration allowed for a high level of consciousness, even at rest. So, when his self-allotted forty minutes were up, he simply opened his eyes.

Falby's mind was immediately racing but *still* he didn't move. Absolute silence and immobility were crucial, especially now.

He'd arrived several hours earlier in the dead of night, under complete darkness, looking like a dedicated jogger to the passing eye.

But there had been no sign of anyone, and his insertion was perfect.

He'd carefully stopped and camouflaged his motorcycle in the dense woods east of Route 213. He'd easily scaled the modest fence at Ocean Beach Park, and within minutes arrived at a pre-determined place, where he'd hidden his equipment the day before.

Now he just had to wait, but patience had always been one of his more honed and valued skills.

Ensconced under layers of brush and leaves, his light body suit further concealed him. The only thing that peeked out into the open world was the end of his customized Barrett M107 sniper rifle. But even that had been modified to look like the extremity of a small tree branch.

He glanced at his watch and smiled at the perfect storm brewing within the hour.

He knew that former President Walker Montgomery would be sailing out of Norwich with an old Navy friend, on their way to Mystic. At the same time, former president Harold Bowman was playing nine holes of golf in Maryland.

Montgomery's sailboat excursion was a security nightmare for the Secret Service and a dream for a seasoned assassin like Falby. The Secret Service would undoubtedly be on the boat, with two or more flanking power crafts and air support.

But the land parameters favored Falby; with several miles of dense woods on both sides of the river that couldn't be adequately surveyed.

Even the roads falling away from the park were ideal. Falby could go north and be on I-95 in minutes or take the arcing 213 across New London and pick the interstate up several points east.

Still, Falby planned for multiple contingencies and was assured that, except for a heat signature, which his body suit all but deflected, he was invisible. The Secret Service could send foot patrols to the water's shore. But barring a federal agent literally stepping on him, Falby was confident in his position.

The Chameleon's name was well-deserved and spoke to his most valued skill: his ability to disappear and maneuver so easily.

Falby glanced at a small monitor, showing a live feed from the seventeenth hole at Chartwell Golf & Country Club. Days before he'd placed two concealed cameras atop a tall oak tree. One showed a high, all-encompassing sweep of the seventeenth hole and the sixteenth green. The other was focused directly on the seventeenth tee box.

It was no secret that Bowman was a punctual man and slave to his regimented itinerary. With a tee time of 8:30 a.m., even with the pomp and circumstance, he would be on the seventeenth hole by around half past ten. A noon lunch with the Maryland governor was planned and his staff would be monitoring the time.

A vibration buzzed on Falby's left arm and his eyes moved to another small screen. It was a grainy video, not meant for precision, but measure; and it showed what he wanted to see: a view south from the bridge on the 2A, just a few miles north of his position.

He saw that Walker Montgomery, an avid sailor, couldn't help but take the wheel of the sixty-foot Hinckley. The monitor showed the unmistakably large bulk of him at the helm. With the cutter under power at about eight knots, it would put him within range in under twenty minutes.

Back in Maryland, Falby also saw the accumulation of Secret Service and local law enforcement on the seventeenth hole, as Bowman's foursome was undoubtedly on the sixteenth.

Falby looked to the third monitor, showing a broad local view of the woods that surrounded him. There was no movement. He was just part of the lush landscape, perfectly embedded in his silent resolve.

Readying himself, the killer palmed the Barrett and looked through the Leupold Mark-IV scope, getting a benchmark read of the river's chop. The Thames was under a hundred yards out and spanned about a mile, so Falby could take the shot any time the sailboat came into view.

The brackish, slate-blue water was at sharp contrast to the green landscape that edged it, and the sunlight cast a sheen on the surface like a glide path. A modest chop rolled in from the sound and folded over the calmer waters inland, forcing lines of whitecaps to the north. Winds were ideal, the sun was chasing away the morning clouds, and the temperature was climbing into the mid-seventies.

Falby had chosen his weapon carefully. The M107 was a manageable fifty-seven inches long and weighed just under thirty-one pounds. It was semi-automatic and fired .50 caliber rounds with a ten-round magazine.

With a trained marksman like Falby, it was lethal at just over a mile, but more importantly the Barrett was designed as an anti-material weapon that could pierce body armor and cut through walls.

His first shot was obvious, but the next several were meant for the boat engines. He didn't think helicopters would come into *immediate* play, but he was well aware of the nearby Coast Guard stations at both Fishers Island and New London and had planned accordingly.

Falby looked to his disposable cell phone. Then he thought of the intricately placed C4 he'd threaded just ten inches under the tee box on the seventeenth hole at Chartwell. He just had to make a phone call to trigger the vibration circuit, and whomever was within twenty feet would have a very bad day.

Falby had obsessed and calculated this moment for weeks. He knew the itinerary of both men but couldn't control the exact timing. But while the golf course explosion could only happen with Bowman in place, Falby estimated a fatal shot for Montgomery within a window of twenty-eight minutes at a lethal eight hundred yards.

He'd calculated it on paper so often; but now in *real-time*, it looked like Bowman's three-minute window would be well within Montgomery's shot time. The Chameleon would kill two former presidents, possibly within seconds of each other in two separate states.

And even he had to admit that was something special, and a new high for what had already been a colorful and deadly career.

CHAPTER 18

Steve Bisciotti laughed at Harold Bowman's attempt to get into his head.

They were on the sixteenth green and with handicaps in play, Bisciotti was up one and looking at an eight-footer for par. At stake were Super Bowl tickets versus a ride on Airforce One. Dudley Dixon and Rob Agresti had a handshake deal to play for a dollar-a-hole and the golf pro had been generous with the handicap.

"I don't know about the Ravens this year, Steve," Bowman started. "The Steelers did pretty well in the draft, and your secondary needs a little help."

Steve Bisciotti knelt a few yards behind his ball, knowing the path would bend left toward the Severn River. "I wouldn't worry too much about my defense, Mr. President. These things have a way of working out."

Bowman let it go and moved behind the pin, whistling "Hail to the Chief."

Dixon looked to Rob Agresti, shaking his head at the obvious breach of etiquette, but the golf pro just shrugged his shoulders and smiled.

A few quiet moments passed, and all eyes were on Steve Bisciotti, as he smooth-tapped the ball with a perfect read and it fell in for par. The others tapped in and smiles abounded, as they headed to their golf carts.

In truth, Harold Bowman was thoroughly enjoying himself. The morning temperature was firmly in the seventies and the modest wind was refreshing.

And why wouldn't he have fun? He'd been treated like a king and was playing a quick round of golf with a couple wealthy donors and a golf pro, who'd promised to fix the slice he'd developed.

Arriving at the seventeenth tee, Harold Bowman was feeling good about himself. Again, ignoring etiquette, he teed off first. He looked to the course's longest par three and decided on a three iron, as he confidently strolled to the tee box.

The Secret Service agents in four golf carts parked on the path, behind the player's carts and emptied quickly, joining the five forward team agents already there.

Still, they kept their distance to Bowman, who had argued more than once that they shouldn't get too close. "It's a golf course, guys," he'd said several times. "Give me a break!"

The other players stayed back. Bisciotti was undecided between a six and a seven iron, Rob Agresti, in charge of scoring, was adding up strokes, and Dudley Dixon was checking his voice mail.

Still, by the time Bowman was on the tee box and into his second practice swing, he had the group's full attention.

And what they witnessed was something they would never forget.

CHAPTER 19

"Just beautiful, isn't it, Charlie?" former president Walker Montgomery shouted to his old friend, as he palmed the large circular wheel of mahogany, and stared gleefully to the open water.

"Sure is, Walk," Charlie yelled back. "Sailing doesn't get much better than this!"

"You bet it does," Montgomery countered, waving a hand all around him. "If we could lose those two flanking protection boats and the five extra guys on this cutter; maybe even kill the damn engines for a pure sail, that would be nice."

Charlie laughed. "Can't do anything about your security detail and neither can you. And we still need to be under power until we cut into the Sound."

Montgomery smiled knowingly, rolling a fat cigar between his teeth. He wasn't altogether kidding. If he could just be with his friend on a three-hour sail—away from the Secret Service, Press, and even his wife—he'd be ecstatic.

A short and stocky man, Walker Montgomery had been a no-nonsense oil tycoon from Texas. A Republican that got things done and didn't mince words.

He'd left office more than a decade prior, after eight years in the White House, with a high approval rating. The economy had reacted well to his trade deals and deficit reduction, and the stock market had swelled because of low interest rates, deeper infrastructure spending, and job creation. He'd increased military spending and reinforced foreign military bases that had been neglected.

Over his tenure, he'd visited each one, delivering galvanizing speeches and pointing directly into every camera, touting that the United States was never more enabled to meet any challenge. The Press nicknamed him "Bulldog," partly due to his short and stocky frame, but also how his pudgy face would crinkle and redden when he was incensed.

"Well, I guess things could be worse," Montgomery said, expelling a cloud of cigar smoke, and looking hopeful.

Gazing up the river, where the darker blue waters of the Long Island Sound met the Thames, he smiled and looked to his friend. "What could go wrong on a beautiful day like today?"

A rare smile formed on Falby's normally expressionless face, as he saw the sailboat come into view, not from the small monitor to his left, but from the scope of his Barrett rifle. A quick look to another screen showed a view from the trees high above the seventeenth green in Maryland. Bowman was walking to the tee box and his imminent death.

Another glance at the sailboat showed a distance of just one-thousand yards and closing. Both targets were in the kill zone. *Oh, the timing!*

Releasing a long breath, Falby readied himself. Peering through the scope he kept measure with the speed of the boat and the slight chop and followed the target for a few seconds before pulling the trigger.

It was a perfect shot, and he saw Montgomery fall sideways, lifeless.

In quick succession he shot three more times, piercing the boat engines on the cutter and trail boats.

Then he reached for a cell phone within a zipped case and simply speed-dialed the only number in the phone's directory.

CHAPTER 20

"**R**emember what I told you," Rob Agresti shouted to Harold Bowman. "If you're really gonna fix that slice, you must keep your right elbow closer to your body. **S**low down your swing and strike through the ball."

Bowman looked up from his practice swings and waved him off, before addressing the ball and steadying himself.

Bowman hit a solid shot, with just enough lift to clear the large center bunker, pin high. But before he could celebrate the effort or even dabble into thought, the ground under him erupted into an intense fireball that swallowed him, with a thundering blast that shot out in every direction.

He disappeared within an inferno of heat and orange flame. Brown earth, shrapnel, and other debris—pieces of Bowman himself—flew in every direction, as the other three golfers and the Secret Service agents hit the ground.

The concussion of force blew the landscape over fifty feet into the air and outward three times more, leaving a cratered scar in the land yards deep.

Through the madness, Steve Bisciotti reacted the fastest, still clutching his golf club and running to where Bowman had just stood. His ears were ringing and his eyes watered, as the heavy smoke engulfed him, but he ran into the chaos blindly.

But Bowman was gone.

The Secret Service agents were quick to follow, shouting to each other. Reality came slowly, as they traded looks to each other in despair.

Their Charge was gone.

A shout came from the right near the tree line. A Secret Service agent was kneeling over some debris and the others rushed over. It was the headless torso of Harold Bowman, his bright red blood still running over seared black flesh. Bisciotti vomited, stumbling a short distance away, as more agents rushed in to bear witness.

Then, another shout sounded from the golf carts.

Rob Agresti was holding his bloodied right arm. And he was looking at the lifeless body of his golfing partner, Dudley Dixon, who'd also been hit by shrapnel.

In Connecticut, Falby didn't waste time looking at the monitor to witness the golf course explosion. Even seconds were crucial, and he couldn't spare them.

Instead, he leaped up from his protected burrow, grabbed a pre-planned backpack, and ran to his motorcycle. Within moments he was moving up the windy road out of the park toward I-95, just a few miles over the speed limit.

If timing continued to favor him, he would be in Manhattan in about two hours. He didn't waste time thinking of Harold Bowman or Walker Montgomery.

They were the past.

Former President Rube Gilmore was the future, and the only thing on his mind now.

CHAPTER 21

Despite the reigning chaos, proper procedure was followed.

Within seconds, the Secret Service at each location secured the remains of the fallen targets and sent detachments to find the assailants. Local law enforcement was instructed to set up roadblocks and air support was on its way.

Within a minute, the sitting president and two remaining *former* presidents were locked down, along with the vice president, the Speaker of the House, and the Supreme Court justices.

The FBI was contacted, and information was immediately disseminated to the security details across all elected officials. Congress was not in session, but the U.S. Capitol and the White House began their evacuation procedures of non-essential personnel. Security sweeps were in process, spanning away from the higher priority threats on both federal and state levels.

Former President Rube Gilmore had just arrived at the New York Stock Exchange for a day visit in lower Manhattan. He'd been scheduled to meet with several young business leaders, two of whom were launching IPO's later in the trading day.

He was about ten minutes into a speech when the Secret Service swarmed him, rushing him into a designated area without windows. The audience, all of whom were men and women of purpose and wealth, were harshly instructed to exit the building.

Rube Gilmore was a tall, thin man, with sandy hair and a wide smile. He was a one-term Democrat from New York. His presidency had been marred with political fallout and conspiracy theory, and he'd decided against running for a second term.

He held his face in his hands as he absorbed the news.

Presidents Bowman and Montgomery had been assassinated simultaneously! Was the country under attack? Was he next? He'd repeatedly asked the Secret Service, but they were too busy fortifying their position and calling in reinforcements to expand and layer the perimeter around Gilmore.

So poor old Rube thought some more, deliberately obsessing about the two dead men, neither of whom he liked. Were they somehow linked to something that caused this or was it just that they were former presidents? Thankfully, he thought, his security detail would be increased, and he felt comfort knowing he'd never been more protected.

Still the thoughts crept in.

One of his favorite Secret Service agents had long ago said that nothing was certain, and an assassin could always find a way. The agent's words now echoed in his head and cracked his spirit. No one could doubt the capability of the people involved in this!

Now cradling his face in his sweaty palms, Gilmore shook his head and shot up from his seat. "I want to speak to POTUS right now! What the hell is going on?!"

"Sir," the closest field agent started, squaring himself against the man. "That's not possible but within the hour, okay?"

Gilmore sat back down, blinking rapidly, his thoughts turning inward once again. He'd been involved in many questionable things. From adultery to back room dealing, and typical politicking to outright lies.

He couldn't help but make a mental list of the people who would want him dead. He'd broken campaign promises and committed fundraising violations, and he'd delivered high profile acquittals and questionable prosecutor opinions for profit as a former D.A. The list grew exponentially as his mind worked, until he started hyperventilating, drawing deep breaths that forced his head to bob from his shoulders.

Hell, his own wife probably wanted him dead!

"I need to get out of here," he stammered, fumbling for the cell phone in his pocket.

"Negative," a Secret Service agent said, approaching Gilmore, and snatching the phone away. The agent removed the casing and took out the battery, placing the separate pieces on a nearby table. "You are locked down."

Gilmore looked up at the man in anger. His face was flush, and his words spilled out without a filter.

"I'm Rube Gilmore you son-of-a-bitch and I demand—"

"Quiet, sir!" the agent demanded. "You're not in control of this situation, and if you want to get out of this alive, I suggest you do exactly what you're told."

The other surviving former president—James Preston—was much easier to secure.

The oldest of them all, 94-year-old Preston had been battling Alzheimer's and was resting comfortably at his home in northern California.

He'd been out of politics for decades and removed from any real media attention for years. And although there had been articles published about him and his medical condition, no interviews or pictures had been taken for at least ten years.

The American people respected the man's service to his country; and with his debilitating condition, they were content to let him live out his days in peace.

Looking at him now—sleeping most of the day in a large sterile room that resembled a hospital, surrounded by a medical team and a loose security detail—one would never have thought how he'd reigned in his day. He was a throwback to another time, vigilant to a fault and dogged with every issue.

Politicians on both sides of the aisle valued his tenure, both as a governor and as a two-term president, but the people adored the love story he'd shared with his late wife, Beth.

As popular as James Preston was, Beth Preston could steal the spotlight from her equally charming husband in an instant. An accomplished actress in her own day, when films were motion pictures of art and their storylines shined with morality, she'd left it all behind to stand by her man.

They were adored by the public and Preston's presidency was celebrated. When they left office and tried to retire to a slower life on the ranch, they were less visible, which left the people wanting more.

The Press became more aggressive in both photograph and interview requests, and the number of reporters swelled at their house gates, until the Preston's agreed to scheduled visits and short interviews to appease the people.

Years later, Preston fell into mental decline. A formal diagnosis came, and the aging couple withdrew into their lives. This time, the public gave pause and respected their privacy, and life outside the considerable compound went on.

Looking at the man now, oblivious to everything around him, he was in the safest place he could be. He hadn't moved from the room in years and was surrounded by thoroughly vetted medical staff and an experienced Secret Service detail. There was a substantial outside perimeter, and it was naturally forbidding and impenetrable.

The head of his security detail was Mike Pritt, a forty-year veteran of the Secret Service. Within moments of the Bowman and Montgomery assassinations, he was at Preston's side, looking the man over and making sure he was okay.

"I've got you, sir," he said softly, using his large hand to brush back the man's white hair. "You're in the safest place you can be right now."

CHAPTER 22

Within the hour, things looked dramatically different at the golf course.

Local police were called in to secure a generous perimeter; and yellow crime scene tape created a giant circle around the seventeenth tee box, or what was left of it.

The community of Chartwell had seven points of entry, and only residents were being allowed in. The country club was closed, and every employee had been questioned and documented before leaving.

The Press had been kept away.

The FBI sent two team leaders, Jack Seargant and James Gibson. They arrived via helicopter, coming straight from the roof of the Hoover building, landing on the twelfth fairway.

Seargant led the Behavioral Science Unit and was one of their most gifted profilers. He'd made the national news with the recent apprehension of the Wolf Man killer, but he was best known for the Island Hopper case the previous year. Gibson was now a team leader in the FBI's anti-terrorism effort and had been a main player in The Last Patriot operation.

Gibson and Seargant emptied the chopper and hurried over to the seventeenth hole, where a dozen federal agents were gathered around several folding tables. A couple of large tents had been erected just off the tee box, and agents in hazmat suits were moving back and forth from the site of the explosion into the tents.

The tallest of the Feds was Steve McCallister, head of the CIA.

McCallister was a gray-haired, physically fit man in his late sixties. His posture and demeanor spoke volumes, and the other field agents looked to him for guidance. A professional soldier, he'd been a proven on-the-ground operator for most of his career. Now, as the director of the CIA, he was still very active in the field, and Seargant wasn't surprised to see him.

"Gibby!" McCallister called out, closing the distance between them with an outstretched hand. "How have you been?" he added, as they shook hands vigorously.

"I'm good, old man," Gibby shot back. "So glad you're here!"

Seargant remained stoic as he let the two men chat. He knew they'd worked together in the past, and the partnership was one of the more successful dual agency operations, as of late.

Turning away, McCallister looked to Seargant, frowning. "Hello, Mr. Director," Seargant said, pre-emptively.

"Jack Seargant," McCallister shot back, eyeing him. "Haven't seen you since mid-May. I believe it was Cape Verde, when you walked right into my surveillance detail and compromised the lives of my men, allowing our target to escape."

Seargant stepped forward with confidence. "I was in active pursuit of—"

"Yeah, yeah, yeah," McCallister stammered, waving him off. "You were the big shot on 'The Island Hopper' case, I know. But I have to ask with what authority were you operating in a non-extradition country?"

Seargant knew this could come up one day. But he also knew that Steve McCallister had his own secrets and wouldn't want an audience in an engagement of morality.

"Speaking of authority," Seargant shot back. "The FBI has taken over this investigation, so why are you even here?"

The Secret Service and local police remained still, eyeing the two men—FBI and CIA—as they sparred. They had received word from their ranking officials at Homeland Security to work with the local police to secure the site and wait for the FBI. But with an FBI chopper on the neighboring hole, and a CIA chopper on the fourteenth fairway, things were getting crowded.

McCallister nodded. "Let's just say the 'The Last Patriot' operation is still ongoing and our number one target, Falby, is still out there. In fact, I would guess this was his work. Both assassinations reek of him. I'd bet on it."

Seargant shook his head, looking to McCallister. He couldn't believe that one man could kill two former presidents within seconds of each other. But as much as he loathed McCallister for his impudence, he couldn't help but entertain the thought.

The CIA director wasn't done. "You should send a couple of drones into those high trees. I'd focus on the ones above and to the left of the green. I'm sure there's at least one camera pointed at this tee box. Obviously, he knew their schedules, and probably dialed this in, while waiting for Walker Montgomery to sail into sight up north."

Seargant couldn't help but agree with McCallister's reasoning, as he looked into the high swaying trees, and the deep blue skies that helped define them.

"And another thing," McCallister said. "I bet you'll find fingerprints all over that camera and they'll match Falby's."

Now Seargant was perplexed. "Why would the perpetrator—even if it *is* Falby—not just wear gloves?"

McCallister grimaced, knowingly. "Because I know this man. His goal may be to kill the former presidents, and quite possibly reach the White House as well. He won't write a manifesto or send letters to the Press, but he also doesn't care that we know it's him. He has over a month's head start and we've only just begun."

With that, McCallister walked toward his chopper with his team.

Jack Seargant called out after him. "Are you going to Connecticut to Montgomery's crime scene?"

McCallister stopped and turned. "Bowman and Montgomery are gone. Rube Gilmore is closer in New York City and more exposed than he may know. I'm going to secure him myself."

Gibby nodded at Seargant before catching up with McCallister. "Then I'm going with you."

CHAPTER 23

Rube Gilmore's face lit up when he saw Steve McCallister, though the feeling wasn't mutual.

When Gilmore was president, he'd worked with McCallister three times and trusted the man completely. The operations were in different areas—Syria, Afghanistan, and Iraq—and the decisions Gilmore had to make were based on information that couldn't be verified. But McCallister had promised him pinpoint accuracy and resolve, with minimum risk to American life and assets.

And all three operations had succeeded. Gilmore took full advantage of them, holding press briefings with inflated, leaked information that increased his polling numbers and bolstered his efforts on foreign policy.

Things went according to plan when Steve McCallister was around, and Gilmore was visibly more relaxed when the director of the CIA and FBI Agent James Gibson entered the room.

McCallister remained stone faced, though his insides were burning with disdain. Still, he had a self-promised directive to secure the man.

In the five hours since the assassinations, security surrounding Rube Gilmore had increased exponentially, though Gilmore couldn't have known it. Still locked down and confined to small quarters at the New York Stock Exchange, he couldn't validate what was happening outside the closed walls.

The four rings of protection had expanded to seven and those teams were tripled. The Secret Service was in charge, but with McCallister on site and James Gibson joining him, a joint operation of extraction was underway.

McCallister studied Rube Gilmore.

The man was disheveled. His blonde shock of hair was sticking out to the side, and his puffy red eyes searched the room like a small child. His defeated posture left everyone wondering how this shell of a man could have once ruled the free world.

Still, he was theirs to protect and as McCallister looked into the eyes of the immediate security team, everyone was ready to move.

He looked to Gilmore. "We're going to get you out of here in the next ten minutes, sir." McCallister said, firmly.

"Where to?" Gilmore shot back.

"The Waldorf. It's close and has the infrastructure we need to secure you until we know more."

Then McCallister turned and addressed the agents in the room, speaking in a low, authoritative manner. "We move in ten minutes. Tight formation all the way."

McCallister paused, looking to everyone in the room and searching their eyes, taking measure.

"We're clear all the way to the Waldorf. And we're gonna move fast."

CHAPTER 24

The Waldorf Astoria is one of the more iconic hotels in midtown Manhattan and has accommodated every president since Herbert Hoover. Prominently located at 301 Park Avenue, between 49th and 50th Street, it extends forty-seven stories above New York City's skyline and hosts 1,413 rooms.

Several of its luxury suites are named after the celebrities who've lived or stayed in them—from the Cole Porter, Frank Sinatra, General MacArthur, and Winston Churchill Suites—to the Royal Suite, named after the Duke and Duchess of Windsor.

But the most expensive and coveted room is the Presidential Suite.

Forward security teams were dispatched to sweep it and prepare for Rube Gilmore's arrival. And right behind them was an entourage of heavily armored SUV's, along with countless more police. Gilmore arrived with a screech of tires and was rushed into the side entrance.

Within seconds Gilmore, McCallister, Gibby, and two Secret Service agents were cramped into an elevator. Piano music sounded from a hidden speaker, but it had the opposite effect and only added to the tense mood. The men regarded each other in silence, waiting for anything to happen.

At the 35th floor, they swiftly walked the narrow hallway and turned right. The door to the Presidential Suite was already open, and a handful of Secret Service agents nodded as McCallister stopped and Rube Gilmore rushed past him.

"Sir, I'm Special Agent in Charge Heather Moore, Secret Service," a woman stated firmly, moving from inside the suite. She was almost six feet tall and physically fit, with a tight blonde ponytail. She was hard but pretty, and wore her Glock tight against her dark, form-fitting pant suit. She looked to McCallister with a flash of recognition, but quickly dismissed him and focused on Gilmore.

"We have you from here, Mr. President," she said, looking back to McCallister. "The FBI and maybe the CIA may be investigating the *assassinations,* but we have your security detail."

Everyone focused on Gilmore. With the initial shock over, he couldn't help but embrace the impressive show of security. And given his massive ego and separation from any real notoriety over the last several years, he reveled in it.

McCallister watched as the man suddenly transformed, becoming more presidential with each passing moment. He regained the color in his face, his eyes held a beaming glare, and he showed determination and fight. The man even seemed to stand straighter.

Clearing his throat, Gilmore nodded to those present. "Well, I hope you all do a better job from here on," he stated, belligerently.

Then, with a steady gait that swelled with false bravado, he moved further into the room and disappeared from sight. He closed the bedroom door behind him, and the agents gathered in the hallway.

McCallister shook his head in disappointment at both Gilmore and Agent Moore. The exchange was too abrupt considering the events of the last several hours, but he had to admit that Agent Moore was correct. The FBI was leading the investigation and the Secret Service had jurisdiction over Rube Gilmore. And if he wasn't so close to FBI agent James Gibson, McCallister himself wouldn't even be involved.

But the director of the CIA understood the big picture and had classified information. He just knew that Falby—the Chameleon—was involved and that *The Last Patriot* operation would likely come back with a mighty roar. He also knew that President Maclemore, the current *sitting* president, would be all over the CIA for help.

So here he was. But his mind was reeling, trying to grasp what had happened.

Until now there had been only four presidential assassinations in American history; and there had been two more in the morning alone! But what everyone feared and what McCallister already knew, was that it was far from over.

McCallister studied Agent Moore for a moment before speaking in a conciliatory manner, trying to find common ground.

"I assume the entire suite's been microwaved and checked for electronics. We've only had access for the last couple hours and this is now a Chinese-owned hotel. Just something to consider."

"We're on it, Mr. Director," Moore responded, knowingly.

"And what about these three designated security rooms?" McCallister asked, motioning to either side of the hallway.

"Checked as well. This is where we'll stay, just like in the past. And there will be an agent at the elevator and one man inside the suite."

McCallister nodded, casually, before turning to Agent Moore. "Looks like Agent Gibson and I have room A4, and you have A2 and A3."

Agent Moore eyed McCallister, incredulously, letting out an exhaustive sigh. "Sir, you're staying here with us?"

"No, Agent Moore, I'm actually going to be *inside* the suite with Gilmore."

"I don't think—"

McCallister was already moving past her; but stopped abruptly at the door to the Presidential Suite. An imposing Secret Service agent stood, steadfast.

"Open it, please," McCallister said, eying the man.

But the agent didn't move.

McCallister braced against the much younger and larger man, his stare burning into him.

"Son, if you don't open this door, I will reach right through you and do it myself."

"Do it, Kevin," Agent Moore called out. "Let President Gilmore inform Director McCallister that he is no longer needed."

With that, the agent turned and removed a key card from his suit pocket. The door opened and McCallister entered, taking in the expansive room.

It was decorated in the Georgian style to mimic the White House.

But McCallister didn't notice the John F. Kennedy rocking chair or the Richard Nixon wall sconces. He didn't care about the stylish, massive rugs under his feet or the original novels by Homer, Shakespeare, Lewis Carroll, and J.K. Rowling on the ornate shelving.

Instead, he quickly scanned and moved around the 2,245 square foot space with purpose, before returning to Agent Moore and her team.

The agent stationed inside the suite was perplexed. "Sir, is something wrong?"

"With all due respect, son, I'm going to be joining you on this overnight detail."

Suddenly, Rube Gilmore emerged from the bedroom on the far side. Gone was the suit he'd been wearing, replaced by an oversized white robe. He crossed the space confidently, with strong stepping and a quick gait. His bare feet seemed to spring up from the thick rugs.

"Director McCallister," he started, eyeing the group. "Is everything okay?"

"Yes, sir," McCallister said. "I was just informing this agent that I'll be joining him for the evening."

"Oh, I see," Gilmore said, enjoying the attention. "And where, exactly would you like to be?"

McCallister motioned to the room Rube Gilmore had just exited. "Standing right outside your door, sir."

Gilmore looked back at the bedroom. "I'm good, Mr. McCallister," he said. "I've been here on three separate occasions and know it well. It's completely secure and as you know I *really like* my privacy."

The words hung in the air, and even Gilmore seemed uncomfortable for a moment. McCallister couldn't help but think of the handful of sex scandals the man had been involved in. How many underage girls, prostitutes, or whatever the man had engaged in? But McCallister didn't stir as the images flooded his mind. Instead, he stood tall and looked to Gilmore, who continued.

"You can stay in one of the outside rooms. It's been a long day and I don't want to feel crowded."

McCallister spoke, but Gilmore was already walking away. Despite the circumstances that forced his stay at the Waldorf, Gilmore seemed to be enjoying himself. McCallister watched him saunter off and close and lock the bedroom door.

"This way," Agent Moore said, placing a heavy hand on McCallister's back and pointing to the exit.

The director of the CIA hesitated, glancing around the room once more. But then, as instructed, he left the Presidential Suite.

"I'll be standing right outside this door in the hallway," he said to the inside agent, who didn't acknowledge the comment.

The heavy door closed and McCallister shook his head in defeat.

The three security rooms were bustling with activity, as the agents filling them tried to get comfortable. Food was delivered and everyone was talking amongst themselves or on phones and laptops. Agent Moore wore headphones and was pointing to a display of monitors, showing all angles of the Waldorf.

McCallister shook his head and moved into Room A4 with Gibby. "Well, at least they *look* productive," he said. "Though I'm not sure what they're all doing."

Gibby remained silent and McCallister continued. "I've got the front door."

And Steve McCallister braced himself against it like an old watchman's guard. His presence was commanding and Gibby, who'd known him for years, garnered more respect for the man.

Agent Moore looked over, and though she wouldn't admit it, even *she* felt better with the director of the CIA there.

Because nothing ever went wrong when Steve McCallister was around.

CHAPTER 25

At 3:47 a.m., a silent vibration went off on Falby's watch. It was intended to wake the assassin if he was asleep, but it was unnecessary.

The killer had been awake for hours and counting the minutes; the excitement washing over him with each passing moment. He'd arrived at the Waldorf Astoria and slipped into the Presidential Suite almost sixteen hours earlier.

Well ahead of Rube Gilmore and his security detail.

He couldn't believe how everything was going as planned. He knew the schedules of his two targets from the day before, and *that* timing had played out to perfection.

And although it was public knowledge that Rube Gilmore would be speaking at the New York Stock Exchange, Falby couldn't have known with certainty that the man would be moved to the Waldorf Astoria's Presidential Suite after the two assassinations.

Falby had put the odds at about 20%; with the more *real* probability of Gilmore being whisked away to a more secure and undisclosed location.

Still, a 20% chance was more than enough for Falby to start his meticulous planning. So, the killer had decided on a Trojan Horse strategy, where he would enter the Presidential Suite in advance and wait for his prey to come to him.

It started weeks earlier when Gilmore's schedule was announced. Falby had legitimately purchased a two-night stay in the Presidential Suite, in complete disguise.

He'd immediately gone to work behind closed doors, spending considerable time on a very specific piece of furniture—a decorative armoire made of solid walnut—that sat inconspicuously in the far corner of the smaller living room.

Falby hated to defile the piece, as it was over three hundred years old and made in France during the time of King Louis XIV. But he was able to remove the back, modify the two lower shelves, add Mylar foil, and create several air holes on the false bottom, just a couple feet away from an air vent.

The entire backing was now retrofitted to be unscrewed from the inside, while still looking intact and formidable from the exterior. It took most of the first day to complete the work. Then he'd practiced getting in and out, until he could do so in under ninety seconds each way.

The first night, Falby had confined himself inside for a full eight hours, testing the space and his own physical and mental agility. It was obviously cramped, but he hadn't expected how hot it would be with the Mylar foil preventing his body heat from escaping.

So, the next day he added several more air holes.

The second night, he stayed in the armoire for fifteen hours—a longer period than required—but the extra time lent confidence to his plan. He entered and exited the piece a dozen more times, honing his motions and moving in absolute silence.

He knew Secret Service procedure; and even though the arrival of Rube Gilmore was unplanned, there were very specific security protocols.

The rooms would be scanned for electrical devices and heat signatures. But although the Mylar foil proved effective in blocking his body heat from detection, it would also leave a black space on the scanning monitor that could raise concern. He hoped that the immediacy of the situation and the age and worth of the furniture itself would be enough to overlook it, but it was out of Falby's control, which was rare.

The other uncertainty was video surveillance. Falby had acquired a Waldorf bellman's uniform and a cloned elevator key days earlier. There were several employees going up and down every floor at all hours. If a trained eye looked for the right thing, it would be evident that someone had entered and not exited the Presidential Suite.

But these concerns were irrelevant now.

It was 3:47 a.m.

And time for strike three.

Falby placed the night vision goggles on his head. Then he methodically removed the six screws from the inside and gently separated the entire wood backing from the enormous armoire.

He rolled his limber body out and laid on the floor, his senses peaking, while he acclimated to the room. He slowly stretched and controlled his breathing, as he removed the Walther P22, with the Gemtech suppressor already attached.

Peering across the room in total darkness, he saw a Secret Service agent sprawled across a sofa, with one shoe on a pillow and the other on the floor. Falby focused on the man's chest, happy to see it gently rising and falling in peaceful slumber.

He looked to the front entrance to see a bright seam of light where the door met the wood floor. Although the lone agent within the suite was at rest, there was a security detail just outside that was certainly *not*.

He would deal with them soon enough.

Falby rose to a controlled stand, still flexing his muscles and thankful to be out of the small space. Then, he walked straight to the Secret Service agent and picked up a decorative pillow. He glanced at the front door about forty feet away, before placing the muzzle into the pillow and putting it on the man's head.

Simultaneously he pulled the trigger, feeling the puff of air that freed the man's soul. The body jerked for a split second before falling limp, but Falby's stare never left the front door. Spent sulfur filled the air, but the distant clock continued to tick, and nothing stirred inside or outside of the suite.

Satisfied, Falby removed several long metal pins and went to work on the door that would bring him to Rube Gilmore. In seconds, a small click allowed the door to creak open, and Falby focused on the large bulk in the center of the oversized bed.

The body moved and Falby was surprised to see the man suddenly tense, as his torso rose. In the darkness, Rube Gilmore couldn't have seen Falby as Falby saw him through night-vision lenses, but the assassin noticed a look of concern—maybe even a premonition of fate—that was soon replaced with fear and confusion.

But it was short-lived, as Falby made no time in pointing his weapon at Rube Gilmore's forehead and firing a single whispered shot that sent the man back into the expensive sheets, very much dead.

Strike three, Falby thought to himself, as he moved from the room and back to the armoire. He removed a small bag and undressed; donning exercise shorts, a Nike T-shirt, running shoes, and a head band. But more importantly, he grabbed the bag of grenades, his trusted Sig Sauer P365, and his *own* heat signature scanner.

Softly moving to the front door, he stopped short, holding his weapon steady and scanning the heat signatures in the hallway and adjacent rooms. Just a few feet away and on the other side of the door his monitor showed the image of an imposing figure.

Falby guessed there was a federal agent, armed to the hilt and almost as big as the door itself. He looked to be about six foot three and about 210 pounds. A big boy for sure, but still no match for the fury that awaited him.

To the right, another agent sat on what looked to be a sofa and to the left about eight others were in different positions, with two standing. Muffled conversation could be heard, but Falby couldn't hear specifics through the heavy door.

Falby placed the scanner on the floor next to his night vision goggles, before removing the first set of grenades.

They were homemade, specific for the task at hand. His was a smaller, more compact unit than the traditional Mills version. While it held the common amount of fragmentation, he'd added a smoking application, with less TNT and white phosphorus to reduce noise. The fuse was kept to the standard 4.5 seconds.

The consummate affect would be 100% removal of the threat, with a layer of smoke to disguise the action. The crucial seconds just before detonation would allow for separation and hopefully his ability to eliminate any agents down the hall, away from the explosions.

Falby took several deep breaths, expelling the air silently, as he closed his eyes and played out the next several moments in his mind.

Then with a steady heartbeat and resolute calm, he opened his eyes, as a knowing look washed over him. He was all too ready to meet what was on the other side of the door.

CHAPTER 26

Steve McCallister stood resolute against the door, just outside the Presidential Suite, staring straight ahead.

In the several hours he'd been standing guard, he'd allowed his mind to wander. It would be impossible not to. But then his thoughts would return acutely to the present, and the current events he was *still* trying to comprehend.

He wasn't sure why he was standing against the door, instead of the younger, more enabled, and polished federal agents in the adjacent rooms. He was, after all, the director of the CIA and not a field agent.

Still, he had an internal calling to be on site and part of the security detail for Rube Gilmore. He knew this wasn't over. If Falby was involved in the assassinations, he wouldn't stop until his mission was complete and that would bring him right to this door.

McCallister involuntarily winced as he thought of Falby.

They called him the Chameleon for his expert ability to move around so easily and undetected. More than once—even in the most impossible and compromising of situations—the man had changed his colors and disappeared, evading capture.

And he'd always made it look so easy.

McCallister tracked Falby to Chile just a few years earlier; and *personally* took him into the CIA's clandestine prison system. But the man had escaped, only to be found, again by McCallister, in Cape Verde almost two months prior. But just before McCallister pounced, explosions rang out and the Chameleon disappeared.

Coming back into the present, McCallister shuffled his feet and stood straighter, looking down the short hall, expectantly. He'd taken three short breaks, each time to walk the thirty paces to the end of the hall and another sixty to where a Secret Service agent was guarding the elevator.

Everything was as it should be in the dead of night. The assembly of Secret Service, FBI, and CIA were in constant contact and even wired into the broader investigation.

McCallister continued a silent watch, scanning the walls and looking straight ahead. All night he'd imagined Falby coming down the hall at him with guns blazing, and in each scenario McCallister dropped to one knee, fired, and emptied his clip.

The vision lent him purpose, and he was ready for anything that would come at him.

But McCallister couldn't have expected Falby to come from *behind* him.

The door opened behind Steve McCallister, but before he could react, he felt pressure and then excruciating pain in his back. A quick blow to the head followed and his body was slammed against the adjacent wall, knocking him out.

Falby stepped over McCallister, throwing two grenades in each of the forward rooms, and spraying silent gunfire into the third, striking three additional agents with head shots. Then he bolted down the hall; turning and running directly toward a surprised agent, who was leaning against the elevator door and obviously distracted in the mundane.

Falby got off two shots as he ran toward him; seconds after the hallway was shaken by the spent grenades behind him. The agent fell but Falby still didn't stop as he ignored the elevator and turned right, bolting down the stairs to the lower levels.

He descended each flight of stairs quickly, then rested at the base of the stairwell, reloading his Sig. He exited forcefully into a small corridor, finding two more federal agents, and eliminating them swiftly.

Then he moved to the right and down another half flight of stairs, leading to the side parking garage. Removing the Lunar 9 suppressor, he placed his Sig inside a hidden waistband holster, then started a light jog and exited the garage.

He was met with humidity and the familiar smells and distant sounds of the city streets. Dressed perfectly for a jog, he started an easy run down 50th street, before weaving through the narrower streets.

After six blocks, he allowed a smile to play on his face, as he paused and leaned down to stretch. His steely eyes searched everywhere, looking for signs of pursuit. But instead, the natural early morning drone of the midtown Manhattan streets was all he heard.

Satisfied, he continued a light jog for several more blocks, finally hearing the first sirens south, moving away from him.

From there, the Chameleon was gone.

CHAPTER 27

"We need police and ambulatory support, and every available agent to the 35th floor now!" Gibby screamed into his mouthpiece. "We have multiple fatalities and Rube Gilmore has been compromised! Suspect is a lone male, armed and dangerous!"

Agent Gibson had been unconscious for a few minutes. His body was numb, and his ears were ringing, as he hovered over Steve McCallister, with blood pouring from his own unchecked wounds.

"Steve!" he yelled, slapping the unconscious man hard.

The seconds were painstakingly long, and time seemed to stand still. A stolen glance to his left revealed wounded men and women, a few moving erratically and making terrible sounds. Most, though, were limp, their bodies blown apart and splayed out in death.

Gibby noticed Agent Moore, her legs blown out and gone, her torso twisted. He looked into her hollow eyes, just as they blinked. A gurgled sound lifted from her cherry lips, and he moved over to her.

"You're fine, just stay with me," Gibby yelled. "Just stay with me."

But she turned to him, her features relaxing as she swallowed hard. "I'm so sorry," she managed.

Gibby held her head in his hands as she uttered her last words. Then her glassy eyes closed, and her chest fell.

He jumped back to McCallister, lifting away burning debris. The smoke was gaining, and pockets of fire were spreading through the hallway, which was now one big room. Instinctively, Gibby grabbed a fire extinguisher and moved it over the flames, as more black smoke crowded the area.

With the fire out, he moved to McCallister again.

"Steve," he yelled, shaking him. "Wake up, man, we've got work to do!"

Suddenly McCallister's eyes flew open. His chest expanded and he gasped for air. A sharp pain erupted from his back, and he turned over, ripping his shirt off. The Kevlar vest had saved him from the gun shots to his back. But the subsequent blasts had knocked the wind out of him and rendered him unconscious.

Gibby left McCallister to check on the others. Most were dead, but a few were becoming more aware through the frenzy.

Gibby looked to the blown-out entrance to the suite, knowing what he'd find. With newfound energy, McCallister rose and he and Gibby limped into the room. The interior was remarkably untouched by the explosions, which were meant for the security detail, and save the black smoke filtering in, the place looked peaceful.

McCallister saw the dead agent on the couch and dashed into the master bedroom. He knew the open door was a tell-tale sign, but he had to see for himself. A bulk of sheets covered the center of the bed, and as McCallister drew closer there was no mistaking the pool of blood on the pillow.

Rube Gilmore was dead, with a single bullet wound to his head. His face was cast in a mask of terror, detailing his final moments, and a trickle of blood ran from the crease of his mouth.

"He was in here the whole time," McCallister managed, looking back into the living room. "Gilmore didn't have a chance!"

Gibby looked to McCallister, shaking his head. "What just happened?"

McCallister shot a look at Gibby, a mixture of pain, anger, and resiliency. "Falby is back and he's playing for keeps."

"Falby? But how could one man possibly—"

McCallister cut Gibby off. "There's no time for 'how's' and 'what's.' We have to secure this crime scene, get medical attention to those agents, and I've gotta get to our only remaining ex-president."

"You think he's gonna go after a guy in his nineties, with severe dementia on his death bed?"

McCallister didn't answer. He was deep in thought, trying to reconcile things.

Gibby continued. "I mean the guy's asleep most of the time and nearly catatonic when he's awake. And now he'll be surrounded by every available Secret Service agent we have!"

McCallister remained silent.

There was no need to waste time on needless explanations or words, and Gibby knew the answers anyway. When McCallister said something, he meant it and there was no stopping him.

McCallister and Gibby moved from the Presidential Suite, thankful to see ambulatory support had arrived. Both were met with EMT's and Gibby suddenly felt dizzy, as a rag was pressed against his bleeding head wound.

Gibby was lucky to survive the blasts, but he'd been hit by considerable shrapnel. He was losing a lot of blood from several deep cuts and an EMT caught him as he passed out.

McCallister waved off any medical attention, as he tested a light jog that quickly erupted into a full sprint down the hallway.

He had to get to James Preston in California.

He was the only remaining former president.

CHAPTER 28

Steve McCallister stared out from the window of the Gulfstream 100, before returning to the notebook he'd been writing in.

It contained every hunch he'd had since Bowman, Montgomery, and now Gilmore's death. Every angle, each working theory. How did they do it? Where were they now, where were they going? And what was the strategy?

Then he focused on what was bothering him. Who or whom? Was there only one assassin or could there be a full team? Could his gut reaction be right; that it *was* Falby, a lone assassin hell-bent on killing the presidents?

But to what end and why? None of the four former leaders held any real power. They were just hallmarks of the past.

McCallister thought of *The Last Patriot* operation and how Falby had worked in plain sight. Could Falby have even more help this time around?

Some turbulence rocked the jet and Steve looked up to the main cabin, where a member of the three-person crew gave him a thumbs up. McCallister glanced at his watch. They were about an hour from touchdown at the Charles M. Schulz—Sonoma County Airport, west of Sacramento.

From there he would be transported by a local team to James Preston's residence. And he would stay until he was absolutely sure the man was 100% safe.

McCallister was met by two members of the San Francisco CIA field team directly on the tarmac. A black Escalade took them through the inner workings of the airport, and with a wave to the guard, they exited and eventually found Route 101 North.

President Preston's estate was an easy forty-minute ride northeast of Cloverdale. As they got closer, the mountains and valleys rose and fell, in a picturesque view that reminded McCallister of a nature calendar.

Trees sprung from the landscape between rock formations, as scattered birds flew high against a deep blue sky. The scenery was breathtaking and McCallister took a brief respite from the atrocities of the last few days.

Arriving at the estate, they were greeted by the Secret Service and identification was presented. A large, red-faced man approached them, and his dismay and frustration were evident.

"McCallister, right?" the man asked, making no attempt to shake hands. "Director of the CIA?"

"Yes, sir."

The man looked down, frowning and the tension was palpable. "Well, why not, right?" the man began. "I'm Special Agent Mike Pritt, Secret Service. And just how can we help you?"

McCallister nodded, cordially. "As you know three of our presidents are down and the one remaining is in your charge. I have a working theory as to who is behind this. I know this man and I know his abilities. I'd like to review your protocols and security detail and hang around for a bit."

McCallister spoke genuinely. He expected a certain level of hostility from the Secret Service but had no intention to infringe.

Pritt realized the same, nodding to the group. "Okay, then. But your weapons stay at the gate."

"Can we walk the perimeter, first?" McCallister asked. "I'd like to get an outside-looking-in perspective."

"Sure thing, we have a couple of golf carts over here and can—"

"Actually, do you mind if we *walk* it? Just wanna capture as much detail as I can."

"Be my guest," the man replied, waving his hand, and beginning a casual stride outside the gate.

McCallister looked to the sky and the surrounding countryside. He'd read all about the sprawling Preston estate on the flight over.

Pritt pointed to the distance. "This place is naturally fortified, with mountains all around and a couple of wide streams flowing through the valley. There are only two roads coming in and there's an electrified fence around the perimeter, with cameras placed as far as six miles."

Two walls protect the estate itself. The exterior electrified fence is fifteen feet tall, with barbed wire and motion sensors. The inner one is more aesthetic, a twenty-foot, steel-braced concrete wall with ivy covering the entire inner face. The perimeter fencing is almost seven-thousand feet enclosing over ten acres.

McCallister stopped, looking to the tall trees and the mountainside beyond them.

"I know what you're thinking, McCallister. With that angle, could a sniper be perched on a tree or on a ridge and take a shot, and the answer is no. We've had Marine snipers out here, as part of their training and no one—not even with the time to do so—could pick a spot that would even come close. And the entire structure and windows are completely bulletproof up to .50 millimeters.

"And as far as a 9/11 scenario, we are so far out of the air traffic patterns that we'd have ample time to respond to a rogue aircraft with Patriot missiles on site."

McCallister continued a slow walk. "It looks like you guys have thought of everything, right?"

"Look McCallister, I'm not gonna take the bait on that, blow sunshine up your ass, or try to prove that we're invincible here, because anything is possible. But between our infrastructure and 24/7 roving patrols, which have quadrupled over the last couple days, I think we're in pretty good shape.

"Also, I don't have to remind you, that President Preston sleeps about twenty hours a day, suffers from prostate cancer and Alzheimer's, and is bedridden. His personal detail—the fourth ring—has also been increased. And other than the two doctors who've been caring for him for over ten years each and the nurses who are also tenured, I can't see anything getting to him."

The tour lasted another thirty minutes, with nothing of consequence exchanged. They arrived back at the main gate and, without another word, McCallister handed his firearm to the guard.

"Thanks for the tour, Agent Pritt. Can we head in to see the man, now?"

CHAPTER 29

McCallister had to admit that Pritt was spot on. The place was well-fortified and secure.

He was led through the kitchen; a magnificent open design, with two Sub-Zero refrigerators, a stove top that would rival any fancy restaurant, and a large granite island in the center of the room. Several staffers went about their duties, oblivious to the federal agents.

As they moved from the main area to the residence, the décor changed. The furniture was more rustic, the feeling more relaxed.

McCallister looked to a wall to see several family portraits, some several generations old, and personal effects from another time. There were leatherbound books on a shelf, a few old vases, and a Civil War era bayonet, rusted and lying dormant on the mantle. A large boar's head hung on the far wall, no doubt a hunting prize from the president's more active days.

Moving down a long hallway, the mood was even more subdued, as McCallister was introduced to the medical team in an adjacent room.

Then he entered Preston's bedroom, and even he was taken back by what he saw.

There had been stories and rumors about Preston's health for some time, but the Press had been respectful. Now, McCallister hardly recognized the man, who four decades earlier was such a charismatic and prolific leader.

Preston had been a robust Republican, his wife a darling of the Hollywood film industry. Together, they were a perfect pair and spoke to the hearts of the American people. But now Preston looked so weak and frail. His face was ashen, and his cheek bones protruded out and were well defined against tight, gray skin. There were tubes running underneath the bed sheets, and oxygen flowing under his nose.

A doctor was bedside, examining his only patient. He looked to the monitor, frowning at what he saw. Temperature of 100.8, blood pressure 136/88, heart rate at 110 bpm.

Without regarding McCallister, he turned to the nurse. "How much O2 is he on?"

"Four liters," she said, nervously.

Dr. Duffy shook his head, looking back to the monitor. Preston's respiratory rate was now twenty-four breaths per minute and his O2 saturation was 86%.

Suddenly Preston was sweating and breathing erratically. The doctor placed a stethoscope on the man's chest, closing his eyes and listening intently.

"His lungs are wet. He needs Lasix to get some of this fluid off," he said under his breath.

McCallister spoke up, moving further into the room. "Sir, my name is Steve McCallister. I'm with the CIA. What's going on with—"

Dr. Duffy ignored McCallister and looked to the nurse. "Increase his O2 flow rate to six liters and give him 40 mgs of Lasix, IV push."

Then he turned to Agent Pritt at the door. "His breathing is getting worse. We may need a medevac outta here."

Finally, the doctor glanced at McCallister, and his eyes grew wide. "Steve McCallister; the director of the CIA?"

"That's right. What's his condition?"

"His respiratory status has progressively worsened over the last few days. He now has pulmonary edema, or fluid build-up in the lungs. It all started with a cough and shortness of breath but has gotten a lot worse. His lungs sound terrible."

"And this is due to what, you think?"

"It's not clear. The fluid build-up could be a result of his heart failing, an infection, or an inflammatory process leading to his acute respiratory distress. Today has been particularly bad and we're struggling to maintain oxygen levels. All day he's been somnolent and only responding to painful stimulant."

McCallister grimaced. "Seems a bit coincidental, though, with the other three presidents being assassinated over the last couple of days?"

"Yes, but he hasn't moved for over eighteen months, with the same medical crew the entire time. And as sick as he is, he's probably the safest of them all."

McCallister was unmoved. "Have you ordered additional tests? Think of every possibility. Run every panel and rush it."

Dr. Duffy looked back at Preston, now agitated and in clear respiratory distress. Suddenly the man's eyes flew open, and he looked around the room with unmistakable fear. His back arched upward, and his body crashed into the side of the railing lined bed. His coughing became even more severe as his O2 saturation fell to 72%.

His condition was deteriorating by the moment.

The doctor reached for the emergency bag, turning to the nurse. "We need to emergently intubate him now! Grab the endotracheal tube and the stylet. I'll start bagging him and see if we can get his O2 saturation up."

But after two minutes of bagging, the O2 remained low, and then fell to 52%. Preston was now unresponsive.

The nurse called out desperately, as the monitor sounded more alarms. "His heart rate is dropping, now in the 30's. I don't feel a pulse!"

Dr. Duffy checked at the carotid, confirming it. "Begin chest compressions."

Steve McCallister watched as the medical staff worked on Preston for over a half hour, with every effort expended.

But everything failed.

And at the end, the only sound was the even tone of the monitor as it rang out in the stale room, confirming James Preston had flatlined.

CHAPTER 30

President Maclemore declared all flags at half-mast for four days of mourning.

And in that time, the nation paused.

Concerts and sporting events were cancelled, work and vacations were interrupted, and a stunned nation fell numb.

The media was exploding with around-the-clock coverage. They tried to cram as much information as possible into their segments, even though the initial investigations were still underway.

But what *was* widely reported was that the former presidents were dead and there were no suspects in custody. After reporting the initial facts, they delved into each man's legacy; with the fringe media branching out into conspiracy theories, and hosting an array of personalities, all of whom cogitated the impossible with excitement and vigor.

President Preston's death was not yet ruled a homicide and the media, along with everyone else, were impatiently waiting the autopsy results. But everyone believed it to be an assassination. The timing alone all but guaranteed it, and it was one more part of the developing story.

After four days of mourning, two days of public viewing would take place in each man's home state capital: Austin, Frankfort, Albany, and Sacramento. Then the fallen presidents would be flown to Washington D.C.

Thousands would line the streets to witness the funeral procession along Constitution Avenue, as it moved solemnly at exactly twenty miles per hour. Keeping with tradition, the transfer of the casketed remains to a caisson would occur at the intersection of Constitution Avenue and 16th Street, the point at which the White House is first visible. From there, the procession would made its way to the Capitol Rotunda.

All four were to lie in state for another two days, before a planned memorial service at the National Cathedral. From there, private ceremonies and burials were arranged, per the families wishes.

And through it all, a stunned nation would bear witness to it all.

CHAPTER 31

Pip Palmer stared at his computer screen, as he picked at the remains of his lunch. With the honey chicken gone, along with the garlic croutons and crisp cucumbers, he flicked the arcing slices of red onions and baby tomatoes aside and tried to find the fresher pieces of lettuce within the plastic tray of salad.

Everyone was called in and Pip had never seen things so busy at the NSA. People were standing around and offering support to one another, while others ran past with paperwork meant for higher stations.

Pip went about his duties with fervor, sitting at the Key, listening to idle cell phone chatter, and switching towers and frequencies at random. His system had a parameter search with over four hundred target words, and he was prompted when six were mentioned in a single thread.

Most of the phone conversations he listened to yielded nothing. There were aspiring novelists discussing ideas, people rehashing news stories about terror-related incidents, and others simply joking around.

To that end, he'd heard everything.

There were couples engaging in phone sex and extra marital affairs, exposing dark, personal secrets. And there was Pip and scores of others within the NSA, deciphering what items should be recorded and then elevating the more serious findings to the investigative level.

Pushing away his lunch, Pip rearranged his headphones and switched to another cell tower, putting his feet up on his desk.

And that's when he heard it and began recording.

At first, he couldn't believe it. He actually recognized one of the voices!

Pip immediately planted his feet on the floor and inched up in his seat. He tightened his headphones, shaking his head, and became wide-eyed with every word.

Then he worked the keyboard and ran targeted diagnostics, isolating the cell tower and affirming at least *one* of the participants. He ran a voice recognition software model with a sample, and it came back at a 99.77% match.

His hands moved furiously over the keyboard as he tried to locate the other caller. The signal was blocked so he opened another circuit, launching one of his own software applications. He was blocked again, which he thought odd, due to the technicalities involved. So, he employed yet *another* diagnostic to identify the specific phone.

While it was working, he couldn't believe what he was hearing!

Then his system beeped, and he was surprised to realize that the unknown person on the line was trying to locate *him*! Pip countered with another one of his software inventions, flipping the signal so it was revolving and untraceable.

Then a specific number appeared on his screen. He'd isolated the second person to a government phone within the Department of Defense. But then his screen showed an alert and he realized that he was now exposed. Whoever he was up against had won the sparring contest and had identified Pip and his location!

Pip was dumbfounded and couldn't believe it. Whoever had tracked him did it so easily and had a technical tenacity that seemed to exceed his own, and that was chilling.

The call ended, and Pip saved the recording to a flash drive, which he quickly removed and placed in his pocket.

His problems were two-fold.

He clearly knew the identity of *one* of the callers and that the other was within the Department of Defense community. But whoever the mystery caller was, knew *exactly* who and where Pip was, pinpointed to his exact workstation.

Pip knew he was required to elevate the threat and bring it to his superior. But with the information on the recording and its far-reaching implications, his human instinct took hold.

And, based on what Pip heard, he'd be eliminated or neutralized if found.

So, Pip, flush with adrenaline, got up from the Key and shut it down.

The person on the recording was dangerous. And he or she, while using a DOD circuit, could be anywhere; even ten offices down, within D.C., Europe, or anywhere across the intel community.

Pip exhaled deeply, his mind racing to every impossible scenario. Then his thoughts settled on the only conclusion.

His life was most definitely in danger.

CHAPTER 32

Pip grabbed his keys and wallet.

Then he stood, unsteadily; scanning his office for anything he may need. He wouldn't be back any time soon.

He hastily opened and closed desk drawers and came across the photograph of Lisa Wellington. There was that smile, postponed in time. The same face he'd been looking at for weeks now. It reassured him, lent him pause and called to him.

He grabbed the photo and left, moving down the long hall with eyes on the floor.

He felt like he was in a movie. An alternate reality.

His body temperature rose. Was his every move under scrutiny? His knees were wobbly, but he tried to maintain a steady gait. Finally, he was outside and walking fast through the parking lot. With the high blue sky as the ceiling, he wondered if he was being watched. How many satellites had *he* moved—even recently—with a flick of his mouse and some targeted taps on the keyboard?

Thankfully, he made it to his car and moved easily to the south gate. He waved at the guards without making eye contact and started east on Route 32. But he felt no safer. Now his enemy could be anywhere, from the satellites high above to the cars flying by on the two-lane highway.

Had he really heard what he'd thought he'd heard? And was it really who he thought it was?

He picked up his cell phone and dialed Seargant, placing the receiver to his ear and checking the rearview mirror. He got lost in the ringing tone and even sped up to pass a slowing minivan.

"This is Seargant," the man announced, flatly.

"Seargant!" Pip exclaimed, hearing his own raspy voice for the first time in hours. "I really need to see or talk to you. Like right away. I mean—"

Pip went silent as two police cars showed behind him, moving fast. "Hold on, actually. I think I—"

Pip placed the cell phone down and slowed, glancing back at the rearview mirror, and moving back into the right lane. The police cars didn't slow and thankfully screamed past Pip, taking the next exit onto 175.

Exhaling loudly, Pip picked up the cell phone again. "Seargant, you still there?"

"Yeah, Pip. What's going on?"

Pip controlled his breathing, thinking things through. He had information directly linked to the presidential assassinations. He knew the identity of one conspirator and the *other* could be anyone within the DOD community!

But then another thought took over. Could he trust Seargant? Could he trust *anyone*?

"Actually, Seargant, it's okay. I came across something and I need to think things through. I'm gonna leave town for a while, but I'll get back to you. I think I know some terrible things about some even worse people, and they know who I am. I'm worried about Sam, my roommate. I think they're gonna come after me and anyone near me, and I don't know what to do."

"Where are you now Pip?"

Another deep breath. "Look, I really like you Seargant, but I don't think I should say anything more. This is really bad!"

"Look Pip, I need you to come to me right now. Things are happening fast. This isn't public knowledge, but Preston *was* assassinated. It was *not* natural. He had traces of ricin in his respiratory system. Enough to kill him five times over."

"My God, they did do it," Pip said, almost to himself.

"What did you say, Pip? *Who* did *what?*"

Pip remained silent as he gripped the steering wheel tighter. He was doing almost eighty.

"Pip!" Seargant yelled through the receiver.

"I've gotta go, Seargant. I just need some time, okay?"

"Pip, you'll be safe with me."

"As safe as Preston was, tucked in his bed, with 24/7 medical attention and Secret Service protection?"

Seargant went silent and Pip spoke again, solemnly.

"To be honest Seargant, I don't think I'll ever be safe again."

And then he ended the call and tossed his cell phone from the car window, driving even faster into a clouded future.

CHAPTER 33

Pip tried to recall every thriller novel he could.

What did the guy on the run do?

He contemplated the next couple of hours, then to tomorrow and beyond. If he lasted that long. He needed to get to Sam to make sure he stayed away from the house. Then he needed his personal laptop and computer bag, some cash, pre-paid cell phones, and supplies.

He needed a car!

If they knew who he was, his car was compromised, and obviously his cell phone was no good. It was on the side of the road somewhere on Route 32.

He raced down Cornhill Street, parking directly across from his front door. Then he darted into the house, knowing there could already be some bad people waiting. Still, he had to be there. Everything depended on it. He ran to the stairs, calling out for Sam, who didn't reply.

He spent a few minutes throwing several changes of clothes, some shoes, and random toiletries into duffel bags. He grabbed his personal laptop, power cord, and computer bag. As a final thought, he ran into Sam's room and went straight for the top shelf of his roommate's closet, removing an old leather bag, which he slung over his shoulder.

A sound came from downstairs and he stopped, closing his eyes in total concentration. His temples throbbed and sweat was pouring from him. His heart beat faster and he couldn't control his breathing.

"Pip?" Sam called out from below. "You home, man?"

Pip ran down the stairs, seeing Sam and rushing by him. "Sam, come with me, trust me. I'm not kidding!"

"Dude, what's going on? Wanna hit McGarvey's or—"

"Sam! Follow me now," Pip yelled over his shoulder, running awkwardly with the bags.

Pip carefully opened the front door, looked up Cornhill Street and ran across the narrow road, ignoring his car. The large parking lot between Main Street and Cornhill belonged to a teacher's association, and towing was strictly enforced. But in the far corner, there was a small, unpaved sliver of land they *didn't* own, on which a small car could fit nicely. They called it the nook.

Sam was behind Pip, trying to catch up.

"Dude! Slow down," he yelled, now running.

Pip got to the car, his heart nearly beating out of his chest. This was the moment of truth. One of Sam's many friends had been trying to sell the car for months. It was a Toyota, about fifteen years old. "Take it out for a spin whenever you want," he'd said more than once. "The doors don't lock, and the keys are under the seat. It's always parked at the nook near your house."

Pip opened the car door and threw in the bags. Then he turned to his friend.

"Sam, I need you to get in right now."

Sam moved to the passenger side, sliding in, as Pip reached under the seat for the keys. The car's engine coughed but eventually came to life and they pulled onto Main Street through the side alley.

On Rowe Boulevard they settled in and Pip's posture relaxed.

"All right, man," Sam started. "Where are we going? What's going on? And I assume we're not hitting McGarvey's for wings tonight?"

"Sam, I really need you to listen. And I need you to suspend disbelief and believe me more than you've ever believed anything. What I'm about to tell you is completely true and we are *both* in very real danger."

"What are you talking—"

"Sam," Pip interrupted, speaking evenly, and taking control. "You really don't know what I do at the NSA and that's great, and in fact, required. But I'm an analyst. One with some pretty special skills and security clearances."

They came to the light at Taylor Avenue and stopped, watching a few government employees from the courthouse scurry by.

"Have you been watching the news lately?"

"You mean about the dead presidents? Of course, it's the only thing on!"

"Well, here's some more news for you. President Preston *was* assassinated. It was ricin. It just hasn't been disseminated to the public yet."

"Really? Then how do you know?" Sam asked.

Pip ignored the question and kept going. "Look, about an hour ago I came across some very important information that only *I* know, and it's about the assassinations. The thing is these bad people know who I am. They know I was listening to them, and I'm exposed."

"Wait, you were eavesdropping?"

"Part of my job, Sam. I was well within my protocols, but that's not the point."

"That's awesome!"

"Sam. I think my life is in danger and because you're my roommate, it puts you in harm's way as well."

For the first time Sam fell silent, as he exhaled loudly and ran his hands threw his long blonde locks. He took the tie out of his hair, scratched his head, and re-applied a tight ponytail. Looking out the window, he shook his head.

"So, what are you gonna do, man?"

"That's the thing. I'm just a computer analyst. And the very people I should go to could be involved. I don't wanna tell you anything because that makes you even more vulnerable. But don't go back to the house, at least for now."

They drove in silence for several moments, both contemplating each other and what they should do. Pip hoped Sam believed him, and more importantly accepted the possible danger. But his friend's silence meant he was still uncertain and clearly not comprehending the situation.

Pip turned into the Wawa on Bestgate Road and hopped out.

"Sam, can I borrow your ATM card? How much do you have in the bank?"

Sam opened his wallet and threw the card to him. "About $800 but take whatever you need. You know the PIN."

Pip ran into the store; quickly buying all five of the pre-paid cell phones on display, a few bags of chips, some apples, a national map, a case of water, and the latest Jeff Gunhus novel. It would be a welcome distraction to get through any downtime.

Using Sam's card, he withdrew $500 from the ATM and then did the same with his own card. Then he used his two credit cards to make cash advances for an additional $4,000.

They drove toward the Westfield Mall in silence. Pip knew they should talk, but he'd already said what he could.

Pip stopped the car at the small lot near the Bow Tie movies.

"So, what now?" Sam asked.

"Now I leave you and you don't tell anyone anything. See a movie, think things through, and walk around. Take an Uber but *don't* go home. I mean it, just spend the night somewhere else and stay away from downtown. Walk in crowds. Be aware of everything. I'll be in touch in a few days."

Sam opened the door and got out. "You got it, buddy. Good luck."

"And tell your friend that I'm buying his car and going to Ocean City for the weekend."

"Will do," Sam said, standing idly and looking at Pip, helplessly.

Pip moved his lips to say something, but just swallowed hard, with a wave.

"Thanks, Sam," he whispered to himself.

And as he watched his best friend amble away and disappear into the mall, Pip wondered if anything would ever be the same again.

CHAPTER 34

Sam entered the food court, pausing to let a family of five pass by.

He was greeted by the typical sounds of low conversation and the bright lights from high above. Pockets of teenagers walked casually, occasionally looking up from their smart phones, as the fast-food vendors worked to feed a gathering dinner crowd. Two young kids ran by with their father in tow, while the mother tended to a baby in a stroller.

Sam walked by the Panda Express, Popeye's, and Chik-Fil-A, where he stopped to sample a piece of spicy chicken, before bounding up the five stairs and checking the movie selections at the kiosk.

There were three new Marvel efforts, two sequels, and a remake; none of which inspired him, so he turned and continued a slow walk toward Macy's with no destination in mind.

Could this all be real? Did his best friend just stumble onto a huge conspiracy that could shake the very foundation of their country? Up ahead a crowd was forming in front of a bank of televisions at an electronic store and Sam quickened his pace, arriving behind an old woman with more bags than she could carry.

"What's going on?" he asked to no one in particular, as he focused on the large flat-screen television in the corner.

"It's a press conference. President Preston died of ricin poisoning," someone said, without turning.

Sam stumbled back, taking it all in. Pip was right about the ricin and knew it even before the Press. But did that mean everything else was true? That only Pip had information about it and their lives were in danger?

Sam shook his head. It was always Pip who was the smart one and now he was gone. Conversely, Sam was just a happy-go-lucky soul enjoying a simple life. *We're all just spinning around on this rock*, he would always say.

Sam kept his eyes low to the floor, as he continued to contemplate things. A toddler screamed and Sam reached to catch a stray balloon starting to float away. The mother thanked him, tied the balloon to the boy's wrist and scurried away.

Sam smiled, watching them go, lost in the normalcy all around him. Sure, the world was going mad, but that was always the case. It was out of his control. Who was he, or even Pip, in the grand scheme of things? He reached for his phone, checking it for the first time in an hour.

There were six texts from friends and a handful of emails. Everyone was meeting at McGarvey's over the next few hours, and they were wondering if Sam would make it.

Sam took one last look around, seeing scores of people entering and exiting the stores, a throng of people moving down the wide halls. A Gin Blossoms song played, and he smiled at a sudden revelation.

Whatever Pip was involved in, no matter what he did at that NSA place, had nothing to do with Sam. He ordered an Uber, responded to a group text, and took a right at the Sbarro's to meet his ride.

He would head over to McGarvey's in downtown Annapolis and meet his friends. He vowed not to speak of what he knew, and a little liquid refreshment was just what he needed. Then, maybe he would just make the short walk up Cornhill Street to check on the house.

The man got the call and immediately started toward Annapolis. Then he made another call, and *that* man also changed direction.

Within the hour, both were in place. One parked near the top of Cornhill Street, the other all but invisible, nearby. Each carried a small arsenal and were ready for the task at hand.

It was exactly 4:34 p.m. Fifty-eight minutes since Pip had stumbled onto the conversation; fifty-one minutes since he'd been logged out of the NSA.

Now it was a waiting game.

The man in the car checked his Glock and placed it in his lap, under a towel. He patted the .380 Beretta strapped to his ankle and then the *other* Glock in his shoulder holster.

All three lent him confidence. With his weaponry, things usually had a way of working out.

CHAPTER 35

Pip's mind was reeling.

He'd told Sam all he could, but would his best friend take it to heart and *do* what was asked?

Pip knew he shouldn't overthink things, but he couldn't help it. Sam was a grown man, even several months older, but he was also unreliable. Sure, he meant well and would never *mean* to hurt anyone or himself. But he often acted like an impish child, as if challenging adulthood and responsibility.

Then came the questions that were competing for consideration.

Should he call Jack Seargant back? What would he say? What *could* he say? And was this really even happening?

Pip relaxed and chose to be optimistic. Sam was probably watching a movie and would Uber to a buddy's house. Pip would reach his destination and get a good night's rest, scan the national news and somehow, with a fresh morning start, things would make sense again. That's how it would be.

So, he concentrated on the yellow lines on I-83 north, feeling relieved with each one he left in the rearview mirror. With every mile of separation from Annapolis, the danger eased, and he felt safer.

He'd been careful to take I-97 north to the beltway and then west to avoid the toll at the tunnel. If *they* were tracking him, he couldn't risk being photographed at a toll booth. He'd been on the other side of that hunt and that meant I-95 north was out.

Pip had been listening to NPR since he'd left Sam almost an hour ago. They'd finally broken the story of Preston's autopsy, though the details were still unclear. Pip shook his head in disbelief, accepting the truth. Four presidents had been assassinated in three days! He himself recorded a conversation that spoke to the core of it all!

How could this be happening?

At least his initial plan was a success, and he celebrated the short list of small victories. He'd gotten out of the NSA with proof on a flash drive. He'd warned Sam, ditched his car, picked up a different one, and even gathered some supplies and cash before hitting the road.

Still, he felt vacant inside.

He'd never been out of Maryland and was naïve to the ways of the world. He realized that Sam and Frog were his only friends, and he was feeling exposed and alone with every tick of the clock.

And that's when he thought of *her*. Lisa Wellington. The Wolf Man case.

As crazy as it was, Pip felt a connection to her, albeit one-sided. They'd never met, but he'd saved her life. He'd memorized every curve of her face from the picture and inferred she was a genuine person. Someone he just *knew* he could count on. He just hoped she could feel the same way.

Was that why he instinctively drove north?

He'd kept her cell phone diagnostics from the Wolf Man investigation, and had her address in Phoenixville, Pennsylvania. He could ping her with his laptop but didn't want to risk a trace signal on her end. So, he drove steadily and decided to consult the map as he got closer.

He estimated reaching Phoenixville just after 8 p.m.

Pip considered what he would say to her but became overwhelmed and flustered. Would he just ring her doorbell, wait outside, or what?

He shook his head, dismissing the thoughts altogether. It would work out, he decided. It *had* to work out. Maybe they could go for a walk and he could just explain everything.

And maybe, just maybe, she could help Pip stay alive.

CHAPTER 36

Lisa Wellington awoke from a late afternoon nap at 7:15 p.m. and walked downstairs for a little dinner and family interaction. Things had been difficult since the abduction, and her family had given her space and time.

She'd quit her job at Walmart and taken the semester off from community college. Now she spent most of her time in her room; resting, listening to music, surfing social media, and organizing her closet, which was always therapeutic.

Her already stressed relationship with her parents and older brother was under more pressure, though in the days after her rescue they'd grown closer. Now, it seemed, no one knew how to treat her, and silence was the easiest measure.

Before the incident, she'd been taking some healthcare classes at the community college, hoping to transfer into a nursing program. She'd worked part-time as a cashier, paid $200 per month in rent to her parents, and things were steady.

They'd reproached her often, wondering why she didn't work harder; why she didn't increase her credit load to speed up her academic plans. Her parents often reminded her that no twenty-two-year-old should be living with their parents. Her older brother, Jerry was out at eighteen; now married with two kids, living in a nice home a few towns away.

But the chidings were reduced after the kidnapping and Lisa was thankful for it. She'd adjusted as best she could, knowing she was selected at random. She was at the wrong place at the wrong time, and although the incident was harrowing, it made her stronger.

Nothing like it had ever happened in her hometown and she was a quick celebrity. But that was also hard to accept, and she didn't like the spotlight. Lisa thought of the other girls the Wolf Man had taken and killed. She'd been given a second chance and owed it to them and to herself to live a good life.

She chose strength over victimhood.

"Hi, sweetie," her mother called out from the kitchen. "Your father's going to be a little late so help yourself to some stir-fry and rice."

Lisa inhaled the evening's offering, smiling. "Did you put some extra ginger in it?"

"Of course, honey. Just how you like it."

Lisa slid into a seat at the kitchen table, the same wooden circular they'd used for decades. She looked around, noticing the yellow wallpaper that had been there forever. She noticed the small cuckoo clock that hadn't worked in years and the wooden shelf her brother had made in woodshop holding exactly nine cookbooks; none of which had ever been opened. Then she looked out the sliding glass door to the open fields that led to the Wohl-Smyers Farm.

"When are you gonna get rid of that damn cuckoo clock? It doesn't work and is cheesy as hell."

Her mother turned, trading glances between the clock and her daughter. "That was a gift from my Aunt Cynthia, and I happen to love it. But if you're too good for it or anything else, why don't you get your own place and buy a fancy grandfather clock or something?"

Silence ruled as her mother returned to her efforts at the stove with an exaggerated sigh.

Lisa chose a different direction. "Amy and I are going out tonight. Probably hitting the Gin Mill; maybe a movie."

Her mother didn't turn from the sesame chicken. "Just stay together and keep your phone charged."

"Will do," Lisa said, walking over and grabbing a plate.

She scooped up some rice and her mother dumped a healthy portion of chicken and broccoli on the plate. Then Lisa grabbed a bottle of water and plopped down at the table. She stabbed at the food with a fork, watching the steam rise from the hot plate.

Then she looked at that damn cuckoo clock, thinking, *I really need to get outta here.*

CHAPTER 37

The Gin Mill sat modestly on Route 23 in Phoenixville and was a local hot spot for the twenty-something crowd of northern Chester County. It doubled as a coffee shop in the morning hours, with free Wi-Fi and plenty of open space. But in the evening, the grill came to life, the music swelled, and the long, wooden bar was always busy until close.

Lisa liked how she could get a burger and a beer for under ten bucks, and play shuffleboard, darts, or pool, in a casual setting. The guy-to-girl ratio favored her, but she had yet to be impressed with the local talent, most of whom would show up straight from work, reeking of their trade.

Her best friend Amy arrived in true fashion; wearing high heel sling-backs, tight jeans, and a loose top that complemented her cleavage and showed her lean midsection. Her brown hair was long and recently curled, and her piercing blue eyes lit up when she saw her best friend.

"Hey, girly girl," she purred, throwing her hand around Lisa's shoulder, and coming in for an extended hug.

"Hey, baby girl," Lisa struck back, smiling wide and eyeing her friend. "You went all out tonight, didn't you?"

Amy took a seat on a stool, resting her elbows on the high-top pub table. "I figure my sister's away, and I have full use of her closet."

Lisa nodded. Amy's sister, LeeAnne, was no doubt one of the prettiest girls in town. She'd been in makeup since she was ten and always had the body of a girl three years older until she peaked—and seemed to pause—at eighteen. Now twenty-six, she'd moved to New York City to follow her stage acting dreams, coming home once a month telling tales that stretched the imagination.

Lisa studied her longtime friend.

They were "besties" since the first day of middle school, when the two twelve-year old girls simultaneously rushed to get the last seat at a cafeteria table. Lisa, awkward and shy, was first to set her tray down. But when she looked to a very confident Amy, she retreated and offered the seat to her.

Amy quickly sat down, and the other girls were captivated by her glamor. Easy conversation ensued, and soon the table was cackling loudly, with Amy at the center of attention and Lisa slowly withdrawing, suddenly the outsider.

Lisa clutched her lunch tray, her head down, as she turned and left. She made her way to the door, hoping the tears wouldn't start until she was alone and outside. Amy eyed Lisa's exit, following her with interest. She saw the girl wipe away tears, before disappearing from view.

Outside in the courtyard, Lisa palmed an apple, contemplating it. But she wasn't hungry and just held it, frozen in despair. Then Amy appeared next to her, placing her lunch tray on a nearby wall.

"You know, it's too nice a day to sit inside, don't you think?" Amy asked.

Startled, Lisa turned. "Yeah, I guess so."

"I'm Amy Helmsley. Just transferred from East Pikeland."

"Lisa Wellington. I went to Barclay."

The conversation started easily and never stopped. They discussed their busy summer, then shifted to boys and school. Both forgot to eat their lunch, and they were even late for their fourth period classes.

Similar lunches followed and a routine was established. A deep friendship was forged, lasting throughout middle and high school. There was nothing off limits and both girls knew everything about the other.

When the Wolf Man abducted Lisa, it was Amy who organized a local search party and held vigils until her friend was rescued. It was also Amy who stayed with Lisa for days after her return, listening patiently about what she'd endured and hugging her through both tears and silence.

The girls ordered Cosmopolitans, which stretched the capabilities of the bartender. But when the drinks arrived, and the girls toasted each other and tasted the refreshing tang of lemon, they settled in and chatted away.

A steady stream of people arrived, and the music grew louder. The sounds of pool balls crashing, glasses clinking, and a low drone of banter filled the room, as the evening found its pulse and the drinks started flowing.

The girls scanned the crowd, waving at several familiar faces. Amy was confident there was no one of interest and searched her phone for local movie listings.

Lisa looked to the crowd in agreement.

But then she saw a young man in his mid to late twenties. He was very small, maybe just five feet tall, and dressed too nice for the Gin Mill, with khaki pants and a white button down shirt. He immediately looked away, feigning interest in a wall of neon beer signs and a trophy case.

He was out of place but not altogether awkward. And when his eyes moved back to Lisa, she knew he was very interested in her.

But there was something else strange.

He was the only one in the bar not looking at Amy. And no one ever looked at Lisa when Amy was nearby.

CHAPTER 38

Sam took an Uber right to McGarvey's—one of the most historic saloons in downtown Annapolis—walking back into the second bar, where he was greeted by the proprietors, Jimmy Mac and Kevin Havens. He ordered a Yuengling on tap and leaned against the live tree growing in the middle of the room, thinking things through.

The cold glass felt good in his hand. He took a couple generous swigs, eventually finishing it a minute later. Ordering another, he moved to the carpeted stairs leading to the open second floor that was rarely used. Sitting on the third stair, he took another healthy swig, looking straight ahead but seeing nothing.

The last couple of hours had been crazy. As much as he loved and respected Pip, with his friend now gone and time dulling the urgency, he was more confused than ever.

Pensive, Sam finished the rest of the beer, feeling the warm effects of the alcohol. He went to the bar and ordered a third, letting it sit on a coaster untouched, and watching the condensation develop and slide down the frosty pint.

He was a nobody. A simpleton. Just coasting through life with wide eyes, collecting memories and barely getting by. How could *he* be in danger?

And wasn't Pip the same? Surely more educated, grounded, and career-driven, but still a normal kid just living his life.

A group arrived, rather loudly, and Sam turned to see a handful of his friends coming at him. They were roaring with laughter and had clearly been partying somewhere else.

Jeffy, in front, shook Sam's hand and moved to the bartender, ordering a round of shots and draft beers. The others greeted him, enthusiastically, taking the empty stools and forming a semi-circle. Sam settled in easily, comforted and warmed by the drinks and camaraderie.

After the fifth round, with two additional shots in him, Sam was telling stories from years ago, holding court with friends, both new and old.

Well into the night, a redhead caught Sam's eye and they moved into the larger bar and talked for almost an hour. But when he returned from a bathroom break, she was gone. Likewise, his friends had moved on, and with a spinning head and heavy tongue, Sam suddenly felt in need of a warm bed.

He'd drank away the thoughts, uncertainties, and warnings Pip spoke of several hours earlier; so, he walked out the front door, stumbling along the uneven cobblestone. He moved past City Dock Coffee and Federal House, taking a right onto Fleet and a slight left up Cornhill Street.

He couldn't wait to grab a cold bottle of water, get into bed, and sleep well into the next day.

The man looked up, watching Sam lumber directly toward him.

He stepped back into the shadows, allowing his target to pass, just yards away. Then, with a comfortable space of separation, the man emerged from his enclave like a ghost, treading lightly, and mentally preparing for the next several minutes.

He sensed Sam was drunk, based on his sloppy walk and bobbing head. A few burps and coughs confirmed it. Still, the man was unmoved and would not waver. He was always over-prepared and wouldn't let up, even if the mark was weaker than expected.

Sam passed under two overhead streetlights, which cast a long shadow extending to the red cobblestone sidewalk edging the street. He didn't notice the series of porch lights conveniently twisted off earlier, forcing more darkness along his path.

So, Sam disappeared into the shadows, ambling along without a care.

CHAPTER 39

Sam fumbled for the keys, pushing the metal into the lock, and shaking it vigorously. Feeling the full effects of the evening, he felt dizzy and leaned into the door to steady himself.

The lock gave way and he withdrew the key, entering and throwing a light switch in the small kitchen.

Dirty plates, utensils, and glasses filled the sink. The house smelled stale, with a hint of trash in the air. He opened the refrigerator and took out a cold bottle of water and moved into the main living area. An old but comfortable couch lined the right side, with a wooden coffee table next to it. Both faced a modest flat screen television and next to it a black woodburning stove.

Sam moved to the couch, kicking off his shoes, and throwing his keys and some crumpled money onto the table. He gazed up the wooden stairs that led to the bedrooms.

"Pip, are you here, man?" he shouted, like he'd done so often before.

He took several gulps of water, emptying the plastic bottle and tossing it aside A satisfying belch followed, and he closed his eyes, swaying slightly.

Then Sam suddenly remembered what Pip had said. The warnings, the crazy story. Through his bewilderment, his mind settled on things that probably mattered. Important things.

Things pertinent to national security.

He felt the gloved hand over his mouth but was impotent in its strong grasp. Before a word could be uttered or another thought birthed, he was violently yanked to the floor and a damp cloth was shoved over his mouth.

Within a few seconds he was unconscious.

He didn't even hear the two gunshots that followed.

CHAPTER 40

Lisa listened patiently as Amy went on about her sister in New York City. She nodded politely hearing all about LeeAnne's auditions, the celebrity sightings, fine dining, and premier shopping.

Still, she was intrigued by the small, somewhat cute stranger who had ordered a Coors Light and was stealing glances at her. His attempts to fit in were unsuccessful.

"Anyway, we should go to New York this weekend," Amy announced, grinning enthusiastically, as if it was the most amazing idea ever. "We'll stay for free with my sister, take in a couple of shows, shop all day, and hit a few clubs."

Lisa smiled back in silent contemplation. She knew Amy all too well. The alcohol always made her chatty. It also freed her mind and made her more prone to creative ideas; usually road trips, starting a new venture, or discussing things that bordered on pure fantasy. Lisa usually nodded and played along.

Two more Cosmos arrived, and the waitress motioned to a couple of guys at the pool table in the corner. "Courtesy of those two Romeos," she said, leaving the drinks, and heading back to the bar.

The girls turned and Amy waved. The men looked to be in their mid-twenties. One wore tight fitting blue jeans, casual brown shoes, and an untucked white shirt. He was clean shaven, with perfectly styled dark hair, and strong facial features that belonged in a magazine. The other was short and stocky, with dirty blonde hair, dressed in jeans and a maroon pullover. He no doubt tried to mirror his friend in fashion, but his efforts had fallen woefully short. His appearance was unkempt and desperate in comparison.

They raised their glasses to Amy and Lisa, then turned to each other and did the same.

"I think you know which one I want," Amy said, winking at Lisa, and finishing her first drink. "Should we walk over and school them on that pool table, or play hard-to-get and have them come over here?"

Lisa remained silent, turning back to the bar, where she noticed the short, young man cast another glance her way.

"I'll tell you what, Lisa announced, rising from the bar stool. I'm gonna check on something over there and see what happens."

Amy didn't seem to hear her, as she scooped up both Cosmopolitans and sauntered over to the pool table, exaggerating her stepping to show off her figure.

Lisa moved directly to the young man at the bar. She knew she wasn't as pretty as Amy, but she could hold her own. Confident in her own manner, she sought laughter and friendship over looks and charm.

And something about this guy intrigued her.

He saw her coming and straightened, looking even more out of place. He looked down, as if scanning his clothing to make sure he looked okay. Then he grimaced and yanked off a work lanyard from around his neck, placing it in his breast pocket.

"Hello, young sir," Lisa offered, turning toward him, and holding her half-empty Cosmo.

The man smiled broadly at her, lighting up like a Christmas tree. Almost too eager, so excited to meet her acquaintance. This surprised Lisa, but she also felt warmth in his honest expression.

He was about five feet tall, with brown hair styled nicely, and pleasant features on a rounded face. He had calming, brown eyes and an overall effect of pleasantness. A little awkward but disarming. Instantly likeable and placatory.

She noticed a scar on his hairline, but he quickly raised a guarded hand to straighten a stray lock of hair, and it was gone from sight.

"Hello back," he offered, extending his hand, and taking hers. "I'm Pip. And it's really nice to finally meet you!"

Lisa stiffened, placing her drink on the bar, as she slid into the stool next to him. "What do you mean, 'finally' meet me?"

Pip looked down as if scolding himself. "I didn't mean anything by it, just that I should have met you ten minutes ago."

"So, what was that lanyard thingy you took off your neck? Is that for work?"

"It's nothing," Pip responded quickly. "Can I buy you a drink?"

Lisa looked over to Amy, who had finished the drink the boys bought and was now holding the second one. Her friend was talking enthusiastically about something and both men were enthralled. The pool table balls were left dormant on the table.

"Sure, I'll have a water and a draft beer."

Pip looked to the bartender and ordered two drafts and two waters, paying with cash and a generous tip that made Lisa take notice.

"So, where are you from?" she asked.

"Annapolis, Maryland. Just passing through on a little business," he responded.

"What brings you to this part of beautiful Pennsylvania?"

Pip was surprised and it showed. He wasn't ready for the question and uncertainty played on his face. He became flustered and noticeably red.

The drinks arrived and offered some distraction. He grabbed the water and drank from it, greedily, before turning to Lisa.

"Sorry," he began flatly. "I'm on a secret mission and can't divulge that just yet."

He spoke in a deadpan tone, and the message was a mixture of humor with a modicum of truth.

Intrigued, Lisa just nodded. "Well, I'm not on a mission. Just a girl out for the evening with a friend who will certainly need a ride home. At that, they both turned to look at Amy, who was now playing pool with the guys and bending over a little too much with every shot.

"I see," Pip said. "Looks like my best friend is probably very similar to yours. In fact, I bet they'd really get along!"

Thinking about Sam, Pip retreated inward. He considered the timing and wondered where he was. Was he safe?

Lisa said something, but Pip didn't hear it. He was somewhere else, deep within his mind and worried about his friend.

"Hello!?" Lisa called out, slapping Pip's leg, and snapping her fingers in the air.

Pip shook slightly, looking at Lisa. "Sorry, I was just thinking of something."

"I asked his name."

"Who, Sam?"

"I guess so. Your best friend that would get along with Amy?"

"Yeah. Sam."

Pip spoke of Sam and Lisa of Amy.

Then they both talked about recent movies and their favorite things. The conversation was light and fluid, laced with funny moments that kept them both smiling.

They ordered more water and a couple cheeseburgers. They monitored Amy, who was having a great time playing pool and winning every game.

A couple of easy hours passed, and Lisa ordered an Uber for Amy, deciding to spend a little more time with her new friend, Pip.

CHAPTER 41

Pip paid the bill and he and Lisa pushed through the crowd, exiting into the warm night.

The heavy front door swung shut and the muted sounds of Journey's *Don't Stop Believin'* followed them outside. It was almost midnight. Several people were scattered across the parking lot, while others had just arrived and were making their way in.

Crickets sounded from the high grass at the edge of the property, and Pip and Lisa welcomed the sounds of nature over the loud music.

"This is me," Lisa said, motioning to a red Chevy Traverse.

"Cool, I'm over there," Pip responded, nodding his chin to the far corner.

Pip's heart was beating fast, his anxiety on full display; but the emotions were masked by the dark night and the distraction of the people walking by. He'd been waiting for this moment all day and it had been playing repeatedly in his mind.

He needed her. He knew that. He couldn't mess this up. But how could he communicate that he'd saved her life? Or that he wanted her to join him on the road, possibly even placing her life in danger *again*?

Pip looked down at his shoes, kicking a white stone and watching it roll into a nearby bush. Then he looked to Lisa, studying the face he knew all too well. With her pumps, she was much taller than him, and it was a quick blow to his confidence.

"I really enjoyed meeting you, Lisa. I really mean that," Pip said, placing his hands behind his back and shrugging his shoulders.

"Likewise, Pip," Lisa started. "But I do have one question for you," she announced, moving directly to him.

With a quick movement she shoved her hand into his pocket and took out the lanyard he wore around his neck earlier.

"I've been wondering about this all night."

Pip was in shock and quickly grabbed it back. "It's nothing. Just my work badge."

Lisa let go, retreating, the situation turning sour.

"Okay, no problem. Secrets are cool too, I guess."

Then she moved to her car, unlocked the door, and swung it open. "I had fun, Pip. Maybe I'll see you around, okay?"

Pip shut his eyes, replaying the last few seconds. Then determination overcame him. He had to act quickly.

"Look, Lisa. I need to tell you something."

She looked up, noticing Pip's face was strained and flush. His eyes moved erratically, as if trying to find the right words.

"Then get in the car. I'll crank the A/C. It's better than getting attacked by bugs in this humidity."

Pip swung around the back and got into the passenger seat. Lisa started the engine, turned the radio off, and the air conditioning blew hard.

Lisa looked to Pip, expectantly, waiting for him to speak. Pip took a few deep breaths, hoping he wouldn't sound like a creepy stalker.

"Nice car," he stammered.

Lisa nodded. "It was a gift from my parents after something I went through. It's a few years used, but in great condition."

Pip nodded, wasting time looking around the interior.

Lisa continued. "But I'm sure you're not here to discuss my car."

Pip expelled a breath of air. "Lisa, I know we just met but I need you to understand two things. First, everything I'm about to tell you is 100% true. You may think it's far-fetched but it's the truth. Secondly, you must not tell *anyone*, because your life may be in danger."

Lisa smiled, incredulously. "Look, you had me at hello. I think you're really cute and I enjoyed our conversation, but you're really trying too hard—"

"Lisa," Pip interrupted. "Again, I'm not kidding, and this is not an act. It wasn't just coincidence that we met tonight."

Pip handed her his identification badge. "Read it."

"Price Irvine Palmer. Senior Analyst. NSA Fort Meade, MD # 05300914."

"Cool," Lisa said, flatly. "So, you're like a secret agent, after all?"

"Hardly, no," Pip countered, his voice low and cracking with complete humility. "I'm a data analyst."

"Okay, so what's up? What's a data analyst do? Why are you here?"

"Recently I was involved with the Wolf Man investigation."

Hearing the words, Lisa was paralyzed in shock. Chills ran through her and she hit the air conditioning button to reduce the blast. She looked to Pip, staring back at her, studying her, compassion in his eyes.

"During the investigation I hacked into several data bases, repositioned satellites two hundred miles above us, and was able to track the Wolf Man to you."

Lisa was still silent, now looking around the suddenly cramped space, shaking her head.

"Lisa, I know what you've been through. I was the one who found the Wolf Man and helped direct Jack Seargant and the police to your location."

Lisa was now breathing heavy, reliving the events in her head. She closed her eyes, tasting the salty sweat on her upper lip. Then her mind continued further into that nightmare. She smelled the manure from the farm pen and her own harsh stink from three days in captivity.

"No, that can't be," she uttered, trying to push away the thoughts. "You read all about that and are just saying this for some reason."

She moved her hands to her face and wiped away tears and perspiration. But when she looked back at Pip and saw the look in his eyes—empathy and complete honesty—she knew in a moment it was all true.

"But that's not all, Lisa. Are you ready for the more important part?"

Lisa swallowed hard, massaging her temples. "I'm not sure I can handle much more."

"I hope you can," Pip said, calmly, unfolding a piece of paper. "Because the girl in this picture looks as tough as nails."

Lisa looked over to see her senior high school yearbook picture. A colored 8 x 10 printout folded into quarters.

"Where'd you get that?" she asked. "A little creepy don't you think?"

"It was hanging in my office. I saw it every day, memorized every detail of your face. You were my only focus when I was tasked to find you. To *save* you."

"And here you are," she said, her voice just above a whisper. "What now?"

"Are you ready for part two?" he asked, moving to the dashboard radio, and turning to National Public Radio.

They sat in silence for a few moments, as the news spewed forth, rehashing the events of the past several days.

"You've no doubt heard about the recent assassinations of the presidents?"

"Who hasn't? It's all over the news!"

Pip took out the flash drive from his shirt pocket.

"Earlier today, I recorded a phone call initiated from inside the DOD to someone we *all* know, detailing all of this."

"DOD?" Lisa repeated, shaking her head. "Someone we all know?"

"Department of Defense. And yes, the other party is a household name that I won't reveal for your own safety."

Lisa scoffed, looking away to a group of people hanging out in the back of a pickup truck. There was a small cooler between them, and they were huddled in a close circle, drinking canned beer.

"And what's this have to do with me?"

"I need your help."

"Pip, I'm not Superwoman. In case you haven't noticed, I'm just a local country bumpkin destined to marry poorly, have a couple of kids, and spend my life getting used to the smell of manure."

Pip was now the silent one, contemplating things. He felt vulnerable and the feeling was cutting.

"Look, I know this is huge and you deserve no part in it. But the truth is, like you, I'm not worldly. I need to lay low, keep moving, and figure things out. I was hoping you and I could go on a road trip and keep each other company. I'm not sure I can handle the pressure of the next several days by myself."

Lisa looked to him. "You want *my* help?"

"Absolutely. Believe it or not, Pennsylvania is the second state I've ever been to. I'm thinking we could just drive and think things through. I borrowed my friend's car, which is too risky to take, so I was hoping we could stash it and drive yours."

"Oh, and now you need a *ride*?" she asked, her voice rising in mock surprise.

It was a well-needed, funny remedy, offering levity to what had been a terse conversation.

"Well," Pip began, awkwardly. "Yeah, I guess."

They both laughed, looking to each other.

Lisa thought of the Wolf Man once more, which sent a shudder through her. Then she regarded the calm young man to her right. Someone she'd just met but who no doubt had saved her life. He was a warm person and she felt an instant connection to him.

And she owed him her life.

Then she thought of that damn cuckoo clock and thought of the next few days. It would be exciting, she thought, going on a road trip with a complete stranger, and just hitting the reset button.

"You said this is dangerous. Explain that."

The bad guys know *who* I am but not *where* I am. I've been off the grid since this afternoon. I'm 100% sure that if I got into your car and hid mine, we would be safe and anonymous. I could also call in the FBI at any point. I just need time to think.

Lisa nodded in affirmation. Then she considered where they could go, finally deciding on the perfect place.

"I'll go, Pip. But on two conditions."

Pip turned, surprised at the sudden turn in conversation.

"Anything you say," he conceded.

"First, I'll need a couple of days to get to know you and plan a clean departure, so my parents won't know."

"And second?"

"We're going to the happiest place on earth. Somewhere neither of us have ever been."

Confused, Pip just shook his head, waiting for their destination.

"We're driving to Disney World."

CHAPTER 42

Seargant always had *that* feeling.

It was non-discriminatory and usually spot on and had played out in both the most elaborate and inane of situations. It had both saved and cost lives; and this time it was both. It was the suspicion that something was wrong; a gut reaction that wouldn't cede until properly addressed.

So, when Pip contacted Seargant earlier in the day, the FBI profiler had detected the elevated breathing and voice patterns and knew something was wrong. Seargant had noted the time: 2:43 p.m. on a Wednesday. He knew Pip was in his car and leaving work early, which was outside of routine.

It was too coincidental that it happened on the heels of the presidential assassinations, and it prompted Seargant to drive to Annapolis to Pip's residence. His Number One, Agent Hartley accompanied him. Earlier, they'd parked the black Escalade at the top of Cornhill Street and walked down and tapped on number 32 to find no answer.

It was a simple yellow, two-story historic home; one of many that dotted the tributaries falling away from State Circle. Hartley leaned to the right and peered down a narrow passageway ending at an old wooden gate, presumably enclosing a small yard.

"Continue calling his phone," Seargant said, looking into the small kitchen window, before backing up onto the street to view the house in total.

"Nothing, Sarge," Hartley responded.

They had run Pip's plates and found his car on the street. Hartley felt the hood. It was warm but not hot. "We missed him by about fifteen minutes," he said.

Seargant shook his head, concerned. "Something's not right here."

Hartley nodded in agreement. "What's the call? Search warrant or wellness check break-in?"

Seargant looked to the house once more, starting a slow walk into the alley directly across from it.

"Neither. Not yet. Let's walk the area because we may be here all night. But this isn't right. I know that for a fact."

Several hours later, it all went down. Hartley was closer but Seargant was the first to engage. They both spotted Sam simultaneously. Hartley was positioned inside a group of trees adjacent and across the street; Seargant beside the Escalade and deep within the shadow line.

Then they saw *him*, the man *behind* Sam.

Seargant guessed he was military. It was dark, so features were hard to see, but the silhouette was large and muscular, and moved with calm, targeted stepping. The man's resolute posture and stride spoke volumes.

Then Seargant looked at Sam, lumbering up the street, no doubt sloppy drunk and unaware. The man was following Sam, so Seargant crouched low and moved along the right side of the road, using the parked cars as cover.

When Sam entered the house and a light shined inside, Seargant saw the man move to the right and into the narrow space between the next house. Seargant glanced to where Hartley *had* been but saw nothing.

Quick moments passed and Sam, and then his pursuer, entered the house.

Seargant ran to the door and Hartley appeared behind him. They burst inside and moved straight ahead with guns drawn, finding Sam on the floor with a large man towering above him.

"Stand down, hands up," Seargant yelled, leveling his Glock at the man's head, his stare unwavering.

Hartley moved to the left and crouched, his own weapon trained on the intruder. The man dropped a small white towel and palmed a gun in his right hand.

The situation favored the FBI, not only in manpower and weaponry, but also in position and timing. The man was surprised and his weapon was low and to his right. Any movement would take a half second too long and prove fatal.

The seconds ticked by audibly on a distant clock, as the three men stood like statues.

"Now!" Hartley shouted. "Drop the weapon!"

"Look guys," the man began, evenly. "We're on the same team here. If you could just lower your firearms and let me—"

Suddenly, the man shifted his weight in a blur of movement, raising his gun and leaning away. But Seargant and Hartley were ready for anything. Two gunshots sounded, and the man fell dead into the wooden coffee table.

Hartley moved to confirm the kill. Seargant knelt next to Sam, fingering his neck, thankful for a steady pulse.

CHAPTER 43

Things finally calmed down around 3 a.m.

Within moments of the shooting, Seargant and Hartley walked the entire house, turning on the lights and opening every door, making sure there were no other threats. Seargant contacted both the Annapolis and Anne Arundel County police to report a shooting in their districts. Then he emailed a report to his team.

Hartley carried Sam upstairs into the front bedroom, and the kid was snoring loudly even before he closed the door. He took pictures of the dead man and fingerprinted him, electronically sending both to their crime lab for proper identification. Not surprisingly, the man carried no identification.

Then Seargant and Hartley contacted their wives to check in. They would be pulling an all-nighter and wouldn't be home until well into the next day.

They cooperated fully with the local authorities, being overly patient. And after providing separate but corresponding accounts of the shooting, the dead man was removed, and most of the police left.

A couple officers remained outside to secure the area and manage any spectators.

Seargant looked at the clock and then back at Hartley.

"It's after three in the morning. Do you wanna take the upstairs bed or the couch down here?"

Hartley laughed. "You wanna stay here?"

"Well, if Pip comes home, we'll be here, and I don't want to move his roommate in the middle of the night."

Hartley nodded in agreement, contemplating the choices, and looking around, as if seeing it all for the first time. Nothing in the place matched, and it was obvious the two occupants brought their separate and limited possessions into the living arrangement.

A Bob Marley poster hung unevenly above the sofa, next to a decorative shelf that held candles and a few photographs. The sofa looked decades old, brown and tan in color, and overtook most of the far wall. The coffee table was too big for the room and probably doubled as a dinner table while watching television.

The wooden floor was littered with pillows, clothing, and random scatterings of trash. There were empty pizza boxes stacked in the corner and empty beer cans on every surface. A few old blankets were balled up and the place smelled musty.

Seargant loosened his tie and kicked off his shoes. "Actually, I'm going to make the call here. You go upstairs and I'll try this couch. Let's get a little sleep and we'll talk to Sam in a few hours."

Hartley cracked a smile. "That kid's gonna be out until noon."

Seargant chuckled. "That kid's coming with us to D.C. at 6 a.m. And he's gonna spill his guts."

The man without a name sat at his large mahogany desk, frowning.

He had access to real-time information and had read both Seargant's FBI incident report, and the watered-down police versions.

Both contained the same information. One dead; an unknown. And with a small arsenal of weaponry on his person. Two headshots by the FBI. A classic case of illegal entry with ill-intent. Self-defense. An open and shut case.

Except *he* knew—and the FBI would *soon* know—that it would not be that easy.

His asset would soon be identified and although the revelation would become classified; the repercussions would shine unwanted light into areas that had been dark for some time.

The man wasn't accustomed to being nervous.

He'd even built a career on it. It was not a normal emotion for someone at his level. But with Pip Palmer seemingly on the run, especially with the information the kid had, and now Jack Seargant sniffing around, things were getting messy fast.

So here he was, hands running through his already tousled hair, re-reading the report that would force another action. The man without a name knew what he had to do. He'd been delaying, hoping for something to happen; anything to bend his way. But nothing was working out.

So, he picked up an encrypted cell phone and dialed a number.

He didn't want to talk to the person on the other end, but he had no choice.

PART THREE

PIP & LISA

CHAPTER 44

The next morning Pip awoke to unfamiliar surroundings. The details of yesterday came back slowly and he frowned at the revelation. He kicked out of the cheap bed sheets and stretched, releasing a long, satisfying yawn.

The motel room was simple. The old bed took over most of the area, a slanting end table held a decades-old clock radio, and thick, yellow drapes swayed gently over the single window, as the small air conditioner coughed below it.

He reached for the remote control, which was tightly bound with tape to secure the batteries. Then he pointed it at the old box television, not feeling optimistic. But it came alive slowly and he switched between the local news channels, eagerly.

Information was essential. There was no national cable news, so he settled on the local effort, hoping they'd switch from weather and traffic to things of greater importance. Not wasting time, he moved to the clock radio and found National Public Radio and settled back into bed, listening intently.

They were iterating what everyone already knew. President Preston was the fourth president dead, and an investigation was ongoing. They rehashed each assassination and replayed the two latest news briefings from the FBI. A presidential press conference was scheduled for 10 a.m.

Pip rose and moved to the small bathroom, his bare feet treading lightly on the worn, brown carpeting. The bathroom floor was worse, with sticky yellow linoleum peeling off dark concrete.

But the shower was forceful, and the hot water felt good as it targeted his waking muscles. Steam consumed the small space, and he breathed deeply, feeling more refreshed by the moment.

Meeting Lisa couldn't have gone better. Despite the circumstances that allowed it, he couldn't have asked for a better outcome. He even liked her as a person.

She was a good listener and very genuine. Their conversation was easy, and filled with funny, lighter moments that buoyed the more serious talk. As the night progressed and the crowd swelled around them, they had instinctively inched closer to each other.

And Pip drank her in, smelling her sweet perfume and noticing the smallest of details. He saw the freckles barely noticeable below her makeup, a small birthmark on her lower neck, and the dimples that formed when she smiled.

But best of all, she'd agreed to his request, which was crucial. He was probably already on borrowed time with his friend's car.

Pip's thoughts turned inward. Although he was well educated and mature for his age, he felt out of place, away from the comforts of work and home. A travel mate would provide some levity and a second mind to help navigate the next several days. With Lisa, he just knew things would be better.

He dried off with a thin towel and dressed quickly. Then he refolded his worn clothes and neatly placed them into a zippered compartment, with everything in perfect order. He walked outside to get some fresh air and get his bearings. Seeing the roadside motel during the day cast little more luster than at nighttime.

The motel was a glorified truck stop, like many others dotting the two-lane highways in this part of the county. It was a one story, wooden structure in the shape of a U, probably once painted white, but now faded and cracking with age.

The parking lot that framed it was riddled with potholes and uneven white lines; and weeds had long broken through the asphalt and spidered across the surface. Random debris littered the area, and a light wind pushed the refuse toward the handful of trucks parked at the far end.

Pip saw a worn, plastic chair and sat in it, sipping from a bottle of water and palming an apple. It was surprisingly comfortable, and he spent some time formulating his plan and passing the time.

Lisa promised to stop by later, so he spent the rest of the day watching and listening to the news, reading the novel he'd purchased, and taking slow strolls around the property.

The knock on the door awoke Pip from an afternoon nap.

Jumping up, he heard Lisa's voice ring out and his heartbeat slowed.

"Pip, it's me," she announced.

The door opened and she entered, carrying a bag of Chik-Fil-A and a couple of chocolate milkshakes.

"Thought you could use some grub," she said, looking around the room.

Pip accepted it, gratefully. "Thank you so much," he said, feeling the warm bag and smelling the food.

"I like what you've done with the place," Lisa commented, in a deadpan tone.

Chewing on a large waffle fry, he nodded. "Yeah, I'm thinking about a hot tub over there and a pool table by the closet."

They fell into an easy laugh and sat on the bed, unwrapping the sandwiches.

"Again, thanks for this. Are you still okay with our road trip? I don't want to press you."

Lisa didn't waiver. "I'm still in and actually excited. I just need to organize a few things and get my story straight with my parents."

"Have you told Amy anything?" Pip asked, worried.

"No and she's actually leaving to visit her sister in New York tomorrow and won't be back for at least four days."

"Good, and your parents?"

"They'll think I'm leaving with her, while I'll be heading south with you."

Pip nodded, his breathing returning to normal. "That's actually perfect. So, tomorrow morning it is, then?"

An image of the old cuckoo clock flashed in Lisa's mind and she grimaced. "Yeah, tomorrow morning we go."

At a few minutes past 8 a.m. the next morning, Pip was apprehensive. Lisa was late and every one of Pip's insecurities were attacking his senses. He was sitting in the weathered, plastic chair just outside his motel room, while every worst-case scenario played out in elaborate fashion in his mind.

He glanced at his watch, nervously, not even seeing the time. Then he craned his neck to a high, blue sky; where large, billowy clouds gathered and moved slowly west. An airplane flew slowly against them, before being swallowed within the puffy whiteness.

Another twenty minutes passed, and Pip checked on his car, parked behind the motel. Maybe she would meet him there. Then he returned to his room and listened to more NPR trying to calm his nerves.

A half hour later he was going crazy, replaying their conversations, and hoping for the best. But anxiety swept over him and the next several minutes felt like an eternity.

Then he heard a car horn and he rushed outside.

Lisa was there, waving from her window.

"Sorry I'm late," she said.

The air escaped Pip's lungs and the color returned to his face.

"I'm so glad you're here!" he shouted, moving to her.

She looked more beautiful than he remembered, with her long blonde hair pulled tight into a ponytail, and a modest application of makeup. The handful of freckles on her nose showed prominently, and he smiled at her, just knowing that things would work out.

"My car is around back," Pip said. "You still have a place to stash it?"

Lisa nodded. "Just follow me. It's about ten minutes away."

And their little adventure began.

CHAPTER 45

Lisa told her parents she and Amy were going to New York City to visit Amy's sister.

Her parents were happy to see her get out, though they were adamant about keeping in contact. She felt guilty betraying their trust, but even if she *was* discovered, it wouldn't be for days, and she was an adult anyway.

But would it be too much to understand that she'd met someone, had a wonderful time, and went on a road trip? She was responsible, and Pip was obviously intelligent and genuine. Despite his story and the possible danger, it just felt like the right thing to do, especially after hearing what he'd done for her.

Pip followed Lisa, first on Route 1 for several miles, and then onto a narrow road, before cutting across a one lane path between two farms. Lisa slowed considerably, and Pip mirrored her efforts, as their vehicles navigated several large holes and uneven tree roots.

Then Lisa took a hard left and disappeared into a high corn field. Pip followed and after several moments, they reached a large clearing with an old barn. It was her great uncle's property, and although he still lived on the three-hundred-acre sprawl, he rarely ventured to this side of the farm.

Lisa parked her car and ran to the barn, moving a lever and swinging the large doors open. She waved to Pip, who parked his friend's car inside.

"This should do, nicely," Pip said, getting out of the car and looking around.

It was more of a dilapidated lean-to, with unpainted wooden slats that looked too brittle and uneven to keep the structure upright.

"I know what you're thinking," Lisa said. "Looks like a strong wind would topple this place, but it's been here for almost a hundred years."

Pip nodded, eyeing an old tarp and some horse blankets in the corner. He moved to them swiftly, throwing several over the car.

Lisa laughed out loud. "What are you worried that the bad guys are gonna somehow track you to me and then to this old farm, and find this thing?"

Pip remained silent, turning back to the now-covered vehicle, looking nondescript under the bulky covers. Then he moved some old pipes and metal scrap—a horde of spent tractor parts from another day—and placed them on top of and against the vehicle, making it appear tented and undefined.

"Actually Lisa, yes. I'm forward thinking to that *exact* scenario, but also to what someone like me, using a satellite a couple hundred miles above us, would see."

Then Pip looked at the barn's wall and the angle of the slats that let in more light than not. Lisa was silenced as the thought hit her too. She swallowed hard, absorbing it all. She'd always thought more in the physical, than the fast moving, cyber world that Pip knew all too well.

"That should do it," Pip said, standing back and admiring his work. "It won't cast a heat signature, and there's no way to know what's under here without a physical search, and that would take a warrant or an abiding resident."

"Or a bad guy who doesn't care about either," Lisa said, softly, still reconciling her thoughts.

Lisa moved outside and opened her car door, plopping down hard. She plugged in her smart phone and searched her music library. Pip got in and fastened the seatbelt. She looked over at him and they were off.

"How was the motel?" she asked. "It's one of the better ones around here."

"Just fine," Pip said, looking out the window, as they turned left, passing a dense row of trees that edged another farm.

But then he looked back at her, genuinely curious. "So, you wanna go to Florida?"

"No; I really want to go to Disney World, which is *in* Florida."

Just saying the words forced a wide smile, as she traded looks between him and the road ahead.

She was naturally pretty, he knew. But there was something else that he couldn't place. There was an internal beauty that seemed to radiate from her when she was happy. Her eyes sparkled and grew wide, like a happy character in a cartoon. She spoke exquisitely, flashing perfect white teeth, and he loved the dimples that showed with every smile.

She jerked slightly to the side to check her side mirror and a long, curly lock of hair fell across her chest. He realized that she was the most beautiful thing he'd ever seen. He was suddenly embarrassed in the revelation, but also worried that he'd come off as someone using her for something inappropriate.

The temperature seemed to rise, and Pip became more withdrawn. He knew he was probably overthinking things, but his mind would let nothing go until he analyzed everything.

Lisa noticed the stale moment and looked over. "What's up, Pip?" she asked. "You want some water or something? I packed a cooler with snacks and stuff."

She motioned toward the back seat, and he reached behind her, unzipping a soft cooler, and gulping down a cold bottle of water.

"Thank you," he said, regaining some composure.

"I haven't eaten since last night and—"

"Don't sweat it, Pip. You're all good," she interrupted.

Lisa turned up the volume on *Let it Go* by the Zac Brown Band. Pip knew it well and they started singing, as they saw the first sign for I-95 south.

And the shy NSA analyst got lost in the song—and in the moment with his new friend—and let go of his uncertainties.

For hours, well into Virginia, the conversation flowed nicely.

Both appeared giddy at the thought of an open-ended road trip and the air was charged with a feeling of optimism and adventure. The afternoon sunlight lit up the road against the dark blue backdrop of a perfect sky, and Pip and Lisa were feeling comfortable, if not united, in their purpose.

In Woodbridge, the traffic dissipated considerably. The speed limit increased, and the landscape continued to fly by.

"I have to ask," Pip said. "What's the story about that farm, where we stashed the car?"

Lisa tightened her grip on the steering wheel. Her head slanted and she stole a quick glance at Pip. Then she bit her lower lip and frowned, uneasily.

"I guess I can tell you, but it's technically a family secret that goes back several decades. The only one that knows about it outside of family is Amy."

Pip was instantly curious. He had no doubt stumbled onto something bigger than an old farm and couldn't wait to hear the tale.

"My Great-Great-Uncle Pete died when he was a hundred years old, about ten years ago. And the farm was inherited by my Great-Uncle, Pete's only son, who's a recluse in his own right.

"One day thirty years ago, for some unknown reason, ol' Pete barricaded himself in the farmhouse for exactly ten years. When the kin asked him about it, he didn't provide any answers. But when everyone kept at him, and in exchange for help in bringing him supplies, which he paid for, he admitted doing something bad. Something he would never speak about or admit, and he decided to sentence himself to house arrest at the farm, where he tended to the livestock and the fields.

"During this time, he was very hard on himself and followed a strict schedule. He was the judge and then the warden and the prisoner. There were specific rules, such as only being outside for work duties, and one hour a day for recreation. He was afforded three square meals each day, no alcohol, and he requested that visitation be limited to weekends. He would conduct business with others from town, as needed, but they would only come to him."

Pip was enthralled. There were more questions than answers and his mind was playing out every probability.

"After his death, did you guys unravel the mystery? Was there any paperwork, a journal, or anything that could help?"

"There was an old ledger he kept for business and around the time a crime would have been committed, $20,000 was withdrawn. That's the highest amount ever paid from his checkbook and there were definitely no equipment or supply purchases to explain it. We don't know and my family decided not to pursue it."

"Do *you* want to know?"

"Absolutely! For us and for someone out there who might need some closure."

"Do you think it was murder or what?"

"Pete was a very nice old man. The kind of farmer who doesn't really exist anymore. He was also married for almost seventy years and was a simpleton. He didn't really drink, and rarely traveled past the county line, except to buy farm equipment or sell some crops. He didn't have a lot of money and frankly didn't care to, with his lifestyle. He wasn't overly religious but was certainly a very moral and grounded man."

"What do you think?" Pip asked, still digesting the crazy story.

"I have no idea."

They both withdrew into thought as the white lines on I-95 flew by. Pip's mind was all over the place. He considered the forensic accounting that could track the details of the unusual payment.

The FBI could investigate missing persons reports from that time, and any cold case police activity. Back dated satellite imaging could be overlayed to look for land disturbance or a possible unmarked grave.

"I guess we all have our secrets, huh?" Lisa quipped. "Do you have any skeletons in your closet Mr. Pip?"

CHAPTER 46

"**S**keletons?" Pip repeated.

"Yeah," Lisa said, turning. "I guess we all have them. Some call them enigmas, mysteries, or even *whispers* of a past forgotten, if you want to get poetic about it. Personally, though, I think they're the things that make us more interesting."

Lisa looked over but Pip was just looking out the window, watching the scenery fly by.

"Okay, I'll go first then," Lisa said. "Or I'll go again, because I already told you about my weird uncle squared."

"Squared?" Pip asked.

"Great-great. Squared. Even we take math up here in PA. Try to keep up with me here."

They both laughed and Lisa continued.

"My family is simple. My brother can do no wrong. Handsome, well mannered, smart, and always has a plan. Things just work out for him. My parents were supposedly cool and hip, but then got married, had two kids, and settled into the rural life and are living a mechanical drone of an existence. Me, I guess I'm just still trying to figure things out."

Pip finally looked over. "There aren't any skeletons in there. Where's the cool chewy part in the middle that makes it a great story?"

"I guess you're right. I have no skeletons, at least none that you don't know about."

Pip grimaced. It was a sore subject and one he wasn't sure how to bridge, given his budding relationship with Lisa. He closed his eyes, moving his hands to the sides of his heads, rubbing his temples trying to find the right words of conciliation. Anything to convey how deeply sorry he was for her; that no one should have gone through what she endured.

But then she spoke, evenly. "Pip, I'm not ashamed of what happened to me with the whole Wolf Man thing. I mean, I don't need therapy or anything. It wasn't my fault, and I don't blame anyone but the monster who did it. I've always been one of those 'cup is halfway full' kinda gals, and I'm just happy I'm still here. If anything, I feel sad for and mourn the other girls who *didn't* make it."

Pip looked over, contemplating her. He didn't know what to say. She was a remarkable and well-adjusted young woman, comfortable in her skin, with so much life inside.

"You're amazing, Lisa. I really mean that. I don't know much about your past or anything, but I must say you're impressive."

"Right back at you, Pip," she said, mockingly. "I mean, after all, you saved me!"

Pip's demeanor changed, as he shifted his weight away from Lisa and again stared out the window, blankly.

"Hey, I didn't mean to embarrass you! I was just trying to say—"

"Jack Seargant of the FBI is the one to thank, Lisa. He came to me two days prior, broke a whole bunch of rules, pissed on anyone who got in his way, and lit a fire under my ass to run his parameters to find you."

"Yeah, but in the end—"

"...He rushed in with the cavalry and saved you. He's the one."

Silence ruled as they both mulled over the sudden turn in conversation.

Then Lisa shook her head. "No, I won't let you do it, Pip. This FBI guy may be the brawn, but you were certainly the brains. There's no way he could have done it without you, and I won't—"

"It was my privilege," Pip muttered, just above a whisper.

Lisa looked over, quizzically. "What?"

Pip let out a sigh, repeating himself. "It was my *privilege*."

Then he straightened. "Everything about me. From how I came into this world, to my childhood, and ultimately who I am now and where I work. I've always been alone and looking out to the world. The only way I give back is anonymously through the Key—that's what I call my computer system—by helping from afar. Actually, that's how I like it.

"And when I took on your case, I didn't just become a part of it, it became a part of me. When I saw your picture and learned about the Wolf Man, I couldn't let it go.

"So, I'll say it again. It was my *privilege* to do it. I happily carried the mantle of responsibility and wouldn't have trusted anyone else to—"

Pip cut himself off. Hearing the words spill from him, he was suddenly struck and silenced by an uneasy feeling of self-adulation. He'd crossed the line into arrogance.

"I mean, I just did my job is all," he sputtered in frustration.

Lisa shook her head in amazement. Pip was such a wonderful person. He didn't like the spotlight and wasn't one for bragging or enhancing his ego. He was a kind soul; someone she knew she could trust with anything.

"Well, it worked out, Pip, and again, thank you."

She planted her left hand firmly on the steering wheel and reached over, taking his hand in hers. She pumped it gently a few times and then held it tight. Pip's palm was moist with perspiration, and she could tell he was uncomfortable, but still affable to the touch.

Several moments passed with nothing more said. The exchange was telling and well needed, and both became more invested in each other and the unwritten future.

"But I do have a major problem with elevators," Pip said, plainly.

Lisa was taken back. It was a strange comment at an even stranger time in the conversation, and she shook her head in dismay.

"Elevators? What problem could you *possibly* have with elevators?"

Pip grimaced, looking down and feigning disgust. "Actually, I have *two* problems with elevators."

Lisa smiled, liking his tone, and wondering where this was going. "Okay, I'll bite. What are your *two* problems with elevators?"

Pip grew enthusiastic, waiting for the response. "First, the one at work has a sign announcing a maximum fine of $25 for carrying a 'lighted tobacco product' inside. It hasn't been updated in decades and obviously hasn't kept up with inflation. The penalty is so minimal that it makes me want to smoke in an elevator. Which begs the question, has anyone ever been fined for that?"

"And it also creates another problem because you don't smoke," Lisa teased.

"That's true, I hadn't thought of that and now it's getting more complicated."

"And what's the second problem with elevators, the horrible music they play?"

Nope, the 'Close' button. I'm convinced that pressing that button repeatedly does absolutely nothing. It just keeps you busy and distracted until the thing closes on its own."

"I think you're overthinking things. If those are your problems, I think you have it pretty good."

They both laughed but Pip withdrew his hand from Lisa's, gently touching Frank and moving his hair to cover the scar. He only wished his life's problems *were* that simple.

Lisa looked at the gas gauge and to an upcoming exit sign. "Time for gas, a restroom visit, and some coffee," she said. "And it's a Royal Farms, so I doubt there are any elevators."

CHAPTER 47

Pip gave Lisa money for gas and waited in the car.

When she was gone from sight, he grabbed a large plastic cup and moved to the back seat, hunching over to relieve his bladder. Then he grabbed a baseball hat, pulled it low over his eyes and exited the car, scanning the area.

He kept his head down and moved to a cropping of grass, emptying the cup, and discarding a couple of bottles in a recycle can. Then, moving back to the car, he started pumping gas.

He knew there were video cameras everywhere. And though he wasn't sure if anyone was actively looking for him, he couldn't take the chance to go inside. Especially now that Lisa was involved.

Minutes later, with Pip behind the wheel, they were back on I-95 south. The engine noise swelled as they merged into traffic into the center lane, settling in at two above the speed limit.

Lisa kicked off her sandals and stretched her feet onto the wide dashboard. She placed a sweatshirt over her lap and adjusted the seat to add comfort.

"Bananas," Pip announced, defeatedly, looking over at her.

Lisa was perplexed. "Should I have gotten you a banana back there, instead of a bagel?"

"No. I mean you asked about skeletons and things like that. I have a lot of them Lisa, I'm not gonna lie."

She looked over and saw a different Pip from what she'd known before. He was fragile and uncertain, vulnerable, and pained.

"Wanna talk about it?" she offered, softly, reaching over to take his hand.

He turned slightly, gently moving his thumb over the top of her hand, delighted in the gesture and the warmth within it.

"Stickers," he began. "I grew up in an orphanage since I was five, when my mother died. I never knew my father. Things were rough there. We didn't have much. Food, clothing, possessions. Nothing. And that's probably why I live how I do. Pretty simple."

A horn interrupted them, as a neighboring car swerved aggressively to exit the interstate.

Pip continued. "Anyway, I didn't grow up with much and still don't need a lot today. That's why I enjoy my work because I can sit behind a computer and peer out into the world from a safe place."

"How long were you there?"

"Until my eighteenth birthday ten years ago. Everyone kept getting picked but me. I was always small for my age and underdeveloped, and I guess I wasn't what anyone wanted."

Pip's voice was strained but controlled. Though he'd never spoken much about his past, Lisa could tell the thoughts had long existed in his head.

"I'm good, though," he continued. "I don't want any of this to be construed as a call for help or self-pity. So many others have sob stories and horrible things from their past. At least I'm alive and well. I mean, look what happened to you!"

Lisa nodded in silence, and both contemplated the conversation. She wanted to hug Pip and tell him he was stronger than he may think. And Pip was feeling emboldened with every passing minute, as he continued to hold her hand.

"Anyway, there was this kid named Carl Fink. He was three years younger but was much bigger and he bullied me. You know how there's always that one banana in the bunch that has a sticker on it?"

Lisa smiled. "Of course."

"Well, he always had to have that one. He considered them free stickers and put them on the wall next to his bed, collecting them like trophies or something. Again, we didn't have much.

"Anyway, one day I had enough, and I was the first one in the kitchen. I saw a fresh bunch of bananas and immediately went to them and peeled off the one with the sticker. It wasn't that I wanted a banana as much as I wanted the one with the sticker. I knew it was petty, but I finally took a stand."

"What happened?"

"I was triumphantly eating the banana when I heard talking from down the hall. I walked over and saw Carl Fink with a duffel bag at his feet and a nice couple in their mid-thirties signing some paperwork. He was being adopted and I lost interest in the banana and the sticker.

"A few minutes later, I was at the window watching Carl being seat-belted into a car with this nice couple. They looked like an instant family. She was beautiful, wearing a pink dress, with long curly dark hair moving in the breeze. The man looked like a model from a fashion magazine; tall and thin, with perfectly parted blonde hair. He wore beige pants, loafers, and a sweater. They were smiling at something I couldn't hear, and the car was filled with balloons.

"I just stared out the window at this post card image, unknowingly squeezing the banana too hard, until the mush dripped down my wrist.

"Then Carl Fink looked at me and smiled. Not a smile that was malicious or triumphant, but one of contentment. He raised two fingers in a peace sign and nodded toward me.

"I was conflicted. A flood of emotions took over and like always, I buried them. I felt a pang of guilt for being jealous of him, I felt selfish for taking the banana with the sticker; and trivialized because it was some coveted prize. And then I felt the familiar sense of dread and emptiness, knowing that I was alone in a system that didn't want me."

"I'm sorry, Pip," Lisa said, warmly. "But I think you turned out really well. In fact, if you hadn't, I wouldn't be here."

Pip blinked away a tear and concentrated on the road.

"I just wanted you to know a little more about me," he offered. "I'm sorry it's not as cool of a story as your uncle squared."

Lisa chuckled, looking to Pip. "No, it's not as cool, but it's a start."

Pip laughed and moved the seat back a little. Then they chatted nonstop well into North Carolina.

CHAPTER 48

The billboard signs for *South of the Border* started over one hundred miles out at mile marker 158.5.

"Reptile Lagoon," Pip, read aloud, now back in the passenger seat.

"Yeah," Lisa started. "I heard it's a bunch of stores, games, hotels, and stuff at the North and South Carolina border."

"I've heard of it," Pip said.

"Free air, water, and advice," Lisa said, reading another sign.

"Should we go?" Pip asked, and Lisa could hear enthusiasm in his voice.

"Of course," she said. "Anything you want for your first road trip."

"Pedro's Sombrero Observation Tower," Pip said, reading another.

"Are you gonna read them all?"

"Of course, it's better than spilling my guts to you."

"I'm cheaper than a therapist."

Lisa regretted saying it and she wasn't sure how Pip would respond. But when she stole a quick glance at him, he was grinning at her. So, she offered her hand again and he took it.

"I guess I am, too," he offered, and she couldn't disagree.

"Maybe we're just two emotionally spent weirdos on the road to madness?"

Pip laughed. "I guess so, but one thing I've learned is that nobody's perfect, and everyone comes from somewhere. We all have baggage and some of it isn't neat and pretty. It's what we do about it and how we choose to live that counts."

Pip heard his own words flow so easily and drew comfort from Lisa's acceptance. He suddenly felt encouraged. Maybe he wasn't meant to be such an introvert, spending so many hours alone behind a workstation deep within the NSA. And maybe he shouldn't just live in the shadow of his friend, Sam.

He chuckled out loud. "I think everything is gonna be just fine."

"Of course, it is," Lisa agreed.

But then reality hit. Memories of the last several days.

Four former presidents had been assassinated. He had vital information and they were on the run. That was real.

Pip thought of Sam and reached for his laptop, logging in. The screen came to life and Lisa glanced over. "I thought you weren't supposed to be on any electronics because they could trace you."

Pip didn't look up. "No one can trace this thing, trust me."

The screen came to life and his fingertips worked the keyboard, furiously. He brought up *The Capital* newspaper online, scanning the headlines for Anne Arundel County.

Then he froze and his entire body shook.

A deadly shooting on Cornhill Street. One dead, FBI on the scene. Authorities are still investigating. And the information was a day old! Pip scanned the article and then re-read it slowly. He reached for one of the prepaid cell phones and called Seargant.

It only took a half a ring. "This is Jack Seargant."

"Seargant," Pip said.

"Pip!" Seargant screamed into the phone. "Don't hang up!"

"Is Sam all right?"

"He's fine. He's right here," Seargant answered, calmly. "What's going on, Pip?"

"I have the same question."

"All I know is you called me a couple days ago and sounded scared. You said you uncovered something important and hung up. It didn't fit, so I immediately went to see you in Annapolis and prevented a deadly attack on your roommate."

"What did the guy want!?" Pip yelled into the phone.

Lisa looked over, scared, and Pip composed himself.

"Just tell me what you know, Seargant," Pip said, more calmly.

"We didn't get that far with the guy. We know he's ex-CIA. A mercenary. These guys don't come cheap. Sam is lucky to be alive, but he's safe."

Pip breathed a sigh of relief, but his mind was reeling.

"Someone out there knows what I know," Pip said just above a whisper.

"And what exactly is that? What's going on?"

"Not yet. I have to think, Seargant."

"Pip, these guys acted in real-time. To come after you that quick, they weren't messing around. I need to know what you have."

But Pip fell silent. He thought of Sam; confused and scared. Not knowing anything and paying the price for Pip's actions.

"I have to go now. But I'll be in touch. I'm out of pocket and playing it smart. I just need time to think things through. Please tell Sam I'll send a postcard."

"I don't know what—"

"He'll understand, Seargant."

Pip ended the call and turned on the radio, looking for NPR. For the next hour, they listened to the rehashed reports of the assassinations. There were no leads. No new information. But there was also no mention of the killing an ex-CIA agent in Annapolis. No reference to Pip and a possible link to anything.

And he didn't know if that was good or bad.

The call over, Seargant put the cell phone down. Then he contemplated Sam, who was watching him intently. After the local police had come and gone, Seargant and Hartley delivered the kid to the Hoover building in D.C., and he'd been questioned thoroughly.

It didn't take long to realize he knew nothing, but he was the only link to Pip, who seemingly could know *everything*. Other than that, and the dead mercenary, Seargant was at a loss.

Seargant peered at Sam. "What did he mean about sending you a postcard?"

Sam laughed nervously, looking to the ceiling, and moving his neck in a circle. "It's a reference to the *Shawshank Redemption*. At the end, Andy sends Red a postcard from where he crossed into Mexico. That means Pip is safe but in transit and he'll be in contact when he lands."

"What information do you think he has?"

Sam scoffed. "I already told you he was rambling on about the presidential assassinations and knowing something. Look, man, I didn't even know what he did at the NSA until now. Is he really a spy or something?"

Seargant studied Sam, seeing a lost soul. Totally transparent.

"No, he's a data analyst. And I hope we can get to him before the other guys do."

Sam sunk into the chair, defeatedly. The words hit him hard. "Mr. Seargant, what can I do to help? Really. If this is all true, I—"

Seargant's phone came to life, and he stabbed at the small unit, placing it to his ear, eyeing Sam.

"This is Seargant.," he stated calmly. "Yes sir, I'll hold."

Empty seconds passed and Sam sucked in a deep breath, looking to Seargant, who suddenly stood.

"Yes, Mr. President," he stated, firmly. "Absolutely. I'll be there in twenty minutes."

Seargant looked at Sam and then to Agent Hartley. "Keep him occupied. I've got a meeting at the White House."

CHAPTER 49

"What's your first memory," Lisa asked, turning the wheel slightly and straightening out in the left lane.

They were in South Carolina and skipped *South of the Border*. The windows were down and the fresh, warm air lent another level of freedom as it washed over them.

Pip glanced over, shrugging. "I don't know. My whole life was pretty much in the orphanage."

"What about before? Any recollection?"

Pip grimaced, looking down. He held his hands together, nervously, and peered outside as a distraction.

Lisa spoke in a playful voice, trying to lighten the mood. "I would apologize for being so blunt, but seeing as you need to work all this childhood trauma stuff out, and we're alone in my car for a fifteen-hour road trip that you talked me into...

"...And because four of our ex-presidents were just assassinated, and you supposedly have some intel to save the world, because you're a brilliant NSA computer whiz who just happened to save my life..."

Lisa glanced at Pip who was still silent. "Anything? Anything at all?" Lisa prompted.

Pip cracked a weary smile. Lisa had a way about her. She eased his insecurities and pulled him out of his shell, illuminating everything within. And while he'd only just met her, he was most definitely falling for her.

He didn't mind speaking to her about his childhood and felt fairly well adjusted to the traumas of his past. Absent Sam, she was the only one he'd opened up to—spoken so freely to—and he felt renewed with every exchange.

What was really on his mind was the endgame. Sam was safe and he now felt he could trust Seargant. But something was gnawing at him and he couldn't place it.

If he'd handed the recording over it would shake the presidency. Things like that weren't easily dealt with. There was always a fall guy, and he knew it would be him.

So, what should he do? The higher ups would probably eliminate the evidence, and everyone tied to it. It was their only play.

"I only remember one real birthday," Pip said. "I turned five and my mom gave me a sandbox with a few trucks to play with. It was just me and her, and she made a beautiful cake. It had white frosting and red letters, matching the tiny fire trucks that were on top and the ones she gave me for the sandbox. There were blue balloons attached to a small picnic table."

"What was she like?" Lisa asked.

"I don't remember much about her. She had dark, shoulder length hair. She was always with me and hugged and kissed me a lot. She was like a blanket to me and I still feel her warmth, even now."

Lisa remained silent and Pip continued.

"She was twenty-one when she was murdered in a drug transaction, and it was never solved. She left me with a note, saying she'd always be there for me, and was sorry she couldn't watch me grow."

"I don't mean to pry Pip but that sounds more like a premonition. Like she knew she wasn't gonna make it."

"Yeah, I've often thought about that. She also wrote that the sandbox was her forever gift to me, and she loved me."

"I'm so sorry."

"So that's the only birthday you remember, even though it was one of the farthest away in memory?"

"I remember because it's the only time I had a birthday cake. After that I was institutionalized, and it never happened again."

Lisa's right hand came off the wheel and she moved it to Pip, whose hands were clasped together on his lap. She held his clenched fists tight, trading glances between the road and Pip's glassy eyes.

"I'm so sorry, Pip."

"I never sausage a thing!" Pip exclaimed, perking up.

"What?" Lisa asked.

Pip pointed to another South of the Border billboard, this time on the other side of the interstate facing north. "I never sausage a thing!"

They fell into a quick laugh, but Lisa stole a glance at Pip, who blinked away tears and wiped at his flushed face. She wanted to reach over and hug him. To tell him—to make him believe—that he was amazing. But no amount of conversation could uncover the exact details of Pip's young life.

Or how it all began twenty-eight years prior.

PART FOUR

A LITTLE MORE ABOUT PIP...
(TWENTY-EIGHT YEARS AGO)

CHAPTER 50

South Baltimore

Wendy called him Pip for two reasons: his initials and his small size.

His given name was Pryce Irvine Palmer, and he was born at only twenty-six weeks at just over a pound. His first six months were spent in incubators; fighting jaundice and other ailments his immune system couldn't defend. It was touch-and-go for most of that time, but miraculously the little boy survived and gained weight.

He was also born an addict; with heroin and crystal meth amphetamine being the favorite pastime of his teenage, sometimes homeless mother. Wendy was a runaway since the age of fourteen.

She was a hardened and tenacious soul who'd already lived a punishing life, with experiences well beyond her years. The drugs calmed her and allowed her mind to accept the sometimes-vulgar things she did to survive the streets.

She didn't know Pip's father. Looking back, she wouldn't even remember how she'd arrived at Mercy Hospital to give birth.

But one thing was clear when she looked into her newborn baby's eyes. She felt an overwhelming feeling of love wash over her. It invaded her soul—her very being—and blew up, shaking her senses alive in a way she'd never known. She was paralyzed in a moment of clarity and just knew that Pip had saved her.

No drug had ever given her the euphoria this innocent boy conveyed so easily.

Within a week of giving birth, she was released to the authorities and in front of a judge. She pleaded her drug charges, promised to be a changed person, and that her little "Pip Squeak" had given her hope she'd never known.

She just knew he would survive, though his road would be long and arduous. And she recognized what *she* had to do. For the first time, Wendy saw a future for herself.

She was given a suspended sentence contingent on a successful stay in rehab. Her court appointed attorney provided a timeline and outlined the procedure for a probation officer, and a path to at least *try* to get her son back.

Sunny Day was a wellness facility in Harford County, simple in its design but determined in its resolve to cure chemical addiction. There were twenty rooms and twenty staff members, most with their own stories of reclamation.

Wendy met with the nutritionist, personal trainer, and psychologist, while also being very vocal during the group meetings. The whole time her medical doctors monitored her health, which improved exponentially. Water and protein-layered salads fueled her, and she'd never felt so focused and alive! She thought of her little Pip nonstop and was assured of his steady progress in neonatal care.

So, upon Pip's release from child support services, and after a successful stint in rehab, she'd petitioned the court and was eventually granted custody of her little "Pip-Squeak." At eighteen, she was set up in public housing, and Wendy was determined to love and support her baby.

She knew there was a long road ahead, but she loved him deeply. The nighttime feedings, the bed wetting that lasted months longer than normal, the stunted development, and medications only brought them closer.

Still, she knew herself. She'd been a drug user, a prostitute, and a thief. She'd lied to the authorities too many times to count and had successfully dodged the law more times than that.

But those days were over.

Still, the painful thoughts and regrets of her past punished her at the most random times; usually at nighttime when silence ruled, and she was alone with her thoughts. But mostly, it was when she would feed Pip and those brown searching eyes just looked right back at her.

But those eyes were without an ounce of judgment or chiding. Just pure innocence and love. And it was in one of those feeding times late at night, when they were locked in a stare, that she finally forgave herself, said a silent prayer, and promised Pip she would take care of him.

Public housing assistance and welfare turned out to be a blessing for a girl who had nothing from the start. She made their small Baltimore row house a home and budgeted accordingly. When it came to managing finances and negotiating paperwork, she was a fast learner. Pip's well-being depended on her cutting corners, and she would never hurt him again.

It was just her and Pip and the months turned to years, as both became healthier and stronger in their love for one another.

On Pip's fifth birthday, his sand box became his kingdom.

It was a crude six by six-foot square in the backyard. Wendy had simply dug a hole, framed it with nearby abandoned railroad timber, and dumped in fresh sand.

After a birthday cake with just the two of them, she brought him outside to show him. It wasn't much, but to Pip it was everything.

There was a bulldozer, fire truck, and dump truck, along with a handful of plastic sand toys. For hours, Pip would design and form roadways, fences, sandcastles, and tunnels. He would sometimes use an old colander and hide rocks to act out finding buried treasure. Sometimes Wendy would place a penny or a piece of wrapped candy in the sandbox and tell him to find his fortune.

His brown eyes would grow large and light up at every challenge.

And through all of his fantasy and adventure, Wendy would sit in her plastic porch chair, drinking coffee or water and watch her miracle develop.

Her little Pip. Her beacon of light for the future.

She'd never believed in love but couldn't deny it now. It was wholesome and clean. It was the purest, most unsullied emotion she'd ever known.

Pip always looked at her, adoringly. He never cast doubts and didn't care if she couldn't afford the best clothes or cosmetics. Didn't care what she looked or smelled like. She took care of him, and he returned it ten-fold with a simple smile.

Despite his circumstances and physical under-development, Pip was an unusually bright child, with a natural curiosity. He rarely became frustrated and was patient in his natural progression and understanding. Together they took turns reading book after book from the local library.

They lived on Bank Street in south Baltimore; unaware of the deteriorating neighborhood that enveloped them. They didn't pay attention to the MARC trains just a stones-throw away that shook their thin walls at all hours. They didn't care about the nearby vagrants or the rodents that scampered just outside.

When it was time for kindergarten, Wendy walked Pip to and from school. She was a proud mother who wouldn't leave until he was safely inside. But she wasn't equipped to handle the silence; and that's when the emptiness crept in.

She took a part-time job at a corner grocery but lost it after complaining about a customer grabbing her inappropriately.

It didn't take long for her to associate with a bad crowd. And although she remained drug free, she became a runner. She knew it was wrong, but the money was right, and she'd do anything to provide for Pip.

Soon she was in too deep.

On a rainy afternoon a money count came up short. She and another runner were brought to an empty warehouse near the sports stadiums and interrogated. She was innocent and ignorant to what happened. She never looked in the bags; just did what she was told. It was her blind naivete that saved her. She never knew she was carrying tens of thousands of dollars at a time.

Still, they killed the young thief next to her and made her witness the execution. Her clothes were sprayed with blood, but she couldn't afford to throw them away. She scrubbed them clean, but when she wore them, she would re-live the experience vividly. She was forever stained.

But she had Pip.

It was a bright sunny day in mid-October when she had the idea.

She left Pip in his sandbox and wrote two letters to her son. One she left on the kitchen table; the other was carefully folded and placed in several plastic bags to be buried in a box, possibly *never* to be found.

And if things went well, there would be no need for either.

Later that day it was done; and it was all she could think about as she nervously watched Pip in his sandbox.

The next week she failed to collect Pip from school. Her body was found soon after and Pip was sent to child services.

He arrived with exactly one suitcase and one letter. The police read it during the murder investigation and released it to the orphanage.

There was seemingly nothing important about it.

Pip would never play in his sandbox again. He entered the orphanage at five years old and didn't leave protective services until he was eighteen.

When he departed, it was with the same old bag and that one letter from his mother. He'd memorized the words years ago and would recite the message several times a week, deep in his own thoughts.

And still, more than two decades later, Pip didn't think it held much importance.

But he was wrong.

Because the words contained a clue to another letter, buried deep within a box. And the information within that one *really* told the tale.

CHAPTER 51

The kindergarten teacher took extra notice of Pip.

She knew he was an orphan and understood the circumstances that had stunted his growth, making him appear much younger than the others. She also knew children could be cruel.

But Pip was physically adoring, with large brown eyes that searched everywhere in silent appreciation. Everything was a mystery to be solved, and he couldn't get enough. He was instantly likeable and made friends easily.

He progressed through the grade levels with ease, earning A's in every subject and maintaining a steady interest in his schoolwork.

At twelve, Pip became the longest tenured resident at the Franklin House Orphanage. Kids came and went, the younger ones with more regularity, and he maintained no real friendships.

He was transferred to a new school for sixth grade. Initially the faculty treated him delicately. It was known and discussed that his mother had been murdered and he had no family. He lived in an orphanage and could carry his entire life in the worn book bag that hung from his narrow shoulders.

The other children now seemed to avoid him.

He was physically different, easily the smallest in his class, looking more like a second or third grader than a sixth grader. But he possessed a certain determination and outlook. He seemed oblivious to his plight or the way others regarded him. If life had dulled or jaded him, it was not outwardly apparent. He was always eager to lend a helping hand to both teacher and student and was naturally optimistic.

Some thought him childlike and made fun of him for trying to curry favor with the teachers. He had no real friends; and as time wore on and new kids matriculated in, Pip's situation, while sad, just became another story.

He met his future best friend, Sam, during a game of roughhouse football. The rules of the game were simple: if you held the ball, you ran until you were tackled.

Sam was tall for a six grader. Standing several inches over his classmates, he was naturally strong, with muscles that seemed to grow weekly. He was a below average student, more concerned with sports and impressing girls than academics.

During the game Pip sat on the sideline reading a book when the football bounced near him. Looking up, Pip smiled into the sun, shading his eyes. He handled the ball and threw it to the group of kids.

"I'm sorry, but I don't want to play, guys," he said, meekly.

Charlie Rose, a mean, stocky kid, managed a grunt. He hung out with a couple other boys, and they claimed to be a gang of three. They ran the school yard and committed small acts of defiance against everyone.

"You touched the ball so either you take it and run, or we simply lay into you right now," he said, cackling.

The other kids were quiet, eyeing Charlie, while Pip remained sitting.

"Sorry," Pip started. "I'm just not into it, but I appreciate you asking."

Charlie moved closer. He lowered his head, as his narrow eyes bore into Pip.

"It wasn't a question. You have three seconds to get off your ass with the ball and run or I'll demolish you where you sit."

Silence ruled as Pip slowly stood. He looked to the other kids, expectantly, but was met with only stares.

He picked up the ball and managed a slow, awkward run to the other side of the field. Pip's wardrobe was mostly second hand and donated; and was often mismatched in both size and color. His shoes were too big and his pants too tight. Both, along with his small size, impeded him and Charlie overtook him easily.

Pip was thrown to the ground in a hard tackle, with the larger boy on top of him, as they both slid in the wet grass. Pip's pants tore immediately; his clothes stained green and brown. His body was bruised, his right cheek scraped, and he almost blacked out.

Charlie bounced up and placed his right foot on Pip, raising his hands over his head like a champion. His two buddies cheered as the other kids watched.

Then a small whimper erupted from Pip, as he rolled over, clutching his side.

Charlie looked down, laughing. "Get up you pussy!" he yelled, scouring at Pip, now in a fetal position.

"Move away!" a voice yelled, as Sam walked into the fray.

"Get outta here. This doesn't concern you," Charlie said, turning to his friends, laughing.

But Sam stayed, moving to Pip. He looked the small boy over, taking stock of his injuries.

"Hey, man," Sam offered, gingerly, touching his shoulder. "Are you okay?"

Pip opened his eyes as tears streamed down his dirty face. He just stared back, impassively.

Sam looked back at Charlie, who was still laughing.

Charlie took the opportunity to unleash another verbal attack. "Do you two need a room or something?"

Sam turned back to Pip. "Listen, I know you have a lot to cry about, I really do, and I'm sorry about what happened. But don't cry now. Go somewhere and do it there, but just not *now*."

Pip wiped away a tear. Then he popped up and stood, wearily, limping past the three boys with Sam in tow.

"See you later, lovers," Charlie called out, snickering.

And that's when Sam turned.

Charlie saw it and squared against him. "You want some of this?" Charlie taunted, motioning with his hands, and acknowledging three against one.

But Sam was undeterred. He sized up Charlie with confidence and clocked him, sending him into the grass. Then he turned to the others, but they were already in retreat.

Sam stood over Charlie, who was holding the side of his face.

"Never again," Sam said, peering down.

But Charlie just glared up at Sam in insolence. Sam bent down and pinned Charlie hard into the ground. He raised his fist and held it high, ready to strike.

"Okay," Charlie muttered, closing his eyes, and holding his hands up in submission.

"Never again," Sam repeated. Then he rolled off the boy and ran after Pip.

Pip never looked back but slowed as Sam drew near. They walked a mile in silence, before coming to a bench and sitting. Pip cried and Sam waited him out. But the smaller boy was resilient and soon they were talking nonstop. Pip had never had a friend and Sam proved a good listener. Pip told Sam about the orphanage and Sam spoke about being raised by a single mother.

Sam had little interest in Pip's computer system, so every day after school, they would go to Sam's house, and with each visit Pip was in awe. There was plenty of food in the pantry and toys and video games were everywhere. Sam had his own personal space, with a bed, plenty of blankets, a dresser, and a desk. There was a baseball signed by the Orioles, a few Ravens posters, and plenty of sports trophies on the shelf.

And there were pictures.

Most were framed and some were thumbtacked to the wall, but there were images of Sam and his mom and dad in happier times.

One day the revelation hit Pip hard. He suddenly realized he'd never owned a picture, not even of himself. But Sam was there with patient understanding and a crude joke, that made Pip laugh.

As time wore on, they continued to complement each other, with Sam being the charming, energetic athlete; and Pip the quiet, reliable, and intelligent type who thought things through and offered different perspectives.

They knew everything about each other and kept each other's secrets. There was nothing they wouldn't do for the other, and the years passed easily.

At eighteen, they both worked odd landscape jobs and attended Anne Arundel Community College. This time it was Pip taking care of Sam with endless tutoring and help with his budgeting.

Pip sailed through the curriculum with more A's, while Sam barely got through with C's. Pip worked as a teacher's assistant for several professors in the computer department, and even tutored on the side. Sam worked the fast-food joints, smoked a little weed, and hit as many parties as he could.

Then they graduated.

Pip walked off the stage with a two-year degree in computer science and wasn't surprised when no one applauded or took notice. He'd grown up knowing the world was a hard and lonely place, and that was a lesson as important as the piece of paper in his hand.

But surprisingly, there *was* someone waiting for him.

"Pryce Palmer, right?" the man asked, with an outstretched hand.

Pip was surprised and shook the man's hand, quizzically looking him over. He was about fifty years old, with a thin goatee, smooth bald head, and soft blue eyes. He was average in size and his brown suit looked like it had seen better days.

"It's actually Pip."

"Pip, my name is Rob Gloekler and I work for the National Security Agency. Your professors have told me about your computer engineering capabilities, and we'd really appreciate it if you'd come talk with us about a possible job."

PART FIVE

No Safe Place
(Today)

CHAPTER 52

President Maclemore stared out the window of the Oval Office, seeing nothing and lost in the thoughts purging his mind.

His itinerary had been wiped clean, replaced by security briefings, calls to and from leaders from all over the world, and off-script speeches to the American people, urging calm and pledging justice.

But between the noise, he found himself increasingly pensive and withdrawn, almost feeling adrift outside his own body.

His thoughts reached to the edges of his mind and landed in the most uncommon places. He recalled dreams he'd had as a child, the decades-old scents of his mother's kitchen stove, and the fresh leather smell of his first baseball glove. And then he'd come back into the present, answering a phone call from the Pentagon, overwhelmed by the constant din of noninformation.

It had been four days since the first two assassinations and there were no credible leads and nothing much learned. At least nothing he could believe.

"Sir?" a voice sounded, breaking the man's concentration.

The president turned. "Oh, hi Ruthie," he responded calmly. "What is it?"

"They're here. Shall I show them in?"

"Yes, right away," he said, straightening his tie.

Then he looked up to see the handful of men he'd requested. Jack Seargant and James Gibson of the FBI, Director of the CIA Steve McCallister, and Generals Bauer and Warren from the Joint Chiefs of Staff.

"Please come in, gentlemen and have a seat. Let's get right to it. Where are we on the investigation?"

James Gibson handed a binder to the president and sat down. "Sir, I'll summarize this briefing, but all the details are in there. We've confirmed that Preston was indeed assassinated in plain sight. It was ricin inside his inhaler and the investigation is ongoing. We don't believe the residence was infiltrated, but rather his monthly supply was compromised.

"President Gilmore's was the most elaborate. The assassin was waiting for him inside a piece of furniture within the room at the Waldorf Astoria and Gilmore came to *him*."

"Let me stop you there," the president interjected. "With Preston, how did the inhalers get into the wrong hands? Aren't they sealed, anonymous, and even controlled by *our* guys?"

Gibby shifted, uncomfortably. "Yes, they are *supposed* to be. Somehow, though, they were intercepted, tampered with, and delivered. We are still investigating."

"And how did they know that Gilmore would be diverted to the Waldorf?"

"Again, sir, we are looking into that as well, but whomever did this knew their schedules. When Bowman and Montgomery were killed, they knew the lockdown procedure. And with Gilmore already in New York, speaking at a Wall Street event, it made sense to the Secret Service to go to the Waldorf."

President Maclemore grimaced, thinking of his stay there just under a year ago. It had been a beautiful evening. After a meeting at the U.N., he and Judy dined at Carmines, then watched *Hamilton* on Broadway—even arriving at their balcony to a standing ovation—before retiring to that same Presidential Suite.

"You're saying the assassin got lucky?"

"It was like chess. He made a premediated move and correctly guessed our counter, having also perfectly planned for that as well. But Gilmore could have just as easily been routed to LaGuardia and flown—"

"Have you questioned the lead guy on his detail?"

Gibby looked to the others before regarding the president. "Actually, sir, it was a woman. Heather Moore and—"

"Let's not mince words. We don't have the time. Has *she* been—"

"She's dead, sir, as are most of her team. Blown to pieces just after the assassination."

The words hung in the air and Maclemore fell silent. The oxygen seemed to be sucked from the room, and the president looked to McCallister, who stood and buttoned the top of his jacket.

"Sir, I was there, and I still feel the effects of that blast, and the two shots fired into my vest. Ironically, they're probably what saved me, because the door opened, I got shot and was pushed to the right, away from the explosions."

The president nodded. "McCallister, you've been around a long time, and I trust you more than you'll ever know. But I must say out loud, that you were present at two of these assassinations.

"I mean, President Gilmore gets killed just a couple of rooms away and you somehow survive the gun shots and the grenade blasts. Then you fly to California just in time to witness President Preston's demise?"

McCallister glared at the president. "What are you implying, sir?"

The president just shook his head and McCallister continued, raising his voice. "I told Gilmore I wanted to be by his side. Hell, I wanted to kill Falby in custody two years ago, but Bowman wouldn't let me just—"

"That's top-secret Steve," General Warren interrupted.

Steve was muted, but he was finishing the conversation in his mind. After the Last Patriot operation ended, then-President Harold Bowman had denied Steve's request to interrogate and kill Falby in private.

Instead, the man was kept from McCallister and eventually escaped. How ironic that the very person who had secretly saved the man was eventually killed by him, and even with Secret Service protection.

The president cleared his throat, addressing the others. "So, you really want me to believe that one man did this? Killed four presidents in three days?"

Jack Seargant now stood, walking to the opposite side of the room from McCallister. "Director McCallister was also present just *after* President Bowman's assassination at the golf course."

McCallister looked to Seargant, who met his gaze and continued.

"And McCallister was correct with his on-site assessment, though I must say I didn't initially believe it. We combed the trees surrounding the area and found a couple of camouflaged cameras. We were also able to salvage and analyze some of the bomb fragments at the tee box."

Seargant placed another report on the president's desk. "Steve was correct in knowing there would be fingerprints all over the cameras. They belong to one man. The terrorist known as Falby."

The president scoffed, incredulously.

Seargant continued. "And here's the forensic report from the sniper rifle in Connecticut. Falby's fingerprints are all over it as well."

The president stood and walked the room slowly, thinking through the information. Then he turned to McCallister.

"Steve, how did you know this man would be so careless?"

McCallister shook his head. "He wasn't being careless; he just doesn't care. He has no problem with everyone knowing he's responsible and wouldn't have wasted a second masking that. He's the most focused of operators. If it's not crucial to the task, he wouldn't waste the time and energy."

"But why?" the president continued. "It would have been so easy to wear gloves and maintain an element of anonymity. Why wouldn't—"

"I know this man," Steve interrupted. "I've hunted him for years and even wrestled with him on a rooftop in Chile. Trust me when I say that he doesn't care if anyone knows, because he's still holding all the cards anyway.

"They call him the Chameleon because he's a ghost. He moves easily and seemingly invisibly, and he's always plotting a way out of every situation.

"He's escaped from every compromising position he's ever been in. Who cares if you have his fingerprints when you'll never find him anyway?"

Seargant chimed in. "Steve, he's just a man and—"

"Yeah, he's just a man, but he's also the most dangerous operator I've ever known."

The president moved between Seargant and McCallister, who seemed intent on debating all day. "I still want his picture everywhere.

Release it immediately. Maybe it'll force an action and lead to a mistake. Anything we can leverage to expose him!"

McCallister shook his head. "Sir, he's always several moves ahead. Whatever you've thought of, he's already planned for and has countered with meticulous planning. Which leads me to something else. I know that you were Harold Bowman's vice president, and you became very close friends. But I implore you not to go to his burial service in Kentucky."

The president was already shaking his head in determination. "My team is confident. Security sweeps are already in motion and your assumption that this is a one-man show is actually encouraging."

"That's my point. You're making a move that is known by the very man who may want to place you in that position."

President Maclemore's ego was stoked, and he couldn't run from the comment. "Look McCallister, like Agent Seargant said, he's just a man and we're the United States government. We don't run, especially when we know his identity."

"Sir, this man has just killed four former presidents, and he's probably assuming you'll be at Bowman's burial."

"And the good guys also know that. He wouldn't be that stupid to try for the big prize. Make no mistake, in two days this country is honoring these four great men at the National Cathedral and afterward, I'm personally escorting Bowman's body to Kentucky to see him laid to rest."

The president turned to the two generals, both of whom stood proudly. "Where are we on military readiness?"

General Bauer spoke in a deep, calm voice. "We're ready to go, sir, and have been working with the Secret Service to bolster their efforts."

McCallister cleared his throat and all eyes moved to him. "Well then, let me go with you, Mr. President."

Maclemore was already shaking his head. "I'm not going to complicate things by traveling with the director of the CIA! It's going to be too crowded as it is!"

Seargant walked a few paces to the president's side. "Sir, I completely understand your perspective and the director's position. But with respect, I'd like to tag along. Just a single FBI agent, along for the ride."

The president nodded approvingly, looking to the others. "Then we're done here, gentlemen. I want this man's many faces and descriptions everywhere. And I want it done now!"

The small group cleared the room, save Steve McCallister, who lingered between the two couches in the center, hoping to get another word in. But the president turned his back on the director of the CIA, walking through the side door and into his personal office.

So McCallister sighed, defeatedly, before excusing himself, as a familiar feeling of dread consumed him.

CHAPTER 53

Southwest of Diana
Webster County, West Virginia

Falby sat motionless in a simple chair.

He'd been back in West Virginia for a few days and was fully rested; after what had been a tumultuous time. In under two weeks, he'd been to twelve states, killed four former presidents, and slept less than four hours each day in short durations.

But he'd done his job.

Other than the drive from New York to West Virginia, he hadn't listened to the news or read a single newspaper. He knew the details firsthand and didn't need to rehash a thing.

But he *did* enjoy replaying the memories in his head.

He thought of Preston in California. It was paradoxical that things had gone so perfectly. He was the last to die but the first to be set in motion. It was also the least intimate, something he regretted, but knew necessary, given the man's condition and fortified security.

No one saw it coming and Falby infiltrated all four perimeters of protection by tainting the man's monthly supply of asthma inhalers.

His contact—the man without a name—had provided a sample of the actual supply, and from there it was an easy matter of manufacturing and adding ricin. It was commonly known that the man needed inhalers several times a day. So, it became a waiting game.

And once inhaled, the ricin took hold immediately.

To his medical staff, James Preston looked to be having increased respiratory problems and flu-like symptoms. Little did anyone know that his death was guaranteed, albeit delayed, for a week.

And in that time, Falby had finalized Bowman's bombing in Maryland, and reached Connecticut to await Montgomery's fateful sail.

The hardest part was the wait at the Waldorf, but it was so satisfying killing Gilmore and then running into McCallister again.

It had only been a moment, but after Falby shot through the door and emerged with the grenades, there was no mistaking the man to be Steve McCallister. The director of the CIA and the man Falby had sparred with in the past.

Falby wouldn't have minded the man dead, but even seconds were crucial, and he couldn't waste time. McCallister wasn't the prize; not then anyway.

A twisted grin erupted as he thought more about Steve McCallister. Their time in Chile was one for the books. Falby had underestimated him and would never do so again. Theirs was a storied game of cat and mouse, and Falby almost hoped McCallister survived so he could relish in killing him.

The phone rang and Falby reached for it, slowly. He hadn't been expecting the call, but the number was one he knew well.

It was the man without a name.

"Yes," Falby stated calmly.

"There's a slight problem," the voice announced.

"Not on my end," Falby said, defiantly. *"Never* on my end."

The voice shook. The words came out quick and there was no doubt the man was becoming unhinged. Falby absorbed every word, committing it all to memory.

"I did some digging," the man continued. "This analyst is a loner. He runs in a very small circle. I went with a hunch and it panned out. He was integral in solving the Wolf Man serial killer case a month or so ago."

Falby straightened. It had been national news and he'd read about it. "Go on."

"I have no confirmation that this analyst is with her, but I'm tracking her phone and she's in Florida as we speak."

Falby grunted. "Then put some human intel on the ground and verify—"

The man cut him off. "The less people involved the better. I need *you* there. I've just sent you photos of them both, the schematics on her phone, the details of her car. This phone is on me 24/7 for updates."

"This is outside our agreement, and you know I have plans to leave within the hour."

"Yes, but the situation has changed. There was no way to know with absolute certainty—"

"Then you must do something for me," Falby quickly inserted.

"And what is that?"

"It's *also* outside our agreement. But I have a side project and if I do this for you, I cannot pursue it."

The man listened to Falby speak for several minutes. He couldn't believe what he was hearing and even agreeing to, but it was certainly within his scope and ability.

"And by the way, send someone *disposable*," Falby said.

The man's grip on his phone tightened, knowing what it meant. But then he released it just as easily, as his mind leapt forward to a sudden opportunity, and he thought of a specific operator.

Jordy.

Why hadn't he thought of him before?

"I understand completely, Falby," the man said, a sense of relief washing over him. "I have the right man for the job. Consider it done."

And the man without a name ended the call.

CHAPTER 54

Jordy was a regular at McDoogals strip club.

The young dancers came and went like a revolving door, and most of the bartenders didn't stay much longer, but there was always Jordy.

Located in Curtis Bay, just outside the Baltimore beltway's southeast stretch, McDoogals is licensed as more of a private club than a bar. It's a gray area that allows patrons to bring their own alcohol and pay an increased fee at the door.

Most days Jordy would sit at his usual corner of the bar, so he could face the front door, with two pool tables to his left. He'd sip his cheap brown swill, deep in thought, eyes down, while the pretty young girls did their thing on a single wooden platform in the center.

He was gracious, and though he never mixed with the girls, he'd over-tip and be courteous, enjoying his time alone. His only outburst had been a few years before, when a group of rough necks from the nearby oil refineries—drunk already—stumbled into the place.

One got on stage and started dancing, while another grabbed a girl and buried his bushy face into her ample chest. She ran to the back and the man erupted in laughter, as he cracked open a Pabst Blue Ribbon.

A weekday afternoon only allowed for a single bouncer, and he was younger and smaller than anyone in the group. Jordy sat motionless, sipping his drink but seeing it all. Crystal, the bartender walked over and tried to quell things, offering a slight smile.

"Listen, fellas. I get that you're here to have a good time and we appreciate that, but you need to calm down if you want to stay."

Quick nods and false affirmations followed, and one of them even offered a halfhearted apology, saying he'd just gotten divorced, and his buddies were taking him out.

Crystal nodded and retreated to the end of the bar, turning up a Mötley Crüe song.

As *Girls Girls Girls* blasted, two pretty young things swayed seductively on stage and the men were appeased for the time being.

Jordy returned to his thoughts.

In his mind, he wasn't in a strip joint, but in the harsh climate of Fallujah in the fire fight of his life.

3rd Battalion, 1st Marines. Commanded by Lieutenant General Richard Natonski, directly under Lieutenant Colonel Willard Buhl.

Jordy's face pained as he took another sip and remembered the frontal assault.

He could taste and feel the grit in his mouth and lungs, as he remembered breathing in the desert air and humping his 130-pound pack. His unit first moved south from the railroad tracks along Phase Line Dave, and then southwest to the Euphrates River.

And they cleared everything in their path.

Several minutes later he was shaken into the present by a large hand on his shoulder.

"I said, 'Hey boy, we're outta beer.' What are you deaf?"

But Jordy hadn't heard a word and the confusion showed on his face.

"What'cha drinking?" the man slurred. "Gimme some of that!"

The large man reached for the drink and Jordy launched into action without thought. He grabbed the man's arm and twisted it, before moving into his body and snapping down, breaking his arm. Then he forced the stunned man's head onto the bar, breaking his nose.

The others were quick to walk over to avenge their friend. But this time Jordy had the benefit of timing and awareness. He moved to the center of the room and lowered his head, watching how the group was moving. He sensed nothing special and took them for simple street thugs.

Jordy was just over six feet tall and even in his late forties was well built. Tattoos covered both of his thick arms and he worked out regularly. His closely cropped hair and humble manner spoke of military, but the Harley Davidson T-shirt, torn jeans, and black boots suggested him as a biker.

Still, he had soft blue eyes and when he offered a rare smile, it was sincere and warming, and allowed a glimpse into a life at war with itself.

The largest of the group stepped forward. He looked Jordy over, shaking his head and trying to get a read.

"Now why'd you go and do that, boy?"

Jordy offered nothing. He just stared back, controlled his breathing, and continued to eye the dynamic of the group, treating them as a whole, not as singles.

What happened next was a fury of movement, but it didn't last long. The large man came at Jordy, throwing two punches that missed wide. Jordy went low and countered, with targeted blows to the man's midsection, feeling ribs break on the fourth strike.

The man went down hard, holding his sides and breathing erratically. The next two came from flanking positions. Jordy met the first head on with an uppercut that sent him back, before a round kick caught the other right in the throat.

Another ran to the pool tables and picked up a stray pool cue. He was short and fat, and swung it wildly, putting on more of an act than anything. He stepped over one of his friends and approached Jordy, cautiously.

He was drunk, and the erratic movement consumed most of his energy. By the time he was within striking distance, he was panting and off-balance. Jordy grabbed the pool cue easily, broke it over his knee, and clocked the man on the side of the head, sending him to the floor unconscious.

Two others looked to Jordy and then to his effectiveness, writhing on the floor. They seemed more winded than Jordy as they helped their friends up and out of the place.

Jordy returned to his spot at the bar, where he took another swig and returned to his thoughts.

The bouncer finally made his way over and helped usher the group outside, watching them drive away.

Crystal walked over to Jordy. "Thank you for that," she offered.

He nodded politely, but then lowered his shoulders, closed his eyes, and finished his drink.

Jordy's phone rang and he glanced at the display, frowning.

Then he quickly rose, feeling the full effects of the bourbon he'd been sipping for the past few hours.

He answered the phone and moved to the door, walking into the late afternoon sunshine.

It was the man without a name.

"Yes," Jordy said.

Then he listened intently to the voice on the other end, closing his eyes and committing every detail to memory.

"I'll do it now, sir."

The call over, he rushed to his classic Mustang, parked directly under the sign for Dave's Automotive Repair. Then he started northwest on Fort Smallwood Road toward I-695.

He didn't like the assignment he'd just agreed to. It was too brazen; too reckless. But by the time he turned right onto Fort Armistead Road, he got confirmation that the $250,000 wire had hit his account.

He reconciled things in his mind and started to plan it through. When he crossed into Essex, he'd mentally assembled everything he needed.

But first he had to leave something for his ex-wife.

He sensed something was off and he had to cover some bases. He owed it to Pam and his little girl.

CHAPTER 55

Pip had been driving since their last gas stop and Lisa was napping, quietly.

Midnight found them crossing into Florida, and within the hour the road arced left, as the bright lights of Jacksonville lit up the dark night. Pip smiled broadly, trading views of the dark road ahead, and the water edging the city to his left.

He'd been mentally checking off the states—Florida being his seventh in one day. And with each new state they entered, each city they drove by, and every bridge they crossed, he gained more confidence in his bidding. A better sense of independence and spirit.

He felt emboldened as they pressed on. Liberated and able to face whatever was in his path.

Pip stole a look at Lisa in the passenger seat, shifting in her sleep. He was so grateful for her. A gift in every sense of the word. She was not only his partner in this crazy endeavor, but one of the most solid people he'd ever known.

In the brief time they'd met, the minutes felt like days, the hours like months and years. It was as if they'd been friends forever.

Now curving to the right, with Jacksonville's city lights in the rearview mirror, Pip tightened his grip on the steering wheel and accelerated into the left lane. Soon they'd be on I-4 heading west and before long, pulling into a motel near Disney World.

Then, they'd get some well needed rest and figure things out from there.

After doing some quick research on Google, Pip decided on the Red Roof Inn on Route 92. It was near Disney World and was cheaper and more secluded than the busier places on International Drive.

The motel was tucked behind the lights of the well-lit road, and close to scores of restaurants and stores. And there was no shortage of out-of-state license plates, meaning that large families would be teeming the area all day long. A crowd favored them, and anonymity could always be found in large groups.

Pip woke Lisa and they checked in, quickly moving their things to a room on the second floor. There were two queen beds and a small bathroom. Heavy beige drapes hung across two wide windows, and some nondescript landscape pictures hung on the close walls.

Pip threw his things onto the floor and shut the drapes tight. He turned up the air conditioning to clear the stale, hot air, then used the bathroom. Then he brushed his teeth and fell into bed, exhausted.

Lisa moved to the other bed, but after slumbering for the last few hours, her mind was racing, and she couldn't sleep.

After a few minutes of hearing Pip's steady breathing and light snoring, she threw on the same clothes she'd just removed. Then she grabbed her purse and key card and exited, leaving Pip to rest.

CHAPTER 56

Lisa gently shut the heavy motel door, trying her best to be discreet. She heard the distinct clasp of the lock and walked the narrow hall in the outside air.

The Florida night felt opposite to the cool, dark room. Even after midnight, the temperature was firmly in the 80's. The air was still, and the only noise came from the humming air conditioning units outside the row of rooms.

She was uneasy about leaving Pip, but he needed rest, especially with everything going on. Orlando was home to Disney World, the most magical place on earth, so she figured she'd be safe, and they needed snacks and cold water. So she hurried to the stairway and bounded down with newfound energy. She'd never been to Florida and couldn't hide her enthusiasm in exploring, even so late at night.

Walking in the shadows, she passed the busy IHOP, and a string of fast-food restaurants, convenience stores, and souvenir shops. All were well lit and frenetic, even at the late hour.

Lisa felt giddy as she took in the colors and sounds. It was so different from her small town in Pennsylvania, and she regarded it all, wide-eyed with wonder.

She walked into a large souvenir shop, with windows that filled the facade. It had an old wooden roof that curved high and swung low in an exaggerated angle. They advertised $2 T-shirts and the lowest pricing on everything Disney.

She walked every aisle, perusing the trinkets. It was a playground of toys, clothing, and knickknacks; a perfect medley of shiny, colorful things representing every magical character from her childhood.

She immediately thought of Pip and frowned. He didn't have a childhood filled with these animated characters, and probably had never seen the Disney classics.

She picked up a Mickey Mouse plush toy, smiling all the way to the cashier.

Next, she walked into a convenience store. She looked around casually, more an attempt at passing time, until she saw a bunch of bananas. Curious, she picked them up and saw a small sticker on one of them, representing the supplier and the price. She thought of Carl Fink from the orphanage and shook her head.

An image of Pip flashed in her mind, and she smiled, recalling their poignant conversations. They'd only just met but she felt a connection she'd never known.

Pip had spoken to her in a way that no one ever had.

Even her long conversations with Amy, her best friend for years— someone who knew everything about her—couldn't compare to the electricity and relevance of their recent talks. She'd opened up to Pip, and him to her, about their deepest secrets, fears, and wants; and with every exchange, they'd become more connected and secure.

He was a rock to her; someone she trusted implicitly. Still, it had only been a few days, and her more cautious side competed with the budding emotions.

She took the bananas and continued walking, coming to the candy aisle, where she scanned the different varieties, disappointed to see the same brands she knew from home.

Then she saw some birthday candles and packaged pastries. She thought of Pip's lost birthdays, and grabbed candles, a lighter, and a pastry, moving to the cash register.

Exiting the store, she turned right and walked a few blocks, still in awe of being in Florida, so many states away from home. Up ahead were the large neon lights of a Ferris wheel and to the right a dormant rollercoaster. She heard yells and saw a group of teenagers laughing at a smart phone screen.

Suddenly feeling the humidity, she removed her light sweatshirt and tied it to her waist. Looking ahead she saw a small motel with a vending machine of bottled water and moved over to it. Parched, she laid her purchases down and fumbled in her purse for a couple of dollar bills. But when she turned to the machine, there was a group of men surrounding her.

The teenagers she'd noticed moments before weren't young boys, but a group of vagrants. Startled, she picked up her bags to leave but the tallest one grabbed her, pressing her into the vending machine.

She dropped the bags and tried to scream but couldn't, with his hand on her throat and his leg pressing into her midsection.

"Go ahead and scream," the man hissed, through crooked, yellow teeth.

Lisa's wide eyes searched his face, seeing a handful of scabs and pockets of scars. He was in his twenties, though his leathery, dirt-stained face added years. His eyes were bloodshot and yellow, and his hair thin and greasy. He had an odor that was arresting, and his stained, baggy clothing hung loosely over his thin, gaunt frame.

Terrified, she looked to the others. All were smaller and stood at a loose perimeter, looking at her like a prize, and she could see they were no less vile or intent in purpose.

"Looks like we have a new one, fellas. You out here workin' all alone, or you one of Ronnie's new girls?"

Now it made sense and the revelation hit hard. A young girl alone in the late night, slowly walking the streets near a cheap motel. She'd been so naïve to think that the innocent magic of Disney extended to the entire area, and now she was in trouble.

She wanted to scream but couldn't find her voice. She wanted to kick and fight, but she couldn't move.

"Hey, Rock," the tall man said, turning to the others. "Is the door to that end room still busted?"

"Sure is, Jack-O," the man said. "They don't use that room. Been broken since I kicked it in last month!"

The others laughed and the man nodded in affirmation. "Then let's have some fun," he said.

So, they easily dragged Lisa into the darkness toward the motel.

CHAPTER 57

Pip opened his eyes with an instant feeling of dread; a glum sense of foreboding that shook him awake.

He sat upright, taking a few moments to assimilate to the dark, to realize where he was. And even through the jagged shadows he could see Lisa was gone. He sprang up and flipped on the lights, checking the bathroom and even the small closet.

But she was gone.

He shook his head in deep concentration. Where could she be? Why wouldn't she tell him? Was she getting ice or maybe some extra towels from the lobby?

Then his mind settled on his worst fear. That she'd left him and driven off. Had everything been too soon or fantastical for her to manage? Had she abandoned him in a crappy motel in Florida?

He felt a deep hollowness in his gut and his throat tightened. He felt sick, so he sat at the end of the bed with his head in his hands, rubbing his face.

He couldn't blame her. As much as he didn't want her to leave, he felt no ill will. But there was something else. A feeling of pain that didn't manifest from exhaustion, need, acceptance, or necessity. It was something he hadn't felt since he was five years old.

Since his mother died.

It was a feeling of losing something special. Abandonment.

He'd connected with Lisa and felt whimsical in her presence. Like the entire world had stopped and they were commanding their own universe. Was it love? He became confused in thought and stood up.

He ran to the window and swiped away the drapes, seeing Lisa's car still parked in the lot. But that initial comfort faded fast. Something was off. This wasn't right.

He grabbed his backpack and raced from the room, running along the exterior hall and down the stairs. Reaching the street, he looked in every direction, uncertain of her path or how long she'd been gone.

He paid no attention to the cars streaming down the road, or the establishments that dotted the four-lane roadway. He just had to find Lisa, so he ran with his eyes moving everywhere in a frantic search.

Lisa regained her faculties, digging in with her heels and twisting her head away from the man's firm grasp.

She was finally able to scream for a couple of seconds before a large, dirty hand was again pushed against her mouth and she was silenced. But then she shifted and swung her left leg around, kicking the man in the knee. He let out a yelp and loosened his grip, and she fell sideways to the ground.

"Then we'll do this the hard way," the man yelled. "Rock, get that door open!"

The kid named Rock ran to the door and kicked it open easily. The others grabbed Lisa's legs and arms, and she was carried into the vacant space and thrown onto a single bed.

She heard the door close, forcing the light to wane and the noise from the street to be muted. And then she was alone with a group of strange men with malevolence. She could hear the close breathing of anticipation as they crowded her, though she couldn't comprehend their whispers.

So, she just closed her eyes and prayed.

The door flew open with such intensity that it was sent off its hinges and stuck into the thin wall.

Then there was light and yelling.

The men were swarming her in a semi-circle, but they all turned to the door. Several had their hands up, defensively, backing further into the room. This allowed Lisa to see what was happening and she couldn't believe her eyes.

Just inside the doorway, with his face twisted in anger, eyes narrowed, stood Pip. And he was pointing a large gun at the tall man in the center.

"Back up all the way to the bathroom," Pip said, evenly.

But the tall one remained steadfast.

"What'cha' gonna do? Kill us all?" he snarled, mockingly.

Then the thug stood straighter, staring Pip down. Gaining spirit, the man looked to the others, becoming jocular, and the mood shifted.

"Look at you; you're barely five feet tall!"

Derisive laughter filled the room, as the gun was seemingly forgotten. The men contemplated the outcomes, and it was clear the situation was turning in their favor. Lisa was ignored in the stalemate, as empty seconds stretched by.

But then Pip stepped closer, cocking the hammer, and standing in a ready formation. "I will kill you and not waste a moment's time thinking about it, you sick piece of shit."

The man blinked quickly and looked away, and there was no doubt that the small man with the large gun meant it.

"Okay, man, we didn't do nothing. She can go."

Pip turned to Lisa, softening. He motioned to the door with his free hand, and she jumped up and ran past him.

When she was safely outside, Pip stared at the tall junkie. "If I ever see you around here again, I *will* kill you. And you others? You can do better."

And although his heart was beating faster than ever before, there was no doubt that despite his small size, Pip was the most commanding and biggest man in the room.

CHAPTER 58

They continued to run, even when out of view.

Passing the same store fronts, they continued for a couple of minutes, and even ran up the motel stairs, eventually finding sanctuary in their tiny room.

Lisa bolted the door and Pip drew the heavy curtains tight. Then they stood in silence panting, enjoying the cool blow of the air conditioning unit.

Pip placed his backpack on the floor and sat on the bed, his head down.

"Damn, Lisa," he said. "Why'd you just leave like that; in a place you don't know, and be with guys like *that*?"

Lisa continued to stand, incredulously. "What?!" she screamed. "You think I *chose* to be with that gang of derelicts?"

Pip shook his head in silence, trying to find the right words and Lisa continued.

"My mind was wired and you were asleep. I've never been here and was excited to get some fresh air and pick up a few things at the store. Next thing I knew, I was grabbed and thrown into that room!"

"Look I didn't mean to imply—"

"I was the *victim*, Pip!"

"I know!" Pip yelled back.

The shouts cancelled each other's intensity, and both fell quiet for several moments.

Then Pip rose and took her hand, speaking to her gently. "I'm just so scared at the thought of you getting hurt and I'm sorry."

Lisa looked at Pip, softening. "Well, then can I say, 'thank you' again for saving me?"

"It's becoming a habit, you know," Pip chided. "I guess you're my Lois Lane, but I'm hardly a Superman."

Lisa smiled, turning inward.

In her mind he was already her Superman. She knew he would never allow any harm to her. He was a good person with a hollowed past, but he'd come through it brighter and more equipped.

"I got you something," she said, changing the subject and raising the plastic bags.

Pip looked to her, matching her smile. "Is it awesome? I mean, I hope that whatever's in those bags was worth it."

"Open it," she said, handing him the first bag.

Pip laughed out loud, as he held up the bananas, automatically looking for the sticker. Raising it like a trophy, he triumphantly removed the sticker and placed it on his forearm like a tattoo. "I'll wear it forever, or at least until it falls off in an hour."

Then she turned, shielding the other bag from him. Moments passed and he waited patiently. She spun slowly and offered him a single lit candle on a pastry.

"Happy birthday to you," she sang in a beautiful voice. "Happy birthday to you. Happy birthday, dear Pip, happy birthday to you!"

Pip took the pastry gingerly, regarding it.

"Thank you, Lisa," he said, solemnly. "But it's not my birthday until March."

"I figure you have a lot of them to make up for, so here's the first of many."

She was smiling, happily, but when she looked at him, there were tears in his eyes.

"What's wrong, Pip?" she asked, even though she already knew.

"No one's ever done this for me, and it was so nice of you."

She sat down on the bed, squaring herself against him. "I know, Pip. You deserved so much better. And I'm sorry again for leaving without telling you."

Pip nodded. "I'm sorry, too. I overreacted. I just have a history of being abandoned."

She gently wiped a tear from his face, massaging it away with a loving touch. It triggered many more, and she patiently continued, until he buried his face into her shoulder and cried, uncontrollably.

She instinctively held him, closing her eyes, and slowly swaying.

"It's okay, Pip. I got you," she whispered.

Her touch and her words were meant to soothe. But instead of acceptance, Pip's body jolted and convulsed. A large groan escaped him; and he sobbed, unrestrained, expelling years of frustration, abuse, sadness, and fear.

Lisa waited him out, uttering words of empathy, as she held him tighter and continued an easy sway.

Soon the moment ceded; and Pip withdrew and stood, looking red-faced with puffy eyes.

"I'm sorry for that. I'm not sure what came over me, but I've never cried like that in my life."

Lisa nodded. "You never have to apologize for being true to yourself. It's totally fine and I understand completely."

"Thank you."

"Now make a wish and blow out the candle. That's how it works."

"I know how it works," he said, laughing through the tears.

"Sometimes you have to get through the tears to find the laughter behind them," Lisa said, automatically. "My grandmother used to say that, and I never knew what it meant until now."

Pip closed his eyes, speaking evenly. "I just had the best day of my life and I wish for every day to be as special."

Lisa shook her head, chuckling. "I guess you *don't* know how it works. You're supposed to keep the wish to yourself!"

He blew out the candle and put the pastry on a side table. Then he turned to her.

"Thank you, Lisa. That was nice."

He stared into her beautiful blue eyes and held her gaze; and suddenly the electricity between them grew. They fell into each other, as a slow kiss turned into a charged embrace.

He withdrew, searching her face, and then continued to kiss her passionately. They laid back onto the bed, as their hands explored each other, hungrily.

"Hold on," he interrupted, jumping up and turning off the lights.

"No problem," she said, grabbing the sheets and turning them down.

Then they hastily removed their clothes and found each other in the dark, impassioned and lost in the moment.

CHAPTER 59

"Where did the gun come from, by the way?" Lisa asked in the dark.

It was somewhere between 4 and 5 a.m., and they'd been talking and making love alternatively. Pip had never experienced anything like it and had trusted Lisa implicitly. He'd confessed he was a virgin, even at twenty-eight, and was naïve to it all. She'd explained that she'd only been with one other man and harbored her own trepidations. So, they took it slow and bonded in the shared experience.

The conversation was easy, and they promised to always be in a safe place with each other on *any* topic. Nothing was taboo, and with each passing moment, their relationship grew.

In the total darkness of a cheap motel room, they found how much they meant to each other. How much they needed each other.

At the same time, they felt the world shrink around them and the bedlam fall away. The future became clearer and more manageable, and they felt like they were in a cocoon. But instead of being pressed or claustrophobic, they wore it like a blanket and regaled in its warmth.

Pip hoped the night would never end. It was the most amazing experience of his life and he'd never felt so free. Likewise, Lisa was feeling euphoric and looking opportunistically to the future. She'd never experienced such comfort in the darkness and only hoped it would continue into the light.

"To answer your question, it's Sam's grandfather's old Colt. It probably hasn't been fired in years, but I know it's loaded and ready to go. The guy was a fanatic about it. I was hoping not to use it, but then you came along."

She sighed and they continued to hold each other under the thin sheets. Then she nudged him, moving her foot over his leg, and rising to straddle him. She grabbed his arms and fell on him, their bare bodies moist with salty sweat.

"Are you ready for some more? she asked, playfully.

He entered her, this time with more patience, familiarity, and intention. They fell into an easy rhythm, gasping for air and clinging to each other, until a sliver of daylight crept into the room.

Then, just after sunrise, their bodies gave out and they faded into a deep sleep.

CHAPTER 60

Just before noon, a noise sounded from outside the motel room door.

Pip jumped up naked, grabbing a T-shirt to cover himself and moving to the curtain. Seeing nothing, he scanned the floor and saw his shorts from the night before. He hurriedly dressed, crouching down, and hoping to hear the sound again.

He inched to the window, opening the curtain further, peering out. To his relief, he saw a housekeeper pushing a cart past the window.

Letting go of the heavy cloth, Pip sneezed, seeing the dust in the bright sunshine spilling into the room.

Another sneeze came and Lisa opened her eyes.

"Bless you," she called out, still wrapped in sheets.

"Thanks," Pip said. "It's these dusty drapes. Sorry to wake—"

Another sneeze erupted and Pip ran to the bathroom for tissues. He splashed cold water on his face and returned, moving a wet cloth across his face.

Lisa sat on the edge of the bed, reaching down for her clothes, which were scattered around, evidence of their passion and urgency. He looked her over, noticing the delicate lines on her back; the smallness of her shoulders, where her hair folded over to the side.

He smiled, his eyes adoringly washing over such a simple, beautiful sight.

Not able to resist, he moved behind her and massaged her shoulders, before planting a soft kiss on her neck.

"Are you all right?" he asked.

Memories from the night came back quickly, and she welcomed his touch. She thought of the group of thugs, briefly frowning, before pushing the images away and concentrating on Pip and their lovemaking.

"I'm fine," she said. "You make everything fine."

They exchanged smiles and Pip laid down next to her.

"I was thinking about something," Lisa said.

"What's that?"

"If you have something of importance about the assassinations, why not just provide it to the feds? You trust Jack Seargant, right? I know *I* do!"

"It's not that easy," Pip said. "It involves some pretty important people, and it won't just go away."

"Okay, but you *know* it's the right thing to do. Can't you just say at the most basic level, that you were just doing your job?"

Pip had been agonizing over that exact course of action, thinking about it nonstop, and then playing out the different scenarios. But hearing Lisa say it lent renewed insight.

"Yes, but my job is also *protecting* the United States. I took an oath to that end. And although it was my job to *find* this information, it's also my job to *protect* it."

"Yeah, but although you're my Superman, you don't have to assume that role for the entire country. This is bigger than you, and if you trust Jack Seargant, maybe he should decide. I mean, he's the FBI, right?"

Pip absorbed her words, feeling a sense of relief. He suddenly realized that he'd been internalizing and perhaps overthinking things. Maybe he'd been acting irrationally.

Gone were the days of someone possessing information that could change the world. If he simply sent it to Jack Seargant and his team, then he wouldn't have the ball anymore. He'd just be the messenger, right?

Hot potato hot potato. Gone.

Pip reached for his laptop, turning it on. Then he picked up one of his burner phones and dialed Seargant's number.

"Pip!" the man exclaimed within half a ring. "Don't hang up!"

"Listen, Seargant. I'm gonna send you what I have. Stay on the line until you hear it."

"Okay, Pip, go ahead."

Silence ruled, even though they both had so much to say.

Pip logged into his laptop, bringing up the file. He attached it to a simple email and sent it into cyberspace with a quick stroke of his finger.

Pip stole away from the laptop and kissed Lisa on the cheek, waiting for Seargant to respond.

"Got it," Seargant sounded. Then he went quiet, listening to the audio.

"Is that who I think it is?" Seargant asked, dubiously.

"Yep."

One voice was altered, masked in a mechanical drone, but the other was easily discernable. Unmistakable.

Seargant was listening to the First Lady of the United States—Judy Maclemore—discuss details of a presidential assassination.

Before it happened.

CHAPTER 61

"Housekeeping," a voice sounded, and Pip moved to the curtain once more.

Peeling it from the wall, more dust fell from the thick folds, but he breathed easier when he saw the maid service cart. Then he sneezed again, moving to the door, unbolting the lock.

The housekeeper was a thick, middle-aged black woman, and she was smiling affably at Pip.

"You all about ready to check out, honey?" she asked in a sweet, southern drawl.

"We're almost set. About a half hour, if that's okay?" he said, returning the smile.

"Well, don't be too long," she said, moving away. "I'll make you my last room to give you more time."

"Thanks so much," Pip offered with a wave, and she continued on her way.

Then he sneezed again, his head jerking downward with the momentum.

But then everything went black, as a short-lived, searing pain ripped through his world, and he fell backward into the room, unconscious and bloody.

Moments earlier, Falby arrived at the motel, driving past slowly before parking a few hundred feet away. Unrecognizable—even to himself—he limped into the lobby in elaborate disguise, scanning for security cameras and sizing up the lone attendant snoozing behind the counter.

"Excuse me," Falby said, shaking the young man awake. "I need to find my two friends. "A young man and woman; they checked in late last night. What room are they in?"

The sleepy lobby worker moved his hands to his face, rubbing his eyes and in no mood for pleasantries.

"You can't just walk in here and expect me—"

Falby flashed his trusted Sig Sauer with a long suppressor attached. The man fell silent, the air escaping him, as he shrunk into his chair.

"You only have nine cars in the parking lot, and it looks like only seven rooms are occupied. But I need to know where my friends are. It's a surprise, you might say."

Falby again made a sweeping look at the security camera. He knew it to be closed circuit and an early model that stored imaging on-site. He wasn't concerned.

"Number twenty-nine, second floor," the man stuttered, his eyes now wide with fear.

"Make me a key," Falby stated, calmly.

The young man got up slowly, walked to a drawer and took out a plain white card, before swiping it into a small machine and nervously punching a couple numbers on the display.

"Here you go. Look I don't want any—"

The man didn't finish the sentence, and Falby didn't wait a moment longer than he needed. Placing the gun back into his jacket, he moved swiftly from the lobby and up the outside stairs to the second floor.

He saw a large housekeeper stopped in front of room twenty-nine, speaking to the occupant.

Falby leveled the Sig at her and fired, pushing away her considerable bulk.

Then he turned to see Pip, who stood frozen in horror, his eyes rising from the dead woman to the killer, who looked at him without emotion.

Then, Pip involuntarily sneezed.

Falby pulled the trigger and Pip's head all but exploded.

CHAPTER 62

Lisa looked to Pip, lovingly, as he stood in the doorway, his dark silhouette framed against the bright sunlight. He was speaking to the housekeeper just outside.

There was some commotion and a strange man appeared just outside of view. Then Pip sneezed and his head jerked backward; his body falling back and landing hard against the floor.

She instinctively moved to him, almost amused. Was he fooling around and playing a joke?

But her face went white, and her skin felt afire when she saw his body convulsing, his blood everywhere.

"Pip!" she screamed, cradling his head, blood spilling out of a dark red hole in his skull.

The stranger entered, calmly scanning the room, before jetting past her to get Pip's laptop. Then his eyes settled on her.

Time stood still. The temperature in the room seemed to rise and the close walls were insufferable. Her movements were in slow motion, her ears rang, and she couldn't force a coherent thought.

She blinked away stinging tears and looked up at the man in her delirium. She saw the barrel of a gun leveled at her but couldn't comprehend the gravity of it.

She wouldn't remember the killer leaving or her crying out for help. She wouldn't recall stepping over the dead housekeeper, or even calling 911.

But one thing she'd never forget was holding a cheap white towel against Pip's head, as bright red blood rushed from the gaping hole that cut across his head.

Jack Seargant's phone rang, snapping him out of deep thought. He glanced at the display. *Unknown caller.*

Hoping it was Pip, he answered, excitedly. "This is Searg—"

"Mr. Seargant this is Lisa Wellington. You saved me from the Wolf Man! Pip's been shot and they just took him in the ambulance!"

Seargant slumped forward, bringing a quick hand to his face. It was a punch to his entire spirit. How could this have happened?

But he recovered and straightened, gaining his faculties, and processing the information. He had so many questions.

"How are you with Pip? Who shot him?"

Lisa sobbed loudly and Seargant softened.

"It doesn't matter anymore, Lisa. No more games. Where exactly are you?"

"Orlando. At a motel off Route 92. They just took him away in an ambulance. Can you get in contact with my parents? And can you call Pip's—"

Lisa fell into an unintelligible blur of words as the sobs robbed her of all communication. Seargant heard the receiver fall away as she continued weeping, unrestrained.

"Lisa! Are you there?" Seargant yelled into the phone.

Moments passed.

"Okay, I'm back," Lisa managed. "I guess Pip has nobody. But can you tell his friend, Sam?"

"Lisa, I need you to remain calm. Get a ride to the hospital. I'll contact the local police and your parents. We're coming to you in the next several hours."

The call over, Seargant emerged from his office, approaching a handful of agents, including Hartley.

"Listen up people. I need you to divide and conquer. Our guy Pip was just shot at a motel in Orlando. Call the police and get the initial report and the hospital he was taken to. I also need Lisa Wellington's parents briefed and flown down. She was the only surviving victim of the Wolf Man killings and it seems they were together, somehow. I also need Sam, Pip's roommate, to be picked up again and brought into the fold."

Agent Hartley, stood. "Are you still going to Kentucky tomorrow with the president?"

Seargant fell silent in thought and blinked a few times, before looking to Hartley. "Right now, you and I are going to the White House."

Hartley was taken back, confusion showing on his face. But he nodded and picked up his suit jacket, following Seargant's lead.

"Anything I should know about?" Hartley asked.

"I'm gonna have a little chat with the president and it can't wait."

Smiling now, Hartley picked up the pace and barely caught up to his boss as the elevator opened and accepted them both.

Falby was on I-95, moving steadily north and out of Florida, when he allowed himself a bit of self-reflection. It was rare that he dwelled on the past. It was the future that was more important and moments like these were generally a waste of time.

But he couldn't get the girl's face out of his mind.

Lisa Wellington.

He felt good about the day's events. He had to kill the motel clerk and a housekeeper, but at least he'd also gotten Pip and secured the laptop.

He'd scanned it for any electronic signatures and GPS and found nothing. So now it was lying dormant on the backseat floor. He obeyed the speed limit and saw the first sign for Savannah, Georgia, content with Florida fading further into the rear view.

The girl's face threw him for a loop.

He remembered the Wolf Man case. It had dominated the news and ended in a rescue.

Falby knew the girl was an innocent player in the game; and as he pointed his weapon and she simply looked back at him—unaware and virtuous—he'd hesitated, letting her live.

A rarity.

A couple of motorcycles raced passed him noisily and he regained focus, quickly admonishing all thoughts of the morning.

President Maclemore was now the only thing on his mind.

CHAPTER 63

The Oval Office
The White House

"We keep this internal for now," President Maclemore said, exasperatedly. "Can you imagine if the Press found out?"

Seargant and Hartley stared at each other in disbelief, before looking back at the president.

"Shall I play the recording again, sir?" Seargant asked, rhetorically. "There's no mistaking the voice of the First Lady on this recording."

"Yes," the president conceded. "It *does* appear so, but we *cannot* be certain at this point. And the other voice is too muffled to determine anything."

"True, but I'd like to ask her a few questions."

The president spun around, shaking his head. "No. I need to speak with her first."

Seargant shook his head. "You know I can formally open an investigation, subpoena her, or even take her into custody right now and—"

"Look," the president said, sitting for the first time in the exchange, trying to act casual and deflate the situation. "Even if it *is* my wife, almost *all* of the talking was done by this unknown voice, and she offers nothing of consequence. The recording itself is illegal. It won't be enough."

Seargant looked incredulous. "But sir, as you know it's conspiracy at a bare minimum, and if—"

"Yes, but may I remind you that you took an oath that extends to the highest level. Protecting the *presidency*, not just the *president*. All I'm asking for is a few days. Let's get through these funerals and deal with this in-house for now. We'll regroup and then loop in the Attorney General if it makes sense."

Seargant walked the room, treading lightly, in deep thought.

All eyes were on him as he moved to the intricate inlayed bookcase, a sampling of leatherbound novels stacked against brass bookends.

Seargant deliberately moved to the south window, standing next to the president, staring past the expansive, manicured lawn. He looked to the Washington Monument, the soft flickering of the two top red lights barely visible through the haze and humidity.

Then Seargant nodded, thinking of George Washington and briefly the entire presidential lineage right up to the man sitting beside him.

"Hartley," he said, almost to himself, without turning around. "Go get the First Lady and bring her to us immediately."

The president exploded from his chair, first jumping toward Agent Hartley before composing himself and bracing up against Seargant.

"Jack, I implore you *not* to do this!"

"Sir, when I said I wanted to speak with her, I wasn't asking for permission."

And Hartley left the Oval Office, as instructed.

Minutes later Judy Maclemore entered the Oval Office, followed by Agent Hartley. She regarded her husband and Jack Seargant, cordially but refused to take a seat when offered.

Seargant eyed her, taking in everything. Her manner of walk was casual and measured, consistent with the well-practiced movements of accustomed scrutiny.

She herself was a two-time senator from Massachusetts, before giving up her political aspirations when her husband was elected vice president under Harold Bowman.

A picture of perfection, her auburn hair was done impeccably, laying just over her shoulders, her makeup flawless. Her posture was straight, and she moved to her husband gracefully, pecking his cheek with a quick kiss before settling her uncaring gaze on Agents Hartley and Seargant.

Seargant guessed she knew why the FBI was here, though he didn't think the president was involved at this point.

"Play the recording, Hartley."

"…But the end game is all that matters, and everything is in place. Everything," a robotic voice said.

"And it'll all be over, soon?" The woman's voice sounded, breaking up.

Seargant stared hard at the First Lady, who didn't stir in the slightest.

"Yes. The results of our planning are finally here."

The recording ran for almost a minute before it ended, but that was the only audio of Judy Maclemore. Before anyone could speak, the First Lady walked slowly to the sofa, sitting down, and crossing her legs.

"And?" she asked.

Even the president stirred, as the three men looked at her.

Seargant spoke first. "Is that your voice on the recording, ma'am?"

The First Lady drew in a long breath, expelling it slowly. "Absolutely not!"

Seargant was expecting the response. "You know the analyst who recorded this has a diagnostic fingerprint that leads to a cell phone at the White House?"

She shook her head. "You have an illegal recording that's obviously manipulated, and we're done here. Feel free to speak to my attorneys and my husband but don't waste my time with this nonsense."

Then the First Lady almost floated out of the room. She moved past Agent Hartley, who instinctively opened the door for her, and all three men watched as several staffers swarmed and fanned out behind her.

Seargant followed her out of the Oval Office, before turning to President Maclemore.

"You have three days, Mr. President. And after tomorrow's service at the National Cathedral, I'm accompanying you to Harold Bowman's funeral in Kentucky."

CHAPTER 64

Agent Hartley arrived in Orlando early in the evening, about five hours after Pip was shot.

Seargant ordered the local FBI office to take over the investigation, and with the motel sealed off, Hartley drove straight to Advent Health in Kissimmee to check on Pip and Lisa.

After flashing his badge a few times, he was on the third floor, and found Lisa surrounded by several police officers in a small conference room. She looked scared and was visibly shaking, telling her story—no doubt—for the umpteenth time.

Hartley stood just out of sight in the hall to get a bearing on the conversation and a quick read on Lisa.

She was a shell of the person she'd been just hours before. Distraught, confused, and empty; she traded emotions between devastation and anger, and everything in between.

Meeting Pip a few days ago was a whirlwind of excitement, topped off by a magical night of romance and love.

But now she was cramped into a small room, with the police incessant in their questioning. Still, she knew nothing, which made the inquiries come even faster, the investigators treating her harsher by the moment.

A young, physically fit police detective was sitting casually on the side of an end table, subtly leaning into Lisa.

"Tell me again who you were there to meet, Lisa. And remember we're here to investigate the *shooting*, not what you were *doing*."

Hartley's position allowed for a peripheral view, and he focused on Lisa, watching her face play out several emotions simultaneously. Fear, confusion, acceptance, and frustration. "I told you, we just got there the night before, and—"

Another detective interrupted, this time a Hispanic female behind Lisa, catching her off guard.

"What about the drugs, Lisa? Our guys are tossing that motel room and we'll find it all, but if you cooperate now, it'll be a lot easier."

Lisa was already shaking her head. "I've never done drugs in my life and if you find—"

"Let me tell you what we *did* find then," the first detective said, mockingly. "An unregistered gun and three condoms on the floor. Was this guy a John, or—"

"He was my friend!" Lisa shouted. "I mean he *is* my friend and—"

"Then let's get back to the part where you drove in from out of state with an unlicensed, loaded firearm. Because that carries a minimum sentence of—"

Agent Hartley had enough and decided it was his turn to interrupt.

"Hello, everybody," he announced loudly, knocking on the door and filling most of the entrance with his bulk. "I'm Special Agent

Hartley with the FBI, and I'd like all law enforcement to please leave. We're assuming jurisdiction."

The first detective stood, enraged. "On what authority!? We have a shooting in our district and an unlicensed firearm at a motel well known for prostitution, drug activity, and violent crime. Our Vice Officers have been—"

Hartley crossed his arms. "There are things at play that are larger than you," Hartley responded. "I understand your frustrations, but your captain has been briefed, and I'll take it from here."

Agent Hartley stepped out of the room and made a sweeping motion with his beefy arm; and the five police officers filed out without a word. Then Hartley entered the room, shut the door behind him, and focused on Lisa, who was looking more scared than ever.

"Hello, Lisa," he started, engaging her with a warm and sympathetic smile. "I'm Special Agent Hartley. I work very closely with our friend Jack Seargant, and I believe everything you've been saying."

Lisa was visibly relieved, and she slumped back into the plastic chair.

"But" Hartley continued. "I *do* need to hear everything once more, and I apologize for that."

Lisa frowned but took an instant liking to Hartley. Then she told her story again, rehashing every detail she could remember. Hartley was patient and she felt comfortable with him. Unlike the local police who were scattered in their direction and relentless with their questions and accusations.

They'd deduced that Pip and Lisa were involved in something nefarious, most likely drugs, and had known the shooter. With the gun, they'd already adopted a narrative that fit and were asking questions to funnel Lisa into that story.

But Hartley knew better. He'd been privy to the recording. He'd spoken with Seargant about Pip and had known about Pip and Lisa's connection during the Wolf Man case.

Hartley believed Lisa implicitly and didn't focus on the 'why' but on the 'who.' Seeking more suitable surroundings, he led her to a comfortable room, with a couch and two leather chairs. He shut the door and offered Lisa a cold bottle of water, which she accepted gratefully.

"Let's focus on the man who shot Pip," Hartley said. "Please tell me about him."

Lisa took a couple of swigs of water.

"He was dressed in jeans and a couple layers of bulky clothing. He had on three light jackets or something. He wore a ski hat, so I didn't see any hair, and his face was tight. He had high cheekbones and almost nonexistent lips. Kind of weird looking, actually, and I couldn't tell if he was thirty or sixty.

"But his eyes were something I've never seen before. They were dead. Gray. Like there was nothing behind them. He'd just killed the housekeeper and pushed her aside, like she was nothing. The way he moved right after shooting her, he wasn't nervous at all. Very purposeful and direct.

"Then he shot Pip and those eyes settled on me. He made no gesture or human-like response, which is *impossible* in that moment!"

Hartley nodded in affirmation, choosing not to write anything down, but remain in the moment with Lisa.

"I know this is hard, but you're doing great. Please continue."

Lisa took another gulp of water. "We just stared at each other. He didn't even blink. Again, like he wasn't even human.

"But then he turned away and rushed by me to grab Pip's laptop. Before leaving, he turned and pointed the gun directly at me. My entire body went cold. It was so surreal, and I was paralyzed. Then those eyes turned away.

"He was gone in seconds, like a phantom, and I was left with Pip on the floor."

Lisa went quiet and Hartley studied her.

"Do you know anything about this guy, Agent Hartley?"

Hartley sucked in a deep breath, contemplating the question, and what he could say. Then he nodded, speaking in generalities, noting that much of the case was privileged information.

"First we have to have a little talk about things. Did you hear the recording, or did Pip say anything about it?"

Lisa was shaking her head before Hartley finished the sentence.

"No, I didn't. Pip didn't want to endanger me, so he sent it to Jack Seargant, and it was only played on his end."

"That's good," Hartley said, relieved.

"Now tell me about this killer," Lisa said, pointedly.

"Well, I can say that you're very special, Lisa," Hartley started. "We're sure it was Falby, who you may have read about over the last few years. He's the one responsible for the bombing of the Golden Gate Bridge and the unleashing of sarin gas at Madison Square Garden, and possibly even the presidential assassinations."

"Oh my God!" Lisa exclaimed. "You really think—"

"Yes, I absolutely do. What Pip came across is that big and it fits."

"But why did you say that *I'm* special?"

Hartley exhaled slowly. "Because Lisa. I don't think he's ever come across anyone he hasn't killed."

CHAPTER 65

Hartley and Lisa continued their conversation, long after the FBI agent documented the facts. She even told him about the gang of vagrants and her rescue, and of course, the gun Pip took from Sam's closet.

For a federal agent, she found him easy to talk to and genuinely concerned for her well-being. Then again, she'd never spoken to an FBI agent, and that sudden revelation allowed for a moment of levity. She'd forced a quick laugh before retreating inward, and the tears came as she thought of Pip.

Agent Hartley was patient and proved to be a good listener. She felt safe with him. She liked the image of him flashing his badge at the local police and sending them away. He'd also worked with the hospital to arrange a room down the hall; and enlisted the local FBI office to bring her things from the motel.

After talking for most of the hour, she turned to him and frowned, awkwardly. "Look Agent Hartley, I have to—"

"You can drop the *Agent* stuff, Lisa. Everyone just calls me Hartley. And after what you've been through, let's make things as easy as possible."

Lisa nodded in shy affirmation. "Thank you and I appreciate you believing me. The truth is I fell in love with Pip in just a few days' time. And although it looks bad, he's only the second man I've ever been with."

Tears welled up in her eyes and Hartley reached for some tissues.

"There's no need to explain anything. From what Seargant told me about Pip, he's an incredible young man."

Hartley's phone buzzed and he looked at the screen, standing.

"Pip's out of surgery," he said. "Follow me."

They raced down the hall and were met by a doctor in scrubs, with a splattering of blood across his chest. Lisa was wide-eyed, searching him for answers.

"I'm Dr. Epstein," he began, motioning his arms downward to reduce the tension. "We removed the bullet and shrapnel fragments; but to get access I had to cut out a portion of his skull to clean things up. With this type of injury, there are many potential complications. He could bleed into the brain, and he'll have some swelling that we'll deal with. There's also infection risk and the possibility of post traumatic seizures. We're trying to control the bleeding and relieve some of the pressure, and we're watching him closely. He's stable but by no means out of the woods."

Lisa interrupted. "Will he live? Will he be okay?"

The surgeon frowned, continuing. "He was shot at point-blank range in the head. I understand he sneezed when he was shot, which forced his head down. The bullet entered at the top of his skull and travelled along the fissure, miraculously missing most of the vital brain tissue. Most of the damage is to the bone and not to the brain itself.

"He's a very lucky man to have survived this far."

"What are the odds?" Lisa snapped. "I need something."

The doctor exhaled and looked to Hartley, who was reading the man's mind. Lisa shrunk into herself, not needing to hear anymore.

"We're doing everything we can."

CHAPTER 66

The U.S. Capitol Building
Washington D.C.

A pinkish hue jumped from the eastern horizon, splitting the dark blue and black, and illuminating the sky in a slow muted glow of fluorescent colors that spilled out from its center.

But the sunrise was lost on the twenty-four honor guards, all of whom were paying close attention to the protocols they'd been so meticulously trained in, as they carefully moved the four flag-draped caskets from the Capitol Rotunda for travel to the National Cathedral.

For days, the news networks covered the constant flow of mourners paying their respects; first at each man's state capital, and then at the U.S. Capitol. A steady stream of Americans treading lightly as they passed the impossibility of what they were witnessing.

Politics were set aside as the population went about their lives in a dim sense of reality. Everything seemed to be in slow motion.

The ceremony at the National Cathedral was four hours long, with each slain president allotted forty-five minutes for a eulogy, bookended by thirty minutes in the beginning and end dedicated to collaborative reflection and prayer.

In the front left row President Maclemore sat alongside the First Lady. Beside them were the three widows, Liz Montgomery, Sasha Gilmore, and Gini Bowman. James Preston's wife had predeceased him, so their two sons and their wives took her place. Filling the fifteen pews behind them sat the lineage of four presidential families.

On the right side sat Garret Scott, the sitting vice president, and his wife Elizabeth, next to Michael Kay, who was Walker Montgomery's vice president. Behind them, sat the chiefs of state, arranged alphabetically by the English spelling of their countries.

The highlight of the memorial was when President Maclemore closed out the service in a poignantly delivered eulogy that briefly focused on each man's service.

At the end, he choked on his words and barely finished a sentence. Then, in an unscripted moment, he stepped down from the podium and solemnly walked to each of the four flag-draped caskets, briefly placing his right hand on each. His lips were moving but no one could hear what he was saying.

Then he returned to the podium, cleared his throat, and looked straight ahead, a statue of control and resolve. A few moments of silence accentuated the pause and an entire nation waited.

"This may have no place at this holy service of remembrance. But today I pledge to these fallen men and to the American people that there *will* be justice. We are not defined by our country's worst moments, but rather how we stand united and throw off such prejudice and shine brighter for it. And to that end I will commit every resource at my disposal to find those responsible and secure our nation."

Every president must plan their own funeral before taking the oath of office; so, after the service at the National Cathedral, each family prepared for their individual interment.

After a private ceremony, Rube Gilmore was to be buried at a family plot at their compound at Pelham in Westchester County, New York. Walker Montgomery would be laid to rest at his presidential library just outside of Terrell Hills, Texas.

James Preston's remains would make the flight back to California, first flying over the Chicago skyline en route, where he was born, before being buried at the Preston ranch, next to his wife.

And Harold Bowman would be honored in Van Lear, Kentucky and entombed at his presidential library, with President John Maclemore in attendance.

CHAPTER 67

Jack Seargant met Maclemore's presidential motorcade at Joint Base Andrews, climbing the stairs to Air Force One just minutes before departure. He moved to the rear of the plane, away from the handful of staff, removed his suit jacket, and plopped down in an oversized seat.

He adjusted an air vent, taking in the grandeur of it all. There were monogramed towels and expensive glassware. The carpeting was heavy beneath his feet, and the seal of the President of the United States was visible on the walls and embroidered into the flooring.

But he was unmoved and closed his eyes, replaying everything in his mind. He reflected on both of the meetings he'd had with the president over the last few days.

He couldn't believe that Judy Maclemore could have information about the presidential assassinations and that Maclemore himself was possibly complicit.

But Seargant also had to agree that the timing couldn't have been worse, so he'd given the man a three-day respite. He agreed it was better to get past the state funerals and allow the country to mourn.

Then he thought of Steve McCallister. Although he'd sparred with the man in the past and theirs wasn't the best of relationships, he had to agree that McCallister was right about this trip to Kentucky.

Was Maclemore the next presidential target and would Seargant himself be witness to it?

When Air Force One leveled off at thirty-five thousand feet, Seargant moved the curtain to peer out the window. He saw two fully loaded F-18 Hornets off the right wing, and two more in the distance.

But they did nothing to quell the nervousness he felt.

CHAPTER 68

Kimberly Hanson was nervous; and she felt it in every part of her body—from her red eyes and dry mouth—to her hollowed inside, leaving her physically and mentally spent. As the highest ranking of Steve McCallister's administrative staff and the only one of those with an office on the seventh floor, she was visibly shaking.

The director of the CIA—her boss—was missing and presumably *had* been for over fourteen hours since he'd checked out of the building the night before.

Standard operating procedure was followed.

His phones were called to no avail. They were pinged, but not in service. She'd elevated it to security, and they were racing to his private residence with an ETA of under two minutes.

She was offered and gratefully accepted a live feed from the forward team. Now she listened, along with the deputy director of the CIA, as they entered Steve McCallister's community in Great Falls, Virginia and raced down Potomac River Road with sirens blaring.

From the street, nothing looked out of sorts. There were two newspapers on the driveway. No vehicles.

The first group of four emptied the van and approached the front, as the others ran to the back. Sporadic radio chatter followed as the teams communicated an "All clear" message and no signs of a break-in. No one was answering the doorbell.

Cursory looks into the windows revealed nothing out of the ordinary. Just an empty house. They picked the rear patio door lock and entered easily, spreading out in search of Steve and Dana McCallister. Or anything at all.

But the only thing they found was a single broken glass on the kitchen floor, with water surrounding it. Initial theories suggested that someone was drinking a glass of water. That person had been taken by surprise from behind. But who was that person?

Questions swirled and hypotheticals were imagined. But one thing was clear.

Steve McCallister—the director of the CIA—was missing.

CHAPTER 69

The Harold T. Bowman Presidential Library
Van Lear, Kentucky

The Harold T. Bowman Presidential Library was completed only two months before his assassination; and although Bowman was very involved in the architectural design and process, he'd only been on-site twice.

Duty called, and with him out of office for two and a half years, he was busy with speaking engagements, philanthropy efforts, and a popular book tour.

The design of the library and adjacent museum was similar to his predecessor's, though Bowman's ego had forced it to be bigger and more ornate. The grandeur flowed from the neoclassical three-story marble building, ornamented by two decorative fountains that framed a large garden.

And that's where Bowman had chosen to be buried; he just couldn't have known it would be so soon.

It was a private ceremony, and the media wasn't invited. Still, over three hundred family members and friends gathered to remember Harold Bowman and his three decades of public service.

The most important guest was President Maclemore, and he was seated next to Gini Bowman and her daughters, as the service commenced, and a man's legacy was celebrated. The Secret Service spilled out from the president in every direction, as Jack Seargant kept a loose distance, waiting for something to happen.

Seargant and the FBI were against the president's attendance, though they had no authority in the matter. Somehow the Secret Service approved the itinerary, but there was no mistaking the increased security presence and hardware.

Pastor Thomas Richmond was a family friend and minister for over sixty years, having baptized Bowman as a child. At 91, he willingly accepted the invitation to speak fervently about the young boy that would become president, and the family he'd adored and left behind.

During the sermon, Seargant's mind wandered.

The thoughtful eulogy allowed images to form in Seargant's mind. When the pastor spoke of Bowman as a young boy, Seargant thought of his own childhood and the deliberation warmed him. But then he frowned, as he remembered himself as a ten-year old boy, seeing his father walk into a convenience store for milk and being gunned down as he interrupted a robbery.

Seargant shut his eyes and shook his head slightly, dismissing the disturbing images. The reason he was in law enforcement. To right the wrong; to bring justice to the disparaged.

His eyes made another measured sweep of the area. Everything appeared normal. Nothing out of place. The pastor continued speaking and the congregation was at full attention.

Still, Seargant couldn't help but wonder what the grand scheme of events were and how they'd play out. There had been many meetings and scores of profiles developed. But everything was a dead end. The crime scenes were just remnants of what *had* happened and offered little insight into the future.

Then there was the CIA and Steve McCallister. The man knew it was Falby from the beginning and FBI Special Agent James Gibson, or Gibby to those closest to him, agreed with Steve's assessment.

Was this a continuation of the Last Patriot operation from years before? A calculated attack on the country? The same players were on the field, with Falby, Steve McCallister, and Gibby.

And then there was the mercenary he and Hartley killed in Annapolis, and the recent revelation he was former Special Forces and even a CIA operative! But the 'why' behind it all still bothered Seargant. What would motivate someone to assassinate the former presidents?

A female harpist played *How Great Thou Art*, and Seargant was back in the moment, following the elegant flow of her fingers on the instrument, and feeling uplifted in the melodic notes of the reverent hymn.

The song was sung at his father's funeral, and as a man, Seargant still remembered the promise his ten-year old self made at his father's casket. To become the greatest crime fighter of all time. To put away all the bad guys so no child would ever feel his pain.

And he had done just that, with the Wolf Man being his latest trophy. Still, his success had brought little closure or contentment to the little boy inside. Every case he closed reminded him of the one still open. His father's.

Seargant delved deeper into thought. As a young man, he was a natural athlete. Fast, agile, strong, and teachable; and he found no better

No Safe Place

place to nurture his budding skills than the high school football team, where he easily beat every record across five counties.

He smiled as he recalled his exploits on the field and his Ohio State scholarship, the sudden difference between college and high school ability. Still, he was in his element, and was a star wide receiver until a knee injury ended his sporting career. But that's when he'd met Susan, his future wife, and she made it easier to leave football and focus on a criminal justice degree.

The hymn ended and Seargant thought of his baby girl, Hailey, who was now three months old. He and Susan had enjoyed nesting with their newborn until the Wolf Man case and now the presidential assassinations had stolen his focus.

Finally, his mind flashed to Falby, the man who was supposedly the sole engineer of this mayhem. It just didn't make sense. Seargant wasn't one to underestimate a foe, but could it be possible? Maybe he wasn't a terrorist, but a paid mercenary. And what if he had some backing?

Seargant's phone buzzed announcing a text message. He politely took a few steps back and disappeared behind a large hedge to look at the display.

It was Hartley and he was direct. "Steve McCallister, director of the CIA, is missing."

And Seargant realized things just got a hell of a lot worse.

274

CHAPTER 70

Dundalk, Maryland

Pam Pilsen felt sick.

But being a military wife, she was used to the feeling; and the sleeplessness and anxiety that went along with it. She'd felt the cutting despair more times than she could remember.

She'd never stopped worrying about Jordy, even after their divorce.

But Pam had to be strong. So, she sat next to her four-year old daughter, Macy, at the kitchen table, and joined her in coloring a Disney Princess picture book.

But adding color to the flowing gowns on the pages couldn't hold her attention or suppress her fears. As a remedy, she walked to the front window and stared out blankly, as the worst-case scenarios ran through her head, unfiltered.

It started at eighteen, when her high school sweetheart and now ex-husband went to Basic Training. It got harder when he was deployed, and even worse because he went Special Forces. From there, she didn't even know where he was most of the time.

But things calmed down when his twenty years were up, and he was finally home. They quickly learned that his pension wasn't enough, and he accepted random contracting jobs from ex-military sponsors.

They had a daughter, which added to the budgeting woes, and the arguments began. Pam quickly found that Jordy was also fighting himself and dealt with his inner demons with alcohol and long stints at strip clubs.

He missed the action of his old unit and confided that he never felt more alive than with his team, when death was never far. He'd asked around for high paying contract jobs and took several, which paid well, and asked for more.

But when Jordy was called away the day before, Pam noticed something different. He'd stopped by the house to let her know but avoided eye contact and was more emotional when hugging their daughter.

He'd be back the next morning. No big deal. Just one of those things.

But he didn't return, and he'd missed their daughter's dance recital.

Pam continued her vacant stare from the front window, thinking of how Macy had shined on stage. She and six other girls had practiced a Taylor Swift song for several months, choreographing every move to perfection. Their costumes—form fitting pink covered in sequins, with large butterfly wings—was the talk of the show.

And Jordy missed it, after promising he wouldn't. Pam shook her head, as if trying to dismiss the situation altogether. Jordy was many things, but unreliable was not one of them. He'd never break a promise, especially when Macy was involved.

Pam returned to see her daughter had finished coloring and was stacking her crayons in a bin.

A forced smile later, she scooped up the little girl and they ascended the stairs to get ready for bed. Theirs was a regimented routine with little variation. First a warm bath and comfortable princess pajamas, then teeth brushing and book reading in bed.

Pam managed to get through it, and Macy only asked about her father twice. Pam deflected each inquiry by complimenting Macy's dancing earlier in the day, and the little girl lit up with excitement.

But now, with Macy in bed, Pam's mind was clear to think more acutely about what was happening. Where her ex-husband had gone, where was he now?

After her third cup of coffee, she realized she hadn't eaten all day, and felt shaky. She quickly ate three stray chicken nuggets from Macy's dinner and gulped down a cup of water.

Then she discarded her coffee and went straight to her cell phone, speeding through her list of contacts and settling on one in particular.

Bill Sanders used to be her husband's Master Sergeant in his old unit.

And she felt some of her stress abate as she made the call.

Bill Sanders took a swig of his Fat Tire beer before lifting up his grill cover and turning over the porterhouse steaks. Grilling was an art form to him, and he regaled in the cut of meat, the precise marinade, and his technique, which charred both sides while sealing in the juices for ideal flavor.

His cell phone rang, and though he didn't recognize the number, his high spirits made him hit the button to receive the call.

Some quick affirmations and pleasantries were exchanged. He'd met Pam Pilsen years ago when she was pregnant, and they'd crossed paths a few times since.

He'd known Jordy like a brother, and they were operators in the same unit. They'd completed more missions than he could remember and had tasted the same dirt through every rotation.

Pam was a nervous bundle of energy and spewed forth her story without pause. Bill remained quiet, taking it all in and walking away from the grill.

Disheartened, he knew it wasn't a coincidence that another member of his old team was killed by the FBI in Annapolis just the week before.

The call over, he dialed a number and left a voice mail for General D.B. Warren at the Pentagon.

Ten minutes later, General Warren listened to the voice mail, and after deleting it, made some well-placed calls.

To the director of the Secret Service, the director of the FBI, and the chief of staff to the president.

CHAPTER 71

When the funeral service ended, President Maclemore walked Gini Bowman into the library to pay his final respects, privately. They sat on a bright yellow sofa in a beautifully decorated room. The doors closed and the pair, who'd rarely spoken, faced each other.

Maclemore reached for her hand, gently holding it, and looking into the new widow's glassy eyes. He was suddenly struck with the reality of the situation, the finality of Bowman's life, and how the two ends of time were now closed.

Much of the week had been mechanical and programed. With the assassinations of the four presidents, he was locked down, but he'd given the mandatory speeches to the American People, promising justice, and other offerings to promote normalcy.

But now, he looked into Gini Bowman's eyes, and he saw pure loss.

She had truly loved her husband, that was no ploy. And the differences in his own marriage were not lost on him. He thought of his wife, First Lady Judy Maclemore, who was attending Rube Gilmore's ceremony in upper New York.

Would she cry for him if the cameras weren't rolling?

But then he spoke, and more of his programmed responses rolled out. He almost didn't even hear it anymore. Like he was just a puppet on display, a wound-up doll with a pull string.

"I'm truly sorry, Gini. He was a wonderful man and even in the political theater, I was so proud to call him my friend and mentor."

Gini nodded. She moved to speak but an awful sound erupted from her throat, as she fell into a sob.

Then the parlor doors flew open and the Secret Service hoisted President Maclemore from the sofa, ushering him from the room.

In the basement, President Maclemore stared into the face of Ben Reidel, agent in charge of his Secret Service detail. Flanking him was his chief of staff, and he saw Jack Seargant in the back of the room on the phone.

"Sir, we've just got confirmation that Steve McCallister is missing," Reidel said.

"What?" Maclemore erupted. "How can that be?"

"We don't know all the details. But he logged out of Langley last night and didn't return to work today. A wellness check revealed him missing. His wife, Dana is also unaccounted for."

"And what does this mean? Are they now after the directors of the intel community?"

The Secret Service agent shook his head. "We just don't know, sir."

The president looked beyond the men to see Jack Seargant.

"Seargant!" Maclemore yelled. "Get over here!"

Seargant looked up from his phone and walked over.

"Who are you talking to?"

"My Number One, sir. Agent Hartley."

"What do you have?"

"We are also confirming that McCallister is missing, sir."

Maclemore frowned, shaking his head in frustration. "Dammit, we obviously know that!"

Seargant returned to the call, turning his back to the president, and walking a few paces away. "Are you sure Hartley? I need to know this is 100%."

Empty moments passed and all eyes fell on Seargant.

"Well, that's even more telling and none of it's good," Seargant said into the phone. "We were waiting for *something*; I just didn't think it would be this."

"Seargant!" the president yelled once more. "What's going on?!"

Seargant ended the call and turned to President Maclemore, his mind twisted in thought.

"Sir, we have a major problem."

"And what is that?"

"This may all have been a game of chess. The four assassinations were phase one and moved some pieces around. But now we have you here in Van Lear, Kentucky and the CIA director is missing."

"We all know that."

"Several days ago, my partner and I were in Annapolis and killed an ex-CIA operative who was moving in on a young NSA analyst. And just now we're learning of another missing operator. Jordy Pilsen. He was a SEAL and also had CIA ties. I think it's tied to McCallister."

"And what do you make of it, Seargant?" Maclemore asked.

"That we're in the beginning of the next phase. That maybe everything so far was a design to not only kill the ex-presidents, but to flush you into a certain place at a certain time.

Reidel spoke up, moving between Seargant and the president. "Sir, we need to re-think your extraction and we're playing catch up here."

Seargant nodded in full agreement, speaking solemnly. "I hate to say this, sir. But with everything going on, there's just no safe place for you right now."

CHAPTER 72

$\mathbf{B}$en Reidel informed the president the extraction was delayed. Then, as darkness fell across eastern Kentucky, it was once again postponed until morning.

The Secret Service was no doubt under tremendous pressure to protect the president. It didn't have to be said that four of their charges had fallen in the past week, and nobody was more aware than Ben Reidel.

With the director of the CIA now missing, there were competing investigations to determine which side McCallister was actually on. Had he been taken or did he willfully walk away?

Could McCallister be compromised?

Reidel was in constant contact with the director of the Secret Service, Victor Hayes, who asked for and received full support from the Pentagon. They were treating the president's exit like any wartime extraction, and Hayes was coming directly to the president.

He landed in one of three VH-60N White Hawks, in a field just west of the Bowman Library. He thought about utilizing the larger Sea

King but decided on the smaller and more agile White Hawk chopper, which was part of a dozen others known as the White Top fleet.

When Hayes entered the room, Reidel was noticeably relieved, and after some pleasantries and handshakes, the director got down to business.

"Where's the president now?"

"Downstairs in one of the guest bedrooms," Reidel said.

"Good," Hayes continued, without missing a beat.

Then he walked the room, eventually settling over a couple of large maps spread across three tables. The first was an expanded look of eastern Kentucky, with the highlighted roads of every tributary and waterway falling away from their exact position. The second, showed the topography of the land and measured distances, for both auto and air travel, to the four nearest military installations, as well as D.C.

"Sir, we've modeled several extraction routes to safely deliver the pres—"

"Let's take a walk, Reidel," Hayes snapped, interrupting him. Then he looked to the others in the room. "It's a little crowded in here."

Hayes turned and quickly exited and Reidel instinctively followed.

They walked the long hallway in silence, before moving through the kitchen and out one of the rear doors to the patio. Hayes was greeted with energy, as he passed each of the Secret Service agents along the way. He'd been one of them decades ago, rising through the ranks quickly, but he hadn't been in the field for a while.

Before long they were walking in the garden and Hayes continued beyond it.

"Sir, is there something—"

"Look, Reidel. I don't have to say that we've had a very bad week. But it will not get worse!"

"I understand, sir. What's our play?"

"There's no doubt we've been compromised. Whether it's Homeland, FBI, CIA, NSA, or something else, I don't know. But the fewer people that know about this extraction, the better."

"I agree, sir. So, we chopper him to Air Force One and—"

"I want to review all your data, and no one will know—not even the president himself—until a few minutes before departure. And when we do, it'll be with full air support."

Reidel nodded, feeling some of his anxiety dissipate. He was happy to share the mantle of responsibility.

And after several more minutes of hushed discussion, the two men walked back inside to brew a fresh pot of coffee.

Seargant wasn't privy to the conversations of the Secret Service, so he used the time to check on his family and speak to Hartley.

Pip was out of surgery, sedated in a medically induced coma. The bullet had been removed, but it was the resulting internal injury and possible hemorrhaging that was of concern.

"But he's alive, right?" Seargant asked, relieved.

Hartley sighed on the other end. "Yeah, technically, Sarge, but you gotta realize he's been shot in the head and—"

"But he's stable?"

"Stable, but in critical condition in a coma, with more tubes going in and out than—"

"Tell me again about the bullet's path."

"It's actually a miracle he even survived. Turns out he was having a sneezing attack because the room was so dank and dusty. The girl said he must have sneezed a dozen times.

"When Falby rushed in, he shot Pip in mid-sneeze. And with the angle of Pip's head going down, the bullet ran across the top of his head and lodged in the back of his skull."

"That's good news then, compared to what I thought."

"The surgeon said this type of thing sometimes happens with deer hunting. He had a hunter come in a few years back who was nearly gored to death by a buck he thought was dead. It was a clear shot to the forehead, but the bullet traveled right over the deer's crown. The buck was knocked down and out for a couple of minutes. But then it woke up pissed off, gored the hell out of the hunter, and ran off without a hitch."

Seargant heard the story, secretly rooting for the buck, and happy to have a glimmer of hope about Pip.

Even after working decades at the FBI, he'd never come across someone as diligent and genuine as Pip. And even though they'd never met in person, he felt a strong connection with the young analyst.

"Anything on McCallister?"

"Nothing, sir. You know he and James Gibson have a special relationship. From what I understand, Gibby's been back and forth from Langley to McCallister's residence; and interviewed everyone in between but has nothing. Financial records are being pulled and scrutinized, but it's too early to know anything yet."

"So, we wait," Seargant said, shaking his head and blowing out a puff of air.

"That's all we can do, Sarge."

"Just keep Lisa comfortable and away from the police and media."

"I've squashed both and she's got her own room here. Her parents are flying in as we speak."

"Good," Seargant said.

Then Hayes and Reidel entered the room and moved directly to the maps.

"I gotta go, Hartley. Keep in touch," Seargant said, ending the call.

Hayes turned to the assembly of Secret Service and presidential staff.

"I need this room cleared, including the entire hallway."

There were some scoffs, but Hayes met them with a harsh glare. Then he looked to Jack Seargant.

"And that includes you too."

CHAPTER 73

Early the next morning, Director of the Secret Service Victor Hayes checked his watch as he looked over the maps sprawled across the table.

After a sleepless night that included poring over them in exhaustive detail, and consulting with Homeland, the FBI, and the Pentagon, four separate extraction routes were planned. The final decision would be made by Hayes only minutes before departure.

Air Force One was sitting alone on a designated runway eight miles south at the Kentucky National Guard, and they also had the three White Hawk choppers at their disposal. The Beast, the president's fortified vehicle, was ready, as was the standard motorcade that included over forty vehicles.

With the director of the CIA missing—and possibly compromised—there was an overwhelming feeling that something nefarious was at play.

The NSA had also reported increased chatter.

Director Hayes sighed, looking up from the maps he'd all but memorized. There were a handful of other team leaders, including Jack Seargant, and all awaited instruction.

"We are in a very remote place which is good and bad," Hayes said. "Air traffic is already suspended over the area, and we'll obviously have heavy air support. In a few minutes we leave for Camp David instead of D.C. This information, decided just now, is something that's unexpected and impossible to be part of a working offense."

The others in the room nodded but Seargant wasn't impressed. "Yes, it's unexpected from both sides," he suggested, tampering the optimism. "The way to Camp David is high over West Virginia."

"We'll have our F-18's flanking the three helos," Hayes said.

Seargant shook his head, looking down. "With respect, sir, may I be in one of the choppers?"

Hayes looked to Seargant, irritated. "I'm sorry Mr. Seargant, but this is a Secret Service operation. You can take Air Force One back to D.C. That's an upgrade for you, isn't it?"

Seargant remained silent as Hayes, Reidel, and the remaining agents moved past him to escort the president. It reminded him of Steve McCallister at the Oval Office just two days before, and the same uneasy feeling eclipsed him.

Something wasn't right.

He hoped to God he was wrong. But unfortunately, he rarely was.

CHAPTER 74

Falby had to give it to his contact. The man without a name.

So far, the relationship had been mutually beneficial and seamless, starting with a phone call he'd received months before.

That phone call had made Falby uncommonly nervous.

It was a couple of weeks after the explosions in Cape Verde, and Falby settled into a remote cabin in West Virginia, renting it for a year and paying up front.

He'd been well on his way in planning the four assassinations, but even with his attention to detail and clandestine methods, he had unknowingly attracted the attention of someone.

His contact. The man without a name.

And that's when the phone call came into one of his burner phones. How the man could have traced the disposable phone to Falby was still unknown. But it got the Chameleon's attention, a testament to his contact's abilities.

The man without a name confirmed some very recent technological advances, some of which he'd invented—including DNA screening with heat signatures and facial recognition applications—that made the human body part of an elaborate expanding GPS grid.

The message was received. Falby was not as invisible as he'd thought. There was no contingency plan, no escape from this kind of scrutiny.

The man without a name went on to describe and prove that he was linked into every U.S. intelligent agency and had the president's ear on topics of national security.

That also got Falby's attention.

He confirmed Falby's exact location, even commenting on the upside-down Weber grill with the broken wheel, adjacent to the cabin. Beating Falby to his own thought process, the man also stated that he could have an FBI HRT Team onsite in no time.

So Falby listened. And for the first time he was humbled.

The two men spoke more in depth and learned how they could benefit each other. So, the weeks turned into months and things went exactly as planned.

Falby arrived back in West Virginia in the early morning hours, immediately checking on the favor he'd been promised and happy to see it was done. The timing was back on track and even afforded him a few hours of well needed rest.

When he awoke, he was alert and on task.

According to his contact, a decision had just been made, and the President of the United States would be flying just southwest of Falby's location. And for something that was planned over two months before, things couldn't have been better.

Falby walked the inside of the cabin like an accomplished military leader who had succeeded on every front.

Station one was where he'd created the ricin and he smiled at the remnants of the oil cake and spent caster beans. The tables at stations two and three were empty; he'd already used the surveillance cameras and had brought the maps with him. And station four was still there: the replica of the wooden armoire he'd built to spec and practiced on.

And now his full attention was on station five, with a handful of maps showing the great states of West Virginia and Kentucky. Another table held contents listing the exact capabilities, long memorized, of the MQ-9 Reaper drones that would soon take flight.

He marveled at the hardware and their deadly capabilities, but even with their payload—all eight of the laser-guided Hellfire II missiles—it would be their three hundred little friends, the DJI Matrice 200 drones that would be more integral.

He breathed deeply.

The president would soon be dead and Steve McCallister was on his way to Falby.

He thought of the protocols and the movements of President Maclemore and what he must be thinking. The logistics of the extraction had just been finalized, which had to be unsettling.

Falby could get to where he had to be in minutes. The mission pattern was already preloaded and could even be modified remotely on a grid that expanded up to seven kilometers, with thirty-eight minutes of flight time.

The truth was, no matter what route was chosen—ironically except for the way the president came into Kentucky—there would be no counter measure to defend what Falby had planned.

Falby opened the cabin door and was greeted by the sounds of nature. Birds sang from unseen places and the high trees—brightly colored yellow, orange, and deep red—swayed gently in a mild wind. The sun was peeking through the foliage, burning off the morning haze and promising a beautiful new day.

A beautiful day indeed, Falby thought.

But not for everyone.

CHAPTER 75

The Harold Bowman Presidential Library was brimming with activity.

Seargant had already walked the perimeter twice and gotten a closer look at the three White Hawks that would be the method of extraction for President Maclemore. He'd also checked in with Hartley, who was at the hospital with Lisa.

Now they were all huddled in the main family room. Dozens of federal agents sipping coffee from paper cups, all ready to go.

Maclemore hugged Gini Bowman and offered more words of sympathy. He then apologized for the chaos his attendance had created and promised swift justice to the party responsible for her husband's death.

"Justice," Gini Bowman murmured. The words escaped her pursed lips, barely above a whisper. Then she frowned and Maclemore studied her. Her face was ashen and hollowed, and she looked to be aging before his eyes.

"Yes, Gini. Your husband was a good man. And I promise you, justice will be served."

Gini's eyes flashed with new life as she looked to Maclemore. "Then you must be going Mr. President. You have a lot to do."

"This way, sir," Hayes said, opening the door of the parlor. "We're ready for departure."

"That's good. What's our ETA?"

"That's what I'd like to speak to you about, sir. There's a lot of internet chatter. Director McCallister is still missing and now we've uncovered some interesting financial activity that begs more questions."

"Back to D.C. by when?" Maclemore asked.

"Sir, I just made the decision a few minutes ago. We're going to Camp David, and it'll be like the Middle East extractions we've done before. We're gonna go fast and hard and fly higher with increased air support."

"I'll leave it to you, Hayes," Maclemore said. "I like the idea of Camp David for a few days, I must admit."

"Shall we, then?" Director Hayes said, looking to the president, and opening the French doors.

The two men stepped into the hallway and were joined by several other agents, as they headed to the foyer.

Outside, more agents flanked the president, ushering him quickly to the three White Hawk choppers. Overhead, two F-18 Hornets roared, and the sound lent Hayes comfort. He knew there were many more in close proximity.

When the president was secured, Hayes took a final survey of the library complex, then to the sky where he knew the three satellites he'd requested added another layer of protection.

But what he couldn't have guessed was those same satellites also announced the exact path of the president's extraction.

And now the president was even more exposed than anyone could know.

CHAPTER 76

President Maclemore looked out from the insulated, bullet proof glass of Marine One, contemplating the array of colors in the distance.

The early morning sky was royal blue in color, and the cloud coverage was moderate, with billowy white cotton balls showing in the east. The dense tree cover rose and fell with the land; a rolling tapestry of deep green, though some showed streaks of yellow, red, and orange.

To his left, Director Hayes was busying himself with paperwork, and two other agents sat quietly in the forward seats. The two pilots were busy at the controls and communicating with other aircraft, all in wide formation, as the choppers flew high and purposefully across West Virginia.

Maclemore dropped his shoulder and regarded the chopper to his right. Then he glimpsed an F-18 Hornet, several thousand feet higher. There were many others in the air with him, all making steady progress toward Camp David in western Maryland.

With headphones on, most noise, both internal and external, were muted, and the president got lost in the rotor's steady hum.

It allowed him a moment of respite.

The day before, the nation put to rest four former presidents; something that seemed impossible to even consider. There were two Democrats and two Republicans, and Maclemore passed the time reflecting on his interactions with each.

He'd been Harold Bowman's vice president, and though they were initially allied for geographic strategy, they formed a natural, common bond in their eight years together. Maclemore recalled when Bowman called him unexpectantly, asking him to be on his presidential ticket. He couldn't stop smiling during the brief exchange and felt giddy as he ran to Judy to share the news.

His mind turned to Rube Gilmore, a man who was unstoppable in his prime. Charismatic and engaging, he was a true politician who could talk to anyone at their own level and build relationships easily. He'd worked the popular late-night shows to perfection and made cameos on Saturday Night Live, one time even surprising Steve Buscemi, who portrayed him in several skits.

But then a handful of sex allegations surfaced, which led to many more improprieties. He didn't seek a second term and quietly left office. It was funny, Maclemore thought, how a man's legacy became more lustrous upon his death, and how politics could fall by the wayside.

Walker Montgomery was a hard man who Maclemore had only met a few times. A stout Republican, he was imposing and quiet, more bulldog than man. His firm handshake and knowing smile stood out. He remembered Montgomery's confidence and natural leadership, which was something the nation needed during the man's tenure.

Then there was James Preston, who Maclemore had never met. James and Beth Preston's life had been a storied love affair several decades removed, and they were cherished by the American people in a way that was uncommon today.

His thoughts were cut short as the chopper shook and lunged to the right, snapping Maclemore to attention.

He pressed the button on his headphones. "What's going on with—" he started, only to have his voice cut off, as he floated up against his restraints. But before he could recover, the pilot pulled out of the dive and the sudden G force forced Maclemore to vomit.

There were shouts in his headphones, and he threw his hands to his head, tightening his grip and struggling to hear.

"We've got a bogie on our six," one of the pilots said. "What the hell are those things?"

"Ripper Lead engaged," another voice sounded from the Hornet escort.

"Two's high over, I'm seeing a bunch of weird stuff on my FLIR, skipper."

"Shackle and head to the choppers. The bogie went past us. Lead's low," another voice yelled.

The pilot of chopper two interrupted. "We've got incoming! Chaff flares and evasive measures!"

A short scream sounded.

"Chopper two is hit. We're going down—"

Maclemore heard an explosion and they swerved right, diving even lower. More G forces followed and Maclemore fought to breathe through short gasps.

"We've got another bogie, southwest twenty miles. Moving to intercept."

"Are those drones?" another chopper pilot sounded. "They're all over us!"

Moments passed and the same pilot, breathing heavily, shouted. "Our tail rotors been hit. I have no yaw control! I'm dropping the collective to gain forward airspeed."

Maclemore was wide-eyed, as his mind reconciled what he was hearing—and what was *happening* just outside his window—as his body was punished by the erratic maneuvers.

Then he heard words that left him cold, realizing it was his own pilot speaking.

"I'm going to the deck. Mr. President, brace for a hard landing!"

Maclemore could see the pilot and co-pilot's arms working the controls frantically, as the chopper took a gut-wrenching nosedive and Maclemore grabbed the seat.

"Ripper Lead, what do you see?!"

"I've got eyes on what appears to be a Reaper drone. It's shot two of the four Hellfire's. And I see hundreds of smaller drones moving in grid-like form surrounding the choppers."

Maclemore's pilot grunted and yelled into the president's headphones. "I've got missile lock indication. It's away; diving to control a possible landing!"

Suddenly a flare cut through the chopper's cabin and a jagged tear ripped through the fuselage, separating the two pilots from the others. The chopper blades were visible just twenty feet above and the noise from the roaring engines was impossible.

A rush of air swept in, and with the increased spinning, the inner walls separated the craft in two. There was a flash of heat as the vessel split and went into total free fall.

Maclemore and Hayes looked to each other in fear as they spun away from the front piece of chopper. Their rotation quickened and

Maclemore shut his eyes against the swirl of blue and green. His stomach tightened and he felt he would pass out when there was a sudden jolt.

Then total darkness.

Falby studied the monitors from inside the tree line. One of the Reapers about twenty miles out had been shot down easily, but it was a decoy anyway.

What was more important were the three hundred Matrice 200's that swarmed the flight path of the three choppers, one of which was carrying President Maclemore. They were carrying C-4 and were targeting the rotors of the choppers in a grid formation on a pre-populated mission route.

Then there was the Reaper sent up only *after* the Matrices were in play.

Falby traded glances from the handful of monitors at his feet, to the skyline where the activity was happening several miles out and closing.

He wore a one-piece hunting outfit and had a deer rifle next to him. His pickup truck was parked just off-road, as was the oversized trailer that had towed the two Reapers. He had a dead deer in his truck bed and the bumper stickers, battered cooler, and fast-food trash that littered the inside were a nice touch.

And he was indeed a hunter, though not the kind he portrayed.

Falby had simulated his attack exhaustively, knowing he'd have about thirty seconds to hit the three choppers before the Reaper's would be taken out. He watched with a bird's-eye view from the camera in the second Reaper, as it swerved up and to the left to engage the three presidential choppers, the whole time being crowded and protected by the smaller Matrice's.

The Reaper wouldn't hit radar until eight hundred feet and that saved him about ten seconds. He picked up another four seconds when he locked on and fired at the first chopper and already engaged the second in perfect succession. The third chopper was more difficult to target, because the pilot now knew they were under attack. Though the F-18's moved to engage, the chopper was flying right into the cubed grid of the swarming Matrice's.

The first chopper swerved in a nosedive of fire as the Reaper itself came under attack from the jets. The Reaper had only seconds but confirmed missile lock and deployed its Hellfire missile once more.

It was destroyed but not before its second missile hit its mark.

Falby looked away from the monitor and up into the sky, seeing a visual of the compromised chopper under a thousand feet high. It was now about a half mile away, spinning out of control in a ball of black smoke and fire.

He'd been able to shoot down two choppers with the Reaper and take down one with the Matrice drones.

The chopper was lost through the trees, but Falby heard a tremendous thud, followed by an explosion. He hurriedly tossed the two laptops and monitors into a trash bag and threw them into the woods, then started a light jog, dodging the large trees and jumping the low brush with vigor.

This was not part of the plan, but pure curiosity drew Falby closer. He couldn't have known that one chopper would fall so close, and he just *had* to get a visual. He didn't know which chopper held the president, but there was a one in three chance, and that was enough.

Minutes later, Falby rushed into a clearing, bearing witness to his efforts. There was a smoldering craft cut in two and the scene was horrific. The spent fuselage was burning fervently, emitting increasing tendrils of black smoke; but as terrible as that was, the eerie silence was even worse.

An F-18 roared overhead, banking right and testing its lowest speed, only to disappear again.

Then a man stumbled from the wreckage, holding his head. He walked slow and unsteady, remarkably the only survivor. He fell but then stood, looking down and patting out a small flame on his tie.

Through the melee, Falby recognized the undeniable form of President John Maclemore.

The fuselage of the chopper exploded and Maclemore quickened his pace, lumbering directly to where Falby stood. The assassin couldn't believe it. He thought he'd killed the president, but here Maclemore was.

And it was the second time his prey had literally come to *him*.

CHAPTER 77

President Maclemore looked up through the frenzy, noticing a hunter in a clearing.

The pain in his side was forcing him more alert by the moment and his first coherent thought was one of survival. So, he started a slow, clumsy walk to the hunter, who met him halfway, slinging a rifle over his shoulder and reaching out to help.

"Oh my gosh, are you okay?" the hunter asked, shaking his head in dismay, and looking over the cuts and bruises on the president's face. "Ya look like you just plum fell outta the sky!"

Overhead, two F-18's roared and banked left and the two men looked up. Then the president stared at the hunter, who was now looking over at the burning remains of Marine One. His eyes traded glances between the pockets of fire and a few dead men, whose bodies were unmoving and bent at impossible angles.

"We were shot down and I gotta get out of here!" Maclemore yelled.

Then he checked his side and tested a deep breath, stopping short with a grunt. "And I think I cracked a few ribs."

The hunter looked perplexed. "I got me some bandages in the truck, but I don't know nothing about no ribs."

Maclemore leveled his breathing, looking back at the crash site, a sense of dread overwhelming him, competing with the pain.

"Look. We don't know if this is over. We have to move!"

The hunter shook his head. "Hey, I don't want no trouble, but there's a police station not four or five miles away. But first you gotta get some bandages or something."

Falby had to suppress a smile at his lame attempt at a West Virginia accent. Then he considered the lie he'd just told. The closest thing resembling authority was more than an hour away!

President Maclemore grew impatient. "Do you recognize who I am?"

The hunter continued a dull stare, looking back and forth from the dead men and the president. "How you expect me to know you if we just met?" Then he let out a quick laugh and shook his head, walking away slowly. "Maybe you *did* fall from the sky, like some alien or something."

"Hey, wait up," the president said, limping after the hunter. "I need a ride to that police station you mentioned."

Falby didn't respond, but turned and offered his hand, which Maclemore accepted. Several minutes later they were at the pickup truck. President Maclemore climbed into the passenger seat, while Falby unhitched the trailer and retrieved some things from a bag.

The chloroform rag subdued the president into a deep lull quickly and Falby dragged him to the back.

Soon they were on a long, windy road, swallowed by the mature trees that camouflaged their movements. The F-18's no doubt *tried* to maintain a visual on the president, but with no eyes on the ground, it was a clean escape.

Falby was a hunter.

And the President of the United States was his prize.

CHAPTER 78

Falby managed a steady speed, as he carefully maneuvered the old, rusty pickup truck down Herd's Bluff and across Milford Road to pick up Route 20. It was a long, windy path, but the roads fell away from the main thoroughfare, and the emergency vehicles surely on their way.

The killer hoped he wouldn't come across any checkpoints, but his story and appearance were plausible. His identification impeccable. But if things became messy, he was more than ready to engage anyone in his path. With it being so close to the end game, his resolve was peaking.

Still, he held back celebrating his victories; focusing on the narrow, snaking road and the greenery flashing by.

He caught a look of himself in the rearview mirror, and lifted his chin, turning. Wearing full camouflage and a weathered Skoal hat, he looked the part of a hunter driving through the back roads.

His face was dirty, he stank of perspiration, and his left cheek swelled with chewing tobacco.

The President of the United States was unconscious in the truck bed, covered with a couple of tarps. He was further hidden by the dead deer partially laying across his legs.

Falby reached for his cell phone and called a familiar number.

His contact. The man without a name.

In the past, he'd answered within one ring, but this time was different. There was no answer. He ended the call and tried again with the same result.

This was no accident—not now—and it forced Falby to rethink what he always knew was possible. What if he was cut off? What if *he* was now the expendable one?

He always knew it possible and had planned for it, accordingly.

Falby reflected more on his contact. They shared common goals and complemented each other's skill sets. The man had discussed the consummate plan, and when finished, would allow Falby to be untouchable and off the grid.

But now the man without a name wasn't taking calls and Falby knew what that meant.

It all made sense.

With the four presidents dead and Maclemore shot down and *presumed* dead, his contact's goals were achieved. Falby suddenly become another loose end and expendable; possibly even a prize to be used to further the man's intelligence career.

But it also meant that no one knew Falby had President Maclemore! If that was known, he wouldn't be cut off.

A few minutes later, Falby called again and received no answer.

He controlled his breathing, his eyes mere pinpoints as he stared ahead at the road. While chaos reigned, he was a picture of calm. His focus turned to plan B. It was regrettable, but now the only way forward.

He hadn't changed the rules, but he sure as hell was going to enforce them.

Falby turned into a hidden enclave, a few miles from his compound.

He put on headphones and picked up a laptop, looking at the live feeds from every direction starting a couple miles from the cabin. Seeing everything undisturbed, he took a few minutes to scroll through the history of each feed, once again seeing nothing out of order.

Camera fourteen showed motion forty-eight minutes prior, but when he looked at the images, he saw a couple of deer walking cautiously across a path. Camera seven showed the happenings inside the cabin, and Falby was satisfied.

So, he threw the pickup truck in reverse and got back on the road, thankful to have discarded the trailer.

Falby slowed and turned left into a narrow trail, barely making it through two large oaks. Then the truck reduced to a crawl, as he maneuvered and rolled over the root systems that led to the cabin.

He tried his contact's phone number once more, but this time it wouldn't even ring. It was as if the phone number didn't even exist and that sealed it.

He sucked in a deep breath and contemplated plan B. It was an option he'd hoped against, even though he'd spent considerable time on its preparation. It wasn't ideal, but it was now necessary, and he went to the closet to retrieve a pre-packed bag.

Then Falby dragged the unconscious president into the cabin and chained him to the wall.

CHAPTER 79

Seargant had a morose, unsettling feeling he couldn't shake.

He was in the back of a Suburban, along with three Secret Service agents, driving to Air Force One for the trip back to Andrews and D.C.

Deep in thought and with a heavy heart, he searched his feelings. Was it that they'd just memorialized and buried four former presidents? Or was it the helplessness stemming from a stalled investigation yielding no credible results?

Maybe it was because Pip was in critical condition in a coma, or even that Steve McCallister—the director if the CIA—was missing! Seargant tried to connect that latest piece of information to the ongoing threat but fell short. Nothing fit.

"So, Jack," the Secret Service agent beside him said. "What's the FBI have so far?"

Seargant blinked a few times into the present. "James Gibson is the lead. So far we're just playing catch up and—"

"Yeah, that's what I thought."

Seargant retreated inward.

He focused on the *how* behind it all. In his experience the bad guys weren't as equipped as expected. And though he would never discount an adversary, he just knew that Falby could *not* be working alone. How could *one* man be able to move so easily, slip through the smallest of cracks and between the tightest timeframes to kill four former leaders, only to disappear?

Then he concentrated on his own emotions. He suddenly felt overwhelmed and helpless. Like he was just a player on the sideline; a voyeur to it all.

He scowled at the source of the stemming dread. President Maclemore! He should have been allowed to escort the president; he never should have taken no for an answer.

Seargant was sure the president was in danger, and although protected by the Secret Service and flanked by heavy air support, he would have felt better being on one of those choppers.

Seargant reflected on Director Hayes and his decision minutes before liftoff. The threat was valid, and that grim reality had shown on the faces of everyone there. This was as real as it got, and the president not flying back on Air Force One was proof of it.

"I'm looking forward to a quick nap on the unit," the same man chirped in, but no one replied.

"How about you, Jack? You've been up all night too, haven't you?"

Seargant looked at the man and spoke evenly. "I'm gonna take this SUV and follow the president's route to Camp David."

"And why would that be productive?" the man quipped.

But Seargant remained quiet, closing his eyes and focusing on the next several hours.

That morose feeling—his gut instinct—was still there and gaining. And it wouldn't cede until he got back on the playing field.

Driving alone in the Suburban, Seargant *tried* to drive eighty-plus miles per hour, but the road was unforgiving. There were sharp turns and grades that both rose and fell, as the windy road cut through the flowing mountains and valleys.

Large trucks slowly made their way, and Seargant was careful to maneuver between them, while keeping an eye on the road ahead and the clock on the dash. Seeking a distraction, Seargant reached for his cell phone and dialed Hartley, who picked up immediately.

"How's Pip doing? Please give me some good news."

"He's still in a coma, critical but stable. But Sarge, it doesn't look good."

"Yeah, nothing looks good," Seargant said, speeding up to shoot the gap between two eighteen-wheelers.

"Everything okay, boss?" Hartley asked. "You sound a little off."

"Yeah, no. I'm just trying to figure things out. I've got one of my hunches and I'm checking it out."

"One of your hunches, huh? Who are you pissing off now?"

Seargant smiled, wishing Hartley was with him. They thought the same and there was no one he trusted more.

"I can't talk about it now, but I'll call you later."

The conversation over, Seargant started to call his wife when his cell phone rang. He looked at the screen, seeing it was James Gibson.

"Hey, Gibby, what do you know?" Seargant asked.

"Marine One was just shot down! I'm racing to the scene now via chopper. Are you on Air Force One?"

Seargant absorbed the information, tightening his grip on the steering wheel and pressing the accelerator. The color rushed from his face and his extremities went numb. A cold feeling tore through his entire being and held him impotent in its grasp.

"Is the president alive!?" Seargant blurted. "What's the status at the scene!?"

"We know nothing at ground level. There may be no survivors. Everything's coming from the F-18's above, but local police are racing there.

"Where?"

"Tioga, West Virginia. Heavily wooded and rural. Population was ninety-eight at the last census."

Seargant was now pushing ninety on a straight away. "I'll be in Huntington in about a half hour, pick me up on that chopper."

"Roger that." Gibby said.

And the conversation ended.

CHAPTER 80

Seargant and Gibby walked the crash site slowly, not believing what they saw. But they were hopeful for what they *didn't* see.

President Maclemore was not among the dead.

The large steel carriage that *was* Marine One was now just a charred shell, cut into jagged pieces and smoldering. The burnt ground surrounding the wreckage created a black scarring of the land, and small shards of wreckage were scattered in every direction.

The entire scene was videoed and photographed, and the bodies of the two pilots, two Secret Service agents, and Victor Hayes were covered with tarps, nearby. A half mile away, a search team found an abandoned trailer, along with trash bags full of computer equipment, and everything was being catalogued.

The other two choppers flanking the president had also been shot down, both within a mile of Marine One, and other forensic teams were working those sites, no doubt experiencing the same feelings of disbelief and resignation.

Roadblocks were up fifty miles out and armed search parties were fanning out in every direction.

Seargant covered his mouth and nose with a damp rag, but it did little to thwart the pungent stench of burnt fuel, metal, and human remains.

Seargant moved to Gibby, who was bending over, examining some shrapnel.

"What do you see, Jack?" Gibby asked, without looking up.

Seargant frowned. "It's not what I see that troubles me."

Gibby straightened and turned. "How's that?"

"It's what we don't see and what we haven't learned from the past week. This can't just be one man. Even Falby would need help."

"I agree, Jack. I think the Last Patriot operation didn't end. It may still be alive and well."

The two men went quiet as they continued to survey the crash site. Seargant's eyes settled on the black tarps covering the five dead men.

"And Gibby. I'll tell you one more thing that I *don't* see. President Maclemore. Whether he's dead or alive, who knows? But he's obviously not here."

An hour later, Seargant and Gibby were heading to the other crash sites when an FBI agent ran over waving a cell phone.

"Sir!" the young agent called out. "You need to take this."

Gibby looked at Seargant and took the phone. "This is Gibson."

Gibby closed his eyes as he listened intently. Seargant watched the man impatiently, searching for any inroad to the conversation.

When the conversation ended, Gibby turned to Seargant. "The NSA uncovered the coordinates of where the president and Falby are presumed to be right now, about thirty-six miles away. Three Hostage Rescue Teams are on the way."

"That's great news Gibby, let's go!"

"But there's one more thing," Gibby added, tempering the excitement. "There are reports that indicate Steve McCallister is a probable suspect in all of this."

Seargant was taken back, processing the information and Gibby continued.

"The director of the CIA has a shoot on sight order on him. He's now wanted dead or alive."

CHAPTER 81

Pam Pilsen hadn't slept well.

Tossing and turning and not getting comfortable, she'd passed the time by watching the digits on the clock turn, obsessing about Jordy. But every thought led to the same conclusion. Her ex-husband was no doubt missing. He would never have missed Macy's recital.

The night before she'd called one of his buddies from the old unit. He'd listened patiently, letting her do most of the talking. He promised to look into it, but she hadn't heard back.

So, her mind wandered further. Was he active again? Off on a mission, somewhere like the old days? She knew the answer was officially no. She also knew he'd agreed to odd requests that required travel at a moment's notice. And he'd never said no. Though divorced, Jordy had a duty to his family and would always provide.

She took care of the finances and noticed several large payments over the last few years. She'd questioned him a couple of times but received the rehearsed answers a soldier's wife was supposed to believe.

But now, thinking of him in some faraway place in possible peril sent a quick shiver through her, followed by a hot flash and perspiration. She slipped out of the sheets, noticing her pillow was soaked with sweat.

The clock turned to 5:46 a.m. Knowing that Macy would be up in about forty-five minutes, Pam moved to the shower, grateful for the warm spray on her weary body.

After, she threw on a robe, treading lightly in the hallway and down the stairs to make some coffee. She surfed the news channels, which continued to cover the different stages of the presidential assassinations and yesterday's service at the National Cathedral.

She settled on Fox News, which was reporting from the White House.

"… and the president is expected back at the White House later this morning, after spending the night in Van Lear, Kentucky, following the burial of President Bowman."

A commercial cut in and Pam muted the television. She withdrew to the kitchen, where she checked the time and headed for the pantry. She stepped onto a stool to reach the fourth shelf and found her special box of cereal. It was her one vise, something carried over from her childhood.

Sundays were for Lucky Charms. Two full bowls.

Lost in the task, her mind settled as she poured the cereal into a bowl, chasing away another yawn. But something was wrong. Only a few pieces fell, and she shook the box. Peering in and using her hand to fan out the plastic within, she noticed an envelope.

Her heart beat quicker.

Of course! Jordy knew she always ate Lucky Charms on Sundays. It must be a cute love note, or some information on his whereabouts. She recognized his handwriting on the envelope and opened it quickly, perusing it. But while it confirmed where he was, it was anything but conciliatory.

Blood rushed to her head, and she felt lightheaded. Empty seconds passed as she re-read the letter, hoping for new information. Tears came and she brought her hand to her mouth to squash the involuntary groans that escaped her pursed lips.

She read the last line repeatedly.

If I'm not back by early morning Saturday to intercept this, then I'm dead. Be strong. It's going to be all right. It's Sunday, so send Macy to your mother's as usual and call Jack Seargant of the FBI. Read him this letter. I also left a detailing of my financial accounts and passwords in your car's glove compartment. I'm so sorry for what I became, but I will be forever yours, sweetheart. And I love you and Macy with all my heart. I'm sorry.
Jordy

Another sheet of paper contained Jack Seargant's phone number and revealed a precise location somewhere in West Virginia. It showed the exact coordinates with longitude and latitude, and further layered with a topographical sketch and altitude readings.

It was crude in design, but had all the pertinent information, including markings for inroads and even the depths of the two streams that ran through the property.

Wherever the place was, Jordy had given it a lot of thought.

Pam heard the door open upstairs and Macy calling out.

Like many times before, Pam quickly transformed into a wall of stoicism. She had to be strong for her daughter. So, over the next hour, she harbored her initial shock and revelation, and got lost in the motions of their morning routine.

She sat with Macy during breakfast, sipping coffee, nervously. Then Macy dressed and brushed her teeth, while Pam prepared her lunch.

It took every ounce of energy to get to her mother's house without breaking down, but she stayed strong. Then, Pam turned back onto the road and rushed home to read the letter again. Maybe she'd misread something.

Maybe Jordy would be home.

But she arrived at an empty house, and before she could clean the dishes, turn off the television, or even consider the letter, her body gave out from exhaustion, and she fell asleep on the couch.

CHAPTER 82

Special Agents James Gibson and Jack Seargant positioned themselves on a high ridge looking down into a valley. Next to them was a sniper who introduced himself as Gut, but had spoken little after that.

From their high perch, they saw a simple hunting cabin about five hundred yards away. The target of their mission; sourced with the highest credibility from inside their own intel community.

Could the most wanted terrorist in the world be inside with the President of the United States?

Looking through binoculars, Seargant scanned every detail. It was a simple structure, no doubt. Maybe eight hundred square feet total, it looked to be more of a wooden lean-to than an actual residence. The timber walls looked old; constructed and reconfigured over time by uneven boards. The roof sagged and thick, green moss took over most of the front side.

But there was no mistaking the large generators against the cabin and the fresh tire tracks leading away. Seargant continued to pan the ground, noticing imprints across the muddy terrain, suggesting recent activity of heavy machinery, or dragging. There was an old Chevy sedan parked behind a woodpile.

"It fits, Gibby," Seargant said. "This is where he'd be."

Gibby was also peering through binoculars, noticing the same details. "What concerns me is how fortified this place must be."

Seargant looked over to Gibby, who withdrew and turned to the sniper on his right and Seargant to his left.

"I know this guy. It's gonna be heavily monitored and booby-trapped. He had a similar place in Jersey a few years back. Heavily secured. And I'll never forget when I had my weapon leveled at him at Madison Square Garden. It was a long corridor without any doors or exits and his hands were up. It was all over. I had him. And then he smiled at me and was so eerily calm, like he'd expected me."

"What happened?" the sniper asked.

"Let's just say that Falby always has a way out. The Chameleon is a well-suited name, so take the shot when you can."

"Roger that, sir," the sniper said, returning to his scope.

Seargant went back to his binoculars. "He's just a man, Gibby. And if he's down there, we're gonna get him."

Gibby tapped his phone. "The HRT's are here."

Seargant's own phone vibrated in his pocket, and he was relieved to see the number. Over the past couple of days, Seargant had contacted the NSA and spoken to Frog, who was the only other analyst Pip trusted.

"Frog, what do you have?"

"Do you have anything new on Pip?"

"No, I don't Frog. I know he's stable and he's getting the best care possible. It's still too early to know."

Frog sighed, then continued. "I did what you said and researched everything about the property. For a simple West Virginia cabin, it actually has a storied past."

"Go on."

"It's had several owners since it was first deeded in 1848. It was part of the Underground Railroad in the mid 1850's and satellite imaging shows two likely entrance points about two hundred yards south and north of it.

"It was a distillery before and throughout the prohibition, and that same tunnel system probably played a role in that as well. So, there are at least a couple tunnels and obviously a point of escape or entry."

Seargant nodded. "Anything else that can help us, Frog? Can you work some of that Pip magic for me?"

"I pulled the utility records, and it shows no spike in usage, but that could mean he's got some generators. There's no landline for the phone, but I can get into any cell on the property. I just need more time."

"That's perfect, Frog," Seargant said. "I appreciate it. How are we with real-time satellite overhead?"

"Five minutes out."

"Thanks, Frog, call me when you can see me from the sky."

Several minutes later Gibby tapped his phone again. "HRT is in place. They've found the two tunnel systems. The one to the south looks to be the primary. It was hidden with a large, fallen tree branch and is next to a rocky enclave. Very hard to find if they hadn't been looking."

Seargant had never worked with the FBI's elite Hostage Rescue Team.

Based out of Quantico, Virginia and formed in 1982, the FBI's HRT is the nation's primary law enforcement *tactical* unit and is responsible for counter-terrorist and strategic operations within the United States. They are directed from the fifth floor of the Hoover Building in D.C., and always available to deploy at a moment's notice to any domestic threat or catastrophe.

They are one of the most capable and lethal counterterrorism and rescue units in the law enforcement community. They have access to the most advanced weaponry, technology, and training; working tirelessly to raid, search, arrest, assault, snipe, or rescue when ordered.

Through binoculars, Seargant scanned the cabin and then in every direction—to the high trees that extended out and up the hillside—to the lower areas where a small stream descended to the south.

"I can't see the HRT guys," he stated, to himself.

The sniper scoffed but didn't move from his scope. "They're out there, sir," he said. "And we're all ready to go."

CHAPTER 83

Minutes later, Frog confirmed satellite coverage.

The cabin was surrounded on every side, with full air and land support for several miles in every direction. Roadblocks were established, jamming devices were activated, and the utilities were ready to be cut.

Several HRT operators were at the entrances to both tunnels, while another team was planning a frontal assault on the cabin. Other HRT personnel were strategically placed with full sniper support at every angle, completely camouflaged.

The voice of the HRT commander sounded in everyone's headset. "Infrared and heat signatures show two occupants in the cabin. One appears to be a bulky male, lying on the ground, unmoving, legs curled, maybe six feet tall. The other is slight and about five feet five inches in height, sitting nearby."

"That fits," Gibby said, turning to Seargant. "President Maclemore is just over six feet tall and weighs about 220. Falby's five feet four and a half inches and about 135."

Gut adjusted his scope, leveled his breathing, and placed his index finger just over the trigger, awaiting instruction.

"Sir, I can take out either target with successive shots. Judging from the simple construction, distance, and low wind, probability is extremely high."

"Hold tight," the HRT commander said. "We have a possible sighting of Steve McCallister, approaching four points off due north."

The comment hung in the air as time stood still.

"Wait, what did you just say?" Gibby managed, incredulously.

"Yes, definitely Steve McCallister. Now due north, about halfway up the tree line and descending."

Gut repositioned himself, speaking evenly. "I have him, sir."

Gibby and Seargant quickly went for their binoculars, amazed at what they just heard and eventually saw. The director of the CIA—Steve McCallister—was walking down the ridge through the trees, no doubt going to the cabin.

The sniper spoke again. "He has a shoot on sight order, is that correct?"

Gibby and Seargant exchanged glances and Gibby answered. "That's correct, tell me what you have."

"I've got a clear head shot for about ninety seconds."

"I need a 'Go/No go' for shot, sir."

And the sniper leveled his breathing, awaiting the order.

CHAPTER 84

Steve McCallister walked the tree line, stumbling here and there, but he managed the descending landscape effectively.

He was well into the devil's lair—Falby's territory—and felt it with every step he took.

Every thought he birthed, each movement he made could be his last, and he felt the unseen camera's eye. He knew from experience that the most wanted and capable terrorist in the world would have the entire area wired, monitored, and possibly even booby-trapped.

Falby would be heavily entrenched. But McCallister was there as instructed.

The director of the CIA winced as his foot landed hard against a tree root, but he didn't slow. His mind, though, reeling from the past two days, was focused on only one thing.

Getting to Falby.

He knew it was a death trap with no way out, but he had to come.

The phone call had come two days earlier.

Steve's personal cell phone rang while he drove home from Langley on Friday night. It was Falby. Words were exchanged and tempers flared. But moments later, Falby stopped Steve cold.

"There are some easy rules and I expect no violations," Falby said, and McCallister was at full attention.

Steve was breathing faster and driving almost ninety on the George Washington Parkway. "I understand. Go ahead."

"Great, this is going *so* well," Falby mused.

But then his tone changed, and he spoke curtly. "You are being monitored in ways you could not even imagine. I'll know *everything* you do until we meet in two days, but I will uphold my part if you do the same. Just follow the rules."

"And what are the rules?" Steve blurted.

"I see you're about twenty minutes from home and traveling well over the speed limit. First you need to slow down and control yourself. A run-in with a cop is not wise right now."

"What rules?" Steve asked again, taking his foot off the accelerator.

Falby went silent, waiting for Steve to slow. The man's eerie presence was felt, as Steve watched the numbers on the speedometer reduce.

"Very good, then," Falby continued. "First, you're not to contact or communicate with anyone from here on out. I'll know immediately. Second, you have no more than ten minutes inside your house to pack a bag of clothes for two days. Third, you will not bring any weapons, phones, or electronic devices of any kind. Fourth, and this is very important, Steve. You'll drive to West Virginia and stay in some motel near Buckhannon until I contact you on Sunday. Until then, stay in your room in total isolation."

The demands were simple, and Steve understood. He was approaching I-495 and changed lanes, slowing further.

"And how do we communicate?"

"Leave your car in the driveway and take the blue one in the garage. There's a phone and charger on the front seat."

"Blue car?"

"Yeah, consider it a gift. Again, stay at a place near Buckhannon for a couple nights. Relax and unwind, you deserve it. Because you're going to need everything you've got come Sunday."

Steve wasted no more time or energy on words. His mind was spinning from the conversation, but his pulse was returning to normal, and his mind started working. If what Falby said was true, following instructions and getting to West Virginia was critical.

"And Steve?" Falby said, as an afterthought. "Please *do* follow the rules. You know I don't tolerate deviation."

CHAPTER 85

Seargant's phone buzzed and Gibby looked over, frowning. They were moments away from a full-on assault on a highly probable target; and Steve McCallister, who had been missing for two days, had literally just stumbled into the picture, all but confirming he was complicit with Falby.

"Can you repeat that, please?" Seargant asked, astonished.

Seargant looked to Gibby, holding up a finger.

"Okay, but how did she—"

Seargant paused, blinking. "Just put her through."

Gibby continued a harsh glare at Seargant, who was listening intently. Several moments passed and even the sniper looked away from his scope and to the men flanking him.

"Hi, Pam, this is Jack Seargant of—"

Seargant was silenced as the caller no doubt spoke in a flurry of words. Seargant listened with a series of emotions playing vividly on his face. Then his eyes flew open.

"And he was in *what* company?"

Seargant stole away from the receiver. "We have a missing Special Forces operator and former CIA asset who was in the same unit as the guy Hartley and I killed in Annapolis on Wednesday."

Seargant returned to the call. "And repeat those exact coordinates, please."

Seargant fell silent. "Thank you, for this Pam. I'll be in touch with you personally in a few hours. I promise."

The call over, Seargant looked to Gibby, puzzled. "That was a civilian woman telling me to come to this exact location, not even knowing I was already here. She found a note from her ex-husband, telling her to call me if he didn't return."

"What's it mean?" Gibby asked.

"Where did you get your intel on this place, Gibby?"

"From us with information picked up from the NSA."

"And my call came from the ex-wife of a possible rogue conspirator. Possibly linked to Falby."

Both men contemplated the new information and Gibby spoke first.

"You killed an ex-CIA spook in Annapolis. And a mercenary who knew *that* guy wants you here? And we also have Steve McCallister of the CIA coming into the mix?"

Speaking of McCallister, both men looked into their binoculars, seeing him making slow and steady progress down a slope toward the cabin.

Seargant nodded. "The NSA is also telling the FBI to come here as well."

Gibby processed the new development. "At least we got the right place then. Falby must be one of the two people in that cabin."

Seargant looked to Gibby. "We're gonna find out in a couple minutes."

The sniper interrupted. "Yes or no, sirs? I need a 'Go/No go' for shot. I'm only clear for the next twenty seconds."

Seargant and Gibby were silenced, remembering the shoot on sight order.

"I need a yes or no go for shot," the sniper emphasized again, as he leveled his breathing in preparation.

McCallister was thinking of Tikrit, another time when he faced certain death.

There were only four of them and he'd just seen the soldier to his left get shot, falling like a rock. Steve went to move but noticed a land mine, before looking at the field in total and seeing how exposed they were.

Then he saw the line of sight where a sniper had taken the shot.

But one of his men was dying or already dead and there was no time to clear the field. It was only fifty feet, but he counted every measured step as he ran. So, if he even got there, he could backtrack the same way.

Blood rushed to his head as the adrenaline kicked in.

In a mad dash he was there, scooping the soldier up and humping him back to cover. Shots rang out, dirt and rock were kicked up by heavy fire, but they made it. A chopper landed moments later, and they were off, radioing in the location of the enemy combatants. On the way back, they saw the air support en route to level the area.

The soldier survived but was medically discharged; and although there were many similar stories, McCallister always remembered that one. How he'd made a difference. That man, who went on to marry and have five children, would live a life.

McCallister exited the tree line and was now exposed and completely vulnerable. The only way was straight ahead to the cabin, which was just about a hundred feet away.

It sat alone in a low clearing, surrounded by a high ridge line and verdant woodland. McCallister looked to the trees and sucked in a deep breath. He had no idea what his immediate future would hold but was ready for anything.

He'd upheld his part of the deal.

Now mere yards away, with the cabin right in front of him, memories flashed in his mind, as he prepared for imminent death. He was a young boy, begging his parents to let him go out and play after dinner, even though it was getting dark. The next-door neighbor kid was a couple years older and in sixth grade. He had a hammer and was breaking rocks in half to look inside. They'd collected them all day and had over a dozen different types to smash.

Then he was in high school. A third basemen on the team. Good times for sure. Next, he was a foot soldier and memories, some intolerable, flooded his mind.

He'd led a good, honest life and was ready.

McCallister shook his head as his resolve spiked. None of that mattered and knowing Falby, it would be fast. But he wouldn't give up and wouldn't go down easy.

He focused on the cabin door as he walked straight toward it, straining to hear anything from inside. He hesitated only a few seconds, before palming the door handle. Then, with his senses peaking, he pushed it open and rushed inside.

And he couldn't believe what he saw.

CHAPTER 86

Seargant looked to the sniper and took out his firearm.

"I don't like Steve McCallister," Seargant said. "I think he's brash and arrogant. But every move he's made and every hunch he's had, has been correct. And if *he's* here, I must think it's for the benefit of the country."

Gut had his finger on the trigger, ready for the shot. "Sir, I have a confirmed 'shoot on sight order' and we have a possible on the perp and the president with live heat signatures. We don't know if this man is another hostile coming to kill the president or—"

"And I'm accepting full responsibility for violating that order."

"You don't have the authority, sir" the sniper replied.

"I have my weapon pointed at you soldier," Seargant said. "It brings me no joy, but it's all the authority I need."

Gibby looked to Seargant, not believing what was happening next to him and in the clearing below. "Let's all take a deep breath," he said.

"I'm calm," Seargant said. "I just want to let McCallister do his thing and then have you give the order to go in right after."

"Gut," Gibby started, using the young sniper's name to ease the situation. "I agree with Jack Seargant. Let's let this play out."

"I'm putting my sidearm back," Seargant said. "And I expect you to take your finger off that trigger."

"Yes, sir," the sniper offered, unmoving.

Then they turned their attention to the activity below. McCallister paused in the clearing, before walking directly to the cabin.

Then the director of the CIA opened the door and disappeared inside.

What happened next was a flurry of activity from every direction.

After McCallister was inside, the Hostage Rescue Teams moved in simultaneously. Two groups went into the tunnels, while others hit the cabin through the front door.

Other operators provided cover, while Gut oversaw everything through his SR-25 C. Reed Knight scope.

Steve McCallister closed the door behind him, regarding the only two occupants in the cabin: President John Maclemore—now awake but disoriented—and Steve's wife, Dana, who was taken from their home on Friday evening.

He tore off Dana's gag, shaking her and looking her over. "Are you okay? Where is he?"

But before she could answer, the door was kicked in and three HRT operators in full tactical gear stormed in. McCallister put his hands up, as he was pushed down next to Maclemore.

"We're clear!" the lead man said.

Simultaneously, a loud bang sounded from the floor in the corner. It was a flash grenade and the sound was deafening. Two more men entered from below, using an access panel.

Then they all yelled in turn. "Clear. We're all clear!"

President John Maclemore was alive, though beaten and groggy. Dana McCallister, who was kidnapped by Jordy two days before, was lying in the corner, unharmed.

And Falby was gone.

CHAPTER 87

Clarksburg, Maryland

Robert Gangier sat comfortably in his black leather chair, staring at three large monitors.

His long, thin fingers were spread out, making wide circling motions on the smooth, mahogany desk surface. Grinning, he watched his master plan unfold from the safety of his own home.

The four former presidents were assassinated in quick order. President Maclemore had been shot down and was dead. Gangier had successfully embedded and layered false financials and other evidence into Steve McCallister's life, forcing him underground with his wife's abduction and allowing for a shoot on sight order.

Then Gangier turned on his main asset, Falby, and now the FBI had the terrorist surrounded in a West Virginia cabin! And this was orchestrated by an aging computer geek, who'd been fired from his first job at Radio Shack so long ago!

He felt giddy as he watched things play out in real-time, both from the satellite images above and the body cameras on some of the principles on the ground. Hell, he was even wired into the feed between the HRT commander and the FBI, though the channel had been dormant.

He saw Steve McCallister walking down the hillside in plain view.

"Shoot him!" he yelled at the screen.

But the shot didn't come and exasperated, Gangier tapped his keyboard to access the body cameras of the HRT operators.

"You have a shoot on sight order, guys," he yelled to himself. "Come on!"

But the shot never came, even as McCallister paused in a clearing and eventually moved toward Falby's cabin.

The HRT cameras—eight in all—came to life, and Gangier turned his attention to them.

The satellite imaging from two hundred miles above was the best picture, so he watched as McCallister silently made his way to the front door, paused, and stepped in.

Seconds later the frontal assault began, coinciding with the rush up from the tunnels. Audio was now on, but all Gangier could hear were the grunts from the men as they ran at full speed. The camera angles were jumpy, but soon all he heard was "We're clear!" and then a close explosion and fog.

"Clear! We're all clear!"

But Gangier couldn't believe what he saw next. The only occupants in the cabin were President Maclemore and Dana McCallister!

The president was alive!

"Where the hell did you go, Falby!?" the man shouted in disbelief.

But then he heard the door close behind him and Gangier turned to look into the coldest, deadest eyes he'd ever seen. Falby made no grand entrance. He didn't speak and his facial expressions didn't manifest emotion.

"How'd you find me?! This is—" Gangier stammered.

But Falby just stood there, ten feet away, as he watched Gangier fall apart. Then he looked past the man and to the monitors showing the cabin scene play out. The cabin he'd left a couple hours earlier.

"Yeah, this is it, do you wanna see what we've done here?" Gangier sputtered, trying to regain control.

Falby glanced back at Gangier, who was now visibly shaking. Falby was still quiet.

"Everything went perfectly; you were amazing! It's great to finally meet you in person!" Gangier was near tears, wide-eyed and begging.

Falby was impassive. His eyes moved back to the monitor, stepping closer. Gangier could now see a large gun in the man's hand, with a long suppressor attached.

"Seems like you have a name, after all," Falby said.

But before Gangier could speak, he felt a sharp crack of pain in his forehead. His thoughts were suspended for a moment before everything went black.

Falby pushed the dead body off the chair and calmly sat down, placing his Sig Sauer on the desk. He rested his hands on his chin and watched the monitors, impressed by the man's elaborate set-up.

His thin lips formed a rare smile as he saw President Maclemore and Dana McCallister, both alive and well, being rescued by the brave men in blue.

Then he focused on Steve McCallister. The director of the CIA had come as promised, unarmed, having followed Falby's instructions. But Falby also kept his promises.

And he wasn't finished with McCallister yet.

Steve was hugging his wife, tightly, not wanting to let go. They were in the corner, huddled together and rocking each other, away from the others. A field medic attended to Maclemore, and after some smelling salts and field dressings, the man was talking coherently.

"Are my guys all gone?" he asked, and the air escaped the room.

"There's no need to talk, sir. We need to get you—"

"Did this really happen?" he asked, gaining awareness. "We were flying to Camp David and—"

The words were caught in his throat as he stopped and rubbed his eyes, shaking his head. "I'm just so sorry. Such a waste of life."

Steve moved away from Dana and crouched next to the president.

"Sir, do you remember anything about who took you? Falby? Anything?"

"So, it *was* him?"

"Yes, 100%. Do you recall anything?"

"No. We went down hard and then I was in a field and a hunter was there. We talked for a minute and then I woke up here."

Dana interrupted. "Maybe I can help. I was taken from my kitchen by a large military-looking grunt. He threw me in the trunk of his car, hooded. We drove here and I haven't seen him since. Then Falby arrived."

All eyes turned to Dana. She looked spent and ashen, looking the full effects of the last two days that saw her abducted, drugged, and held in chains.

"This man, Falby, was like a robot," Dana continued. "He had no emotion, even his movements were calculated. I watched him, not wanting to make eye contact."

Seargant and Gibby entered the cabin, looking to the group with relief.

Gibby spoke first. "We need to get the president outta here now. This place could be wired to blow and—"

McCallister interrupted. "Duly noted, Gibby, but not plausible."

"And why is that?" Seargant asked. "This guy has killed four of our presidents and can—"

"The answers lie in what he *hasn't* done," McCallister said, calmly.

"And what's that mean?" Gibby asked. "What's up with the riddles?"

McCallister went on. "He could've killed my wife but didn't. She wasn't the goal, I was. And he could've killed President Maclemore at any time, but he didn't."

"Not true!" Seargant erupted. "He shot him down! It's an absolute miracle he's even alive!"

"Yes, it may be, but something changed between Marine One being shot down and right now. When Falby discovered Maclemore survived, the script flipped for some reason, and he kept the president alive."

Gibby and Seargant were silent as they thought it through.

Then Steve McCallister stood, and everyone listened. "Sometimes it's more of a statement to hold someone's life in your hands and *not* take it. He wanted me more than anything else and he fled before I got here. I don't know the answers yet, but we need to figure that out."

Back at Gangier's home, Falby was impressed by the quick summations he was witnessing.

Steve McCallister was correct.

Maclemore stopped being the target once Falby was betrayed by Gangier. And that act of treachery had saved both Maclemore and McCallister's life, while ending Gangier's and changing Falby's.

But again, Falby was just reacting to the changing game. While regrettable, it just delayed what Falby had in store for Steve McCallister.

CHAPTER 88

President Maclemore mended quickly and even seemed to strengthen after his attempted assassination. He'd given a press conference the day after he was shot down and held in captivity.

He renewed his promise to the American people that justice would be served; especially to the memories of the four American leaders who'd been assassinated, and to the families of those who'd lost their lives protecting the presidency.

Robert Gangier's body was discovered the following morning during a safety check, after he failed to arrive at the NSA. Fingerprints and Gangier's own security cameras proved that Falby had committed the murder. It took little time to connect the dots.

The weeks passed, as the recent headlines faded into the background and the American people resumed their lives.

Then there was a wildfire in California and a senator was caught in a sex scandal in New Hampshire. Chicago had a record number of shootings for the month and there was a breakthrough in Middle East peace talks. The pulse of the world moved on and optimism returned.

Upon completion of his investigation, Special Agent James Gibson delivered it to the Attorney General, with a copy to President Maclemore. For something that had shaken the United States to its core, it was remarkably brief at just over two hundred pages, with three binders of supporting documentation.

The best analysts at the NSA, including Frog, picked apart Robert Gangier's life, and done a remarkable job of unraveling his cyber world. It was determined that during the Last Patriot operation, Gangier was a silent co-conspirator, though even Falby didn't know that.

Things got more involved, when it was discovered that Judy Maclemore and Robert Gangier graduated high school together. They'd even dated for a few months, something a then-young Robert had never recovered from.

In Gangier's mind, he would aid in Falby's revenge plot to assassinate the four former presidents, as long as Falby would assassinate the *current* president. Gangier knew that Judy Maclemore was unhappy in her marriage, and he wanted to be with her.

Gangier's telephone calls with the First Lady were limited to five; one of which was recorded by Pip. The others were documented by Gangier himself in a private video diary. They all started about a year before the assassinations, just after their forty-year high school reunion, where they reconnected.

He detailed how they both had too much to drink at the reunion, and their conversation was easy and carefree, just like when they were young. She remarked that she was in a loveless marriage and though she'd always sought power and money, she hadn't laughed in decades.

He confided that he'd always loved her.

Judy Maclemore was dismayed, but played along, because it was just a harmless crush. She hadn't felt desired in years and welcomed the adulation. It was an exciting distraction from her mechanical existence in the spotlight.

As their conversations progressed, she shared her fantasy of leaving her current life and starting over. She'd buy a cottage in Maine near Ogunquit and paint, read, walk the beach, and nest in oversized blankets by a fire every winter.

Gangier's ego got the best of him after Gilmore's assassination; and when he'd called the First Lady, he spoke too much of his ties to Falby. They would be free soon enough, he'd assured her, and this was documented and recorded by Pip.

Gangier went on to say that while her husband was now the most powerful man in the world, he'd been embedded for decades. He was wired into every tentacle of the United States intelligence community, and he was just as lethal.

The First Lady confided to the FBI that she'd learned of the assassination plot too late to help, and that she had no idea it would extend to an attempt on her husband. She was also fearful for her *own* life, noting that she could be killed easier than a former president.

The FBI pressed her over three days of questioning, and she'd passed a lie detector test. The DOJ agreed to close the investigation and seal it.

Robert Gangier was painted as the mastermind of the assassinations, using the terrorist known as Falby to aid his cause. Falby was well known for his past terrorist activity, and with Gangier's inroads to the intelligence community, it was an easy fit.

Part Six

End Game
(Three Months Later)

CHAPTER 89

It happened at 4:03 a.m. on a Tuesday morning.

The only evidence of the dream was the brain activity monitored and stored in the machinery adjacent to Pip's bed. But the random blips and flickering lights were lost on Lisa, who was sleeping on the couch in the corner of the hospital room.

Physically, Pip stirred. His left leg straightened, and his arm fell from the covers and off the bed. His eyes flickered, but remained closed, before he went limp again. But mentally, he was alive, and the dream was as real as any waking moment.

He was a child, maybe five years old. His mother was a blurred image. Too far to see, but close enough to sense her warmth and love. More than that, he felt secure.

He was safe. He was content. And it was a glorious feeling lost on him for so long. He regaled in it. Basked in it. In his dream, his arms opened wide, and he felt the presence of overwhelming love and support.

"I love you, my little Pip," he heard, as his mother moved toward him, hugging him tightly.

"I love you too, mommy," he replied. "I've missed you so much," he sputtered.

Then his arms went to his sides, falling into the cool, coarse sand all around him. "Oh Pip," she said. "You and your sand box. You know you're the king, right? My little prince and king at the same time."

Pip looked to the fire truck to his right. He felt its rigid edges and moved it across the sand, creating a path.

"And someday, Pip, I hope you realize this sandbox and what's *beneath* it is very important. Remember, mommy loves you and I've left something special for you. You like finding the buried treasures I put in the sand."

"I love you too, mommy," he said.

Then the blurred images became clearer. Ambiguity gave way to sensation, as the bright lights and piercing sounds deluged him. His eyes grew wide as he took everything in simultaneously. His body convulsed as his mind tried to reconcile the new reality.

"You're awake!" a female voice sounded. "He's awake!"

Doors opened and several voices sounded. A flurry of activity followed, overwhelming him, and he fell back into darkness.

Lisa sat next to Pip, just as she had for the last few months, gently holding his hand, and looking at his pale face.

"Pip can you hear me?"

She placed her left hand on his forehead, massaging him, lovingly. The bandages had been off for weeks, but there was no mistaking the path of the bullet from the top of his forehead across his head. His hair had grown back spotty.

Lisa asked the same questions relentlessly for two days, ever since Pip briefly slipped out of the coma. But the doctors remained cautious, telling her not to get her hopes up.

While it was a good sign of physical strength, it could also have been an involuntary action. The brain scan was still showing an uncertain level of activity, and there was no guarantee of anything.

Lisa's parents had stayed with her for the first week after the incident. Hartley left after the first few days. Sam made a brief appearance but had also left. Her friend Amy visited twice. Everyone tried to convince her to return to Pennsylvania. Pip was receiving the best care possible and there was no telling if he would ever recover.

But Lisa remembered Pip's worst fear.

Abandonment.

And she would not leave him for anything. A nurse overheard one of the fights between Lisa and her mother.

"But you've only known him for a few days for God's sake! I know this is terrible but get on with your life!"

The nurse was moved by Lisa's simple response. "Mom. I love him and I will not leave him. I will not be just another thing in his life that went away."

The nurse lived just a mile down the road from the hospital and offered Lisa a free place to stay in exchange for walking her dog during extended shifts. Lisa agreed and had fallen into a rhythm of walking back and forth to the hospital, staying with Pip, and caring for the dog.

But for now, she was alone in the hospital room. Waiting and praying for her Pip to come back to her.

CHAPTER 90

Lisa's head dropped to her chest, forcing her awake.

It was another sleep-deprived night, and she moved her hands to her tired, red eyes. She sighed deeply, expelling much of the frustration she'd been harboring.

It had been three months since Pip was shot, and although his physical wounds had mostly healed, there was little progress neurologically. Lisa was dejected and starting to accept that Pip may never regain consciousness.

The world was moving on outside the hospital window, and Lisa knew she had to eventually find her place in it. She looked to Pip and took his hand; and just as she'd done several times each day, held it lovingly against her face, hoping to magically will her life force into him.

And then it happened. He opened his eyes.

Pip looked at her for a couple of seconds and her world stopped. Then recognition flashed across his face, and he moved to speak.

"Lisa?" he asked, in words barely above a whisper. "What happened? Where am I?"

She unknowingly dropped his hand and straightened, looking around the empty room, unsure.

"Help!" she screamed, automatically. "I mean, he's awake. Pip's awake!"

Not wanting to lose him again and hoping he wouldn't return to sleep; she pumped his hand several times and moved closer. Several medical staff rushed in, pushing her away.

"You're awake," the lead doctor announced, touching Pip's face, and flashing a light into his eyes. "Can you hear me? What's your name?"

"Pip," he answered.

"And what's your birthday?"

"March 19."

"What's your favorite food, color, and sports team, in that order?"

Seconds passed. All eyes were on the patient.

"Lemon Chicken, green, and the Orioles."

"One more question, Pip," the doctor said. "Who's this person right here?" he asked, motioning to Lisa.

Lisa moved to the bed and Pip looked her over as tears welled up in his eyes.

"She's the most beautiful girl in the world," he answered. "And her name is Lisa."

Smiles and celebratory affirmations followed, as Lisa cried and paced the room, excitedly. The doctor sat and turned to the monitors still attached to Pip, reading the information.

"Son, I think you're going to be just fine," he said with pride.

Pip tried to sit up but caught himself. "Speaking of Lemon Chicken," he started. "Do you think—"

The doctor stood. "Yes, I think we can make that happen!"

Then Pip leaned back into bed. "And some water, please."

CHAPTER 91

Pip was released a week later.

Remarkably, he was expected to recover cognitively, though his sense of smell and taste were diminished, due to the path of the bullet across his frontal lobe to the olfactory cortex.

The bigger challenge was now muscular. He hadn't moved in months, but the physical therapy was working, and he gained strength daily. His hand-eye coordination was also off, and a psychologist had seen him three times to discuss the emotional trauma. Still, the team of doctors agreed that Pip's recovery was highly probable, and he was a strong, well-adjusted, optimistic man.

After a fresh shower and some new clothes, Pip was ready to go. Lisa had a surprise and couldn't wait to let him know.

Pip emerged from his room to cheers and clapping, as a nurse slowly pushed him in a wheelchair down the hall. The medical team who treated him were unknown to him, but they all showed up for his release. There were balloons, cards, and smiles as he was pushed toward the elevator.

He was appreciative and welcoming of the surprise accolades, and his smile was contagious, as everyone cheered and some wept.

Then his broad smile was replaced by open astonishment as Jack Seargant walked over to give him a hug. The two men embraced for several moments, before pulling away and regarding one another, as everyone else fell away.

"It's nice to finally meet you in person, Pip," Seargant said. "I thought I should be here when the hero was released."

"Thanks, Seargant, but I don't think hero is any way to—"

"Well, let me see, then," Seargant said, cutting him off. "As I recall, you caught the Wolf Man. You uncovered key evidence in an assassination conspiracy and made the correct decision to keep it to yourself. Then you went on the lam, before releasing it to the proper channels and getting shot by the most dangerous terrorist in the world."

Pip looked down, awkwardly, but Seargant didn't let up. "And now, in true Pip fashion, you're humble. If you're not a hero, I'm not sure who is."

"Thanks, Seargant, really," Pip said, reaching for Lisa's hand and squeezing it, affably.

"And true heroes deserve something special," Seargant continued.

Pip looked to Lisa, shaking his head. "Sorry, but I have everything I need right here."

Seargant nodded, looking at the young couple. "I guess you do, but you don't have this."

Seargant produced an envelope, fanning it in the air, and presenting it to Pip. "These are two full day VIP Park Hopper passes to Disney World. You have full access to all four parks, as well as the meal plan, to make your experience as magical as possible."

CHAPTER 92

Pip and Lisa spent the next two days at the Disney parks.

Pip's movements were limited, and he used a scooter much of the time. But he was adamant about walking the wide Main Street at the Magic Kingdom, and taking his time in the shops, bakeries, and game rooms along the way.

Their pace was slow, but they were in no hurry. They had the rest of their lives ahead of them. They cheered for the children running through the crowd and didn't mind the lines, as they took in every moment and absorbed the wonder of it all.

They got personalized Mickey Mouse ears and bought T-shirts and candy. They enjoyed the Monsters Inc. Laugh Floor and Buzz Lightyear ride, choosing to avoid Space Mountain and instead try the much slower People Mover and Carousel of Progress.

They continued to the Beauty and the Beast ride, and the irony was not lost on Pip. He'd been holding Lisa's hand most of the time and she was no doubt the most beautiful girl he'd ever known.

Since he'd been out of the coma, he'd spent considerable time looking at himself in the mirror. Frank the Scar, which had ridden high on his forehead against his hair line was now gone, replaced by Falby's work, as a red ribbon of scar tissue extended over his head. Although it was much larger and physically dramatic, he was glad Frank was gone.

Still, he thought of Lisa as his Beauty, and him the Beast, as he touched his head and looked away. Lisa sensed his withdraw and immediately knew why. They were standing directly in front of a picture of the Beauty and the Beast.

She wanted to console him and tell him how images are only skin deep, and the real measure of a person is what's inside. She thought about telling him she didn't mind his new look, and it even served as a reminder of their beautiful night together. But instead she waited him out. And when he turned to speak, she reached over and kissed him passionately.

"You're the most beautiful and wonderful man I've ever known Pip. And I'm so thankful for you," she said.

"Even though I have this ugly—"

"There's nothing ugly about you, Pip."

And they kissed again.

They shared another charged kiss at Cinderella's fountain, before going on "It's a Small World" and entering the Haunted Mansion. Then they went to The Hall of Presidents, which proved a somber visit. There were flowers in front of the doors, and several attendees openly wept at the introductions of Presidents Bowman, Montgomery, Preston, and Gilmore, as their life-like figures were memorialized on stage.

Later, they enjoyed a pizza, rode the log ride twice, and travelled in the open-air train back to the main entrance.

They took the monorail directly to Epcot Center, and slowly strolled every country, sampling the beers and delicacies each had to offer. By the time they reached Mexico, evening had come, and the interior lights shined brightly. They walked down to the water and talked, lost in each other.

Later, the fireworks started in perfect assimilation to the uplifting music that sounded from all around. Likewise, the water in the center of Epcot lit up and was shot from cannons, synced to the music, lights, and fireworks high above.

A feeling of warmth and contentment embraced Pip. The events of the past few months were pushed from his mind, and he took in the moment. Likewise, Lisa felt astounded by the magic of it all, and squeezed Pip's hand. No words were needed.

Pip reached over and kissed her cheek. She leaned into him, closing her eyes, enjoying his touch.

"I love you," he said. "Truly, I do and thank you for staying with me. I felt you."

She moved to say something, but the words were caught in her throat.

Instead, they looked up; and even as the fireworks lit up the sky in bounty and splendor, they failed to deliver the magnificence they felt within themselves.

The next day they slept in but got to Hollywood Studios by noon. Weary from the day before, Pip accepted the use of a motorized scooter, but still walked half the park. Then they took a shuttle to the Animal Kingdom and did the same.

They left Florida, choosing to take the auto train out of Sanford, and then drive Lisa's car from Lorton, Virginia to her home in Pennsylvania. Pip stayed in the same motel from months earlier, and they even met Amy for dinner and drinks at the Gin Mill.

But the scene took on a different feel.

Pip and Lisa were now a couple. They laughed as they reminisced about where they first met at the bar, and they talked with Amy about their incredible journey since. Amy, who usually eclipsed Lisa, was enthralled by their tale and in awe of how they were involved in such a worldly event.

Lisa had another surprise for Pip. She pointed to the door and Pip's friend Sam walked in.

The two friends embraced, and Lisa wiped away a tear. Amy immediately sized up Sam, who was dressed casually in ripped jeans and a faded Pacman T-shirt. But the ensemble only complemented his relaxed swag and laid-back manner.

When Pip and Sam withdrew from each other, Amy took notice of Sam's electric blue eyes and chiseled features.

"I'm Amy," she announced, loudly, extending her hand, ceremoniously.

Equally intrigued, Sam accepted her hand and kissed it. "So nice to meet you, Amy," he said, softly.

With the adoring gesture, Amy was hooked.

"Here we go," Lisa said, but Amy and Sam were oblivious, as they walked to a dart board.

Pip ordered a couple of beers and sent them over, as Lisa and Pip talked about what was next, equally lost in each other.

CHAPTER 93

President Maclemore gripped the podium tightly with both hands, looking to the press corps. Then he glanced over the dozen or so people in the wings, including the First Lady, Jack Seargant, Steve McCallister, Pip, and Lisa.

He steadied his breathing, blinked a few times, and then stared directly into the cameras for the nationwide address.

It would be different from any speech he'd ever delivered.

"Ladies and Gentlemen of the Press and distinguished guests, I have a message for the American people, and I will *not* be accepting questions after. Please respect that.

"Three months ago, our country was rocked by the sudden assassinations of four great leaders. Men, who had stepped into the role of civil service and executed their duties with pride and diligence for the American people. They were callously murdered.

"We now know there was a security breach within the National Security Agency. We are confident that there were only two players: Robert Gangier who was the Deputy Chief of Central Security Services at the NSA, now dead, and Falby, the terrorist we know from his actions at the Golden Gate Bridge and Madison Square Garden, among others.

"Through his post and clearances, Gangier was able to communicate and supply this terrorist with everything needed to carry out the assassinations. He was also able to orchestrate the shooting down of Marine One and its flanking escorts, which led to me being held hostage, briefly.

"And for my rescue, I again thank our intelligence community and the FBI. They are a testament to what this country stands for; a group of brave men and woman who stand firm and resolute in the face of evil.

"We now know that Falby murdered Gangier and is on the run. But make no mistake, the full force of the United States and even the intelligence agencies of our allies are dedicated to finding him."

Seargant nodded, feeling the confidence the president conveyed. He glanced sideways to the First Lady, Judy Maclemore. She stood steadfast, no doubt hearing her husband's words, but not listening. He wondered how many speeches she'd heard. If she even had any feelings beneath her hardened cosmetic exterior.

Picking up on his stare, Judy Maclemore glared back at Jack Seargant and a knowing smile crossed her face; a silent show of disdain to the man who wanted her arrested in the Oval Office months ago.

Seargant discounted her and looked to Steve McCallister and then to Pip and Lisa, who looked transfixed by the president. Then he gazed at the crowd, seeing everyone drawn to the president's captivating words. Many reporters in the press corps were leaning forward in their seats in anticipation.

"But that's not the entire story," President Maclemore continued, looking down, uncomfortably.

An image of the four flag-draped coffins flashed in his mind. Then he thought of his own security detail and the tremendous loss of life with *his* attempted assassination. Next came a vision of Gini Bowman and the promise he'd made to her in her parlor.

He'd been in turmoil since reading the final report by James Gibson, and in times of crisis, he was reminded of the words his father lived by. *Integrity is a gift to yourself.*

He looked to the press corps and hesitated further, shuffling the papers on the podium, and stalling for time.

Then he thought of his history lessons from so long ago and the words he'd memorized from Lord Denning. The man had described the Magna Carta as "the most important constitutional document of all time. The foundation of the freedom of the individual against the arbitrary authority of the despot."

First drafted by the Archbishop of Canterbury, Stephen Langton, the Magna Carta was agreed to by King John of England at Runnymede on June 15, 1215.

What Maclemore had drawn from it, was that no one—not even the *king*—is above the law, and it upheld the individual and their freedoms above everything.

The Attorney General agreed not to seek charges against his wife and sealed the entire file. But Maclemore's moral compass couldn't let it go.

All eyes were on the President of the United States as the empty seconds continued to tick, embodying the discomfort within the silence.

"You see, the American people deserve the truth; and all too many times, through the guise of national security or the selfish intervention by third party interests, it is denied.

"On the day of James Preston's assassination, a young NSA analyst came across and recorded a brief telephone call between Robert Gangier and my wife, the First Lady of the United States."

The entire room gasped, and the president fell silent. The temperature seemed to soar, and even Jack Seargant shifted uncomfortably, unsure of what was happening. Judy Maclemore expelled a long breath, more in frustration than dismay. She stiffened and stared straight into her husband, who continued to address the nation.

"My wife knew Robert Gangier in high school, and they became very good friends. But when Judy graduated and went to Yale and Gangier to MIT, the relationship, though mainly one sided, didn't end.

"This audio recording appears to show conspiracy, but that is not up to me to decide. So, I ask that my wife be remanded into custody. I've already spoken to the Department of Justice, and the Attorney General."

Another gasp from the crowd erupted, and even the Press seemed unsure of how to act, now being part of the news. President Maclemore turned and looked to Jack Seargant and nodded, and Seargant didn't hesitate.

Walking to the First Lady, he gingerly leaned over. "Ma'am, let's make this as easy as we can."

Judy Maclemore continued a hardened stare at her husband, even as she was led away. And the president looked right back, a wall of stoicism. Camera flashes followed them out of sight.

Then Maclemore looked to the floor, taking a moment to compose himself, and wiping the sweat from his brow.

"During my presidential campaign, I promised the American people transparency.

"When I assumed the office of the presidency, I ran on a platform of change. But there are certain aspects of the American fabric that I will *never* change. Words like truth, justice, integrity, and piety do not lose their luster over time. Nor are their meanings subject to translation or diminution."

President Maclemore's tone took on a sudden bravado. His words were as riveting as any campaign speech he'd ever delivered.

"And though I may face an impeachment trial, and this may prevent me from seeking a second term to the office you've entrusted me to execute, I leave that to the American people."

Maclemore cocked his head back and brought his hands to his face. Then he grabbed the sides of the podium and looked directly ahead.

"To the American people, I say this unequivocally. I had no knowledge of my wife's affiliation to any of this, and I'm sorry I didn't find out until it was too late."

The president hung his head, solemnly. The Press erupted in loud shouts of questions that no one could comprehend, and Maclemore had no intention of answering.

Then he walked away from the podium and out of view.

Like everyone else, Pip and Lisa were shocked. They were pressed against the wall, as the president walked past them.

A large Secret Service agent walked directly to Pip and Lisa. "Mr. Palmer, Ms. Wellington. Can you please come with me?"

CHAPTER 94

Pip and Lisa were escorted through a long hallway, with ornate sconces and oil paintings of rural landscapes on the walls. Then they walked down a set of stairs, maneuvered through a narrow corridor, and turned left into the Oval Office.

It was much smaller than they'd thought, and they looked to each other in silent surprise. But the wonder of it all—from the Resolute Desk, embroidered presidential seal on the thick carpet, and opulent furniture; to the lighting, textures, and palatial accents—was astounding.

President Maclemore walked in from his personal office, as Jack Seargant entered through the main door. Pip and Lisa stood in dismay, feeling the mounting pressure.

"So, you're the NSA analyst who uncovered it all?" President Maclemore asked, rhetorically.

"Yes, sir," Pip replied. "And this is my girlfriend, Lisa."

"Hi," Lisa barely managed.

The president nodded to her in silence. "I understand you've both been through quite a lot, and I want to personally congratulate and thank you for a job well done."

Pip and Lisa were taken back and couldn't withhold their wide smiles. "It was my pleasure, sir." Pip said.

"And I was just along for the ride, but I'm so glad I went," Lisa offered.

Seargant cleared his throat. "Pip Palmer is a little modest. May I speak for him, Mr. President?"

"Go ahead, Jack, what's up?"

"Pip was instrumental to me apprehending the Wolf Man killer. And that brought him to Lisa. Then Pip recorded the phone call, which put his life in danger. He fled with Lisa to Florida, trying to stay off the radar, but was eventually found and shot in the head by Falby."

"Then we have something in common, Pip," Maclemore said, solemnly. "The same man *tried* to kill us both."

The conversation took a darker tone as everyone contemplated the statement. Nobody wanted to follow those words, and the president continued.

"Well, Pip and Lisa. I just wanted to meet you and let you know that you're very much appreciated."

The young couple nodded in silence, still looking around, awkwardly.

"Is there anything I can do to show my gratitude?" the president asked.

Lisa was shaking her head dismissively, but Pip's face was twisted in thought.

"Actually, there is something Mr. President," Pip said. "But it really involves Jack Seargant."

Then Pip and Lisa told the tale of Lisa's great-great uncle who imprisoned himself on his property for ten years; and the decades-old mystery that perplexed her family for so long.

And even Seargant and Maclemore were intrigued.

CHAPTER 95

A week later, the roaring sounds of engine and turbine tore across the Wellington family farm.

Pip and Frog had worked tirelessly on both satellite imaging and forensic accounting. They tried to uncover everything they could about a man who'd been dead for over twenty years, Lisa's Great-Great Uncle Pete.

But they had the help of a dedicated FBI team and Seargant himself, as well as the Wellington family; all of whom were happy to help the process. Everyone was eager to uncover the truth, for a storyline to emerge.

The FBI forensic accountants hit resistance immediately. The Farmer's Credit Union had overhauled their computer system twice since Pete's accounts were closed. And most of the older printed financial records were lost when the bank was sold and renamed.

But then they found an old library card in a discarded desk in the barn.

The family confirmed that a library card was out of character for the old farmer, and it offered a benchmark date to launch from. The FBI backtracked and explored a sixty-day window, looking into the national missing persons registry and longtime outstanding warrants.

The working theory was that Pete used the local library to research newspaper reports of any drifters who had gone missing. It was hypothesized that to commit himself to ten years of self-isolation, an act of manslaughter or worse would be involved.

Everyone agreed they should be looking for a body in an unmarked grave.

Aided by overlapping satellite imaging, the FBI field team unanimously decided to take a hard look at the parcel of property in the southwest corner of the land. While the farm in total was over two hundred acres, much of it was designated for farming and infrastructure, and not ideal to bury a body.

Unfortunately, Seargant was not new to the process. But this time was different because he'd been invited.

Cadaver dogs were deemed useless after so long; and taking soil samples to detect human deterioration of tissue and blood was out. So, they imaged the property using a magnetic gradiometer and ground penetrating radar. It only took a few hours to find something of interest.

Five feet down, in the designated area, a long wooden coffin was discovered, and the machines went to work. Pip and Lisa watched the backhoe retreat and two FBI agents in full protective gear jump into the hole. Everyone waited patiently as the box was secured and lifted.

Seargant moved to Pip, Lisa, and her parents, grim-faced.

"I understand we were invited here, and we appreciate that. But this is now a crime scene, and what we find in that box is likely not going to be a pretty sight. That said, I need you to move behind the tape, please."

Two FBI agents staked a perimeter and were now rolling out the yellow crime scene tape, outside of the retreating family members, which also included Lisa's brother and his wife.

A few minutes later, a crowbar cracked open a crude wooden coffin. Inside, there was a badly decomposed body, male, with longish dark hair and a scraggly beard. He appeared to be a twenty-something vagrant, still dressed in blue jeans and a flannel shirt. A large backpack was at his feet and there were stems that were probably once flowers across his chest.

In the distance, the family stood in silence, not believing what they were witnessing. Pip and Lisa were holding hands. Lisa was thinking of every possibility imaginable. Pip looked mesmerized by the heavy machinery and the hole in the ground, trading glances between both.

Then he had a rare flash of thought from his childhood.

He remembered the dream he'd had in the hospital. The digging reminded him of a very pertinent memory, long suppressed.

His sandbox. Of course!

Pip closed his eyes in concentration, channeling every ounce of energy into recall.

The sandbox. It was more important than he'd thought.

He fought hard to remember arriving at the orphanage at five years old. The adults were so tall and fussing over him, and a policeman patted his shoulder and wished him the best.

The cop left Pip with the letter from his mother. It was only half a page and Pip memorized it. But he had thought little about some the words as an adult; what they truly meant.

If something happens, I hope you can forgive me. But remember all the times in the sandbox and the fun you had exploring and digging.

The memories of his mother were sparse, but he still felt her warmth and comfort, and the fun of finding the buried treasures she'd leave for him in the sand.

Pip tore away from Lisa, walking away, his hands running through his hair, as he contemplated things further.

Lisa moved over to him, curious.

"Oh my God, Lisa. I have to go back to Baltimore!"

"But we just found a dead body on—"

"Yeah, I know," Pip said, dumbfounded. "But I think I've just uncovered something that's even crazier."

CHAPTER 96

$\mathbf{P}$ip was talking nervously, as he and Lisa exited 295 in Baltimore, paused at a stop sign, then took a quick right onto Fern Street. It had been a couple of days since finding the dead body, and it was still at the forefront of their conversations.

"I just can't believe they identified the guy so fast," Pip said.

"Yeah, I know. I feel so bad for his family, but at least now everyone has closure."

The sixty-day window was spot on, and the FBI linked DNA to a twenty-four-year-old drifter from Indiana. The man was no angel, and his lengthy police report listed petty theft and burglary offenses, one domestic violence charge and two arrests for possession of heroin.

He'd left Indiana after missing a court appearance and learning of a warrant for his arrest. His family said he was a loner and always spoke of living off the grid, somewhere south. That's where they thought he was.

An autopsy was performed and found two broken legs, a punctured lung, and trauma favoring the left side. All injuries were consistent with being struck by a car, and it was hypothesized that the old farmer accidentally hit the man as he walked down the road, probably thumbing his way to a warmer place.

Pip and Lisa had been living together in Annapolis for a couple weeks now. They fell into an easy routine; one of comfort and love, and even Sam benefited from a woman's touch around the house. Lisa acclimated well, and Pip appreciated how flexible she was in dealing with Sam.

Lisa adopted a motherly role and was happy. She brightened up the place with new window treatments and swapped the mismatching, dank furniture with comfortable twin couches and a love seat. Within a day, the old décor was replaced with a nautical theme, as pictures went up on freshly painted walls, and accent candles graced newly hung shelves.

The three roommates agreed to a monthly food budget and Lisa was quick to assign household chores. The fridge now held a proper, fresh supply of fruits and veggies, and Sam and Pip were happy to eat from matching plates with real silverware.

Lisa successfully transferred her credits to Towson University and was taking nursing classes part-time; and Pip fell back into his duties at the NSA.

Turning onto Bank Street, they parked under a broken streetlight in front of his childhood address. A place he hadn't been to for over two decades. The narrow row homes that hugged the road were mostly hollowed out and many were burned; and small groups of drug addicts wandered aimlessly throughout them.

"This doesn't look good," Lisa said nervously, searching one alarming detail to the next. "Maybe we should have brought Seargant with us."

Pip remained vigilant, taking it all in.

A couple of memories came to him, as he looked to the sidewalk that curled away and led to the train tracks behind the houses. He grinned as he remembered running down the sidewalk into his mother's embrace. He looked to the utility pole and the lines that ran above, seeing the bright blue sky. He remembered flying a kite on this very street.

"This is where I lived with my mother," Pip said, almost to himself, turning off the ignition and opening the car door.

Lisa got out and joined him, again looking around, nervously. She studied Pip, noticing a calm wash over him. He sucked in a deep breath, as a look of contentment played on his face.

"I'll grab the shovel," he said, opening the trunk.

The block consisted of over twenty row homes, and none were occupied. The one in question—216 Bank Street—was burned out. They stepped through an open space in the front and continued to the rear, where the back wall was gone.

Just like in his memory, the train tracks were behind the house and a tall fence separated them from the row homes. The back yard wreaked of garbage and urine, and every breeze carried the stink and affirmed the deterioration around them.

"The sand box would have been over here," Pip said, pointing to an old mattress and a few tires scattered around.

It took a few minutes to clear the area. He thought of the fine sand running through his fingers and the bright red trucks from so long ago. And for someone who was orphaned, with more bad memories than good, he smiled thinking about his young, self-engaging play.

Then he started digging.

"This is kinda fun, right?" he asked Lisa, who took on the role of lookout for their little endeavor. "I feel like a pirate, wondering if there really is something under here."

"Do you really think that's what she meant in the note?" Lisa asked, suddenly turning around as a light rail train raced by just over the fencing, shaking the ground.

Unfazed, Pip continued, making good progress and gaining momentum.

"She clearly wrote about the sandbox in the letter; and knowing that it would be read by others, she offered some language that spoke to something of interest buried underneath."

"And you really think it's still here," Lisa asked, looking around.

Pip looked up. "Despite what's happened around here, I doubt that anything *underground* has been touched. I mean, it looks to be intact, and this is where the sand box used to be."

Some shouts sounded from the street and Pip and Lisa instinctively crouched in silence. The noise rose for several moments and then stopped, as a small group of vagrants walked by.

"I sure wish Seargant was here," Lisa said in a whisper.

"Sometimes you have to do things for yourself. And I don't want to waste the guy's time. Who knows if we'll even find anything?"

Pip resumed his efforts and the pile of dirt beside him grew larger. He fell into a rhythm and Lisa went quiet to encourage faster progress. Several minutes passed and Lisa became antsy. Pip kept going and even removed his shirt, as the bright fall sun shined down on them.

Another train screamed by and the wind kicked up, swirling some nearby trash. A voice called out from another burned-out structure and Pip and Lisa looked over.

"What are you all doin' over there?" a man yelled.

Lisa was awe struck and Pip took control. "BGE service, sir. Digging and testing a new line."

Then Pip went back to work, hoping the man would be satisfied. Several minutes passed and Pip was feeling the uneasiness of their cause. The prospect of their efforts was loosely alluded to in a letter written by his ex-junkie mother nearly twenty-five years earlier, and while the ground below looked untouched, this could all be for naught.

The man yelled again, this time louder and Pip and Lisa ignored his call. Pip doubled his intensity, blocking everything out.

Then the shovel hit something hard and stopped.

He knelt and used a gloved hand to remove some rocks and debris, clearing away a rectangular package bound in plastic. He reached down and removed it. It was about fifteen by fifteen inches and had weight to it. There were several layers of protective plastic wrapping, and it was bound tight with duct tape.

He looked up to Lisa, seeing her silhouetted against the bright sun above her, but his breath was taken away when he saw two larger shadows flanking her.

CHAPTER 97

Lisa was too captivated by the discovery to notice the two men behind her.

She smelled them before she saw them and turned suddenly.

They were both white, in their twenties, with dirty faces, yellow teeth, and bruises and scabs on their arms. The filth looked permanent and their sunbaked skin made them look much older.

Images of the men who grabbed her in Orlando flooded Lisa's mind, and she swiftly moved next to Pip. They were swaying and disheveled; clearly drug-users and possibly even mentally unstable.

Pip didn't waste time as he grabbed the box and shovel and pushed Lisa to the side.

"Run!" he yelled.

The inability of the men to react offered the fleeing couple every advantage. Pip and Lisa were at the car quickly and speeding away before the men ran clumsily into the street. Pip maneuvered between debris and potholes for several blocks before slowing and checking on Lisa. She was out of breath and looking behind them. But when Pip took a quick left and created a few more blocks of separation, things eased.

Pip turned on the air conditioning and hit the radio.

They drove in silence, even as they merged onto I-695. It wasn't until they were on Route 10 heading south, when Pip glanced at the box on the car floor.

"Are you all right?" he asked, gripping the steering wheel tight.

Lisa nodded, looking out the window. "You certainly keep me on my toes, Pip!"

They erupted in nervous laughter.

"What do you think is in there?" Lisa asked.

Pip shook his head. "Whatever it is, we're keeping it a secret, at least for now. We've come this far together, and this is just another part of it."

"It belongs to you, Pip. It's all for you."

Pip took Lisa's hand. "It may be an important part of my past but I'm sharing it with an important part of my future. Whatever it is, it's *ours*."

Thankfully, Sam was out when they arrived home.

Pip marched into the house and threw the switch for the kitchen light, looking for scissors in a drawer. Lisa shut and locked the front door, peering out the window for any sign of trouble.

They moved to the sofa and Pip went to work cutting the tape and plastic that had preserved the box for so long. No words were spoken as their anticipation grew, along with the wrapping on the floor.

Moments later Pip placed a simple wooden box on the coffee table.

He fell silent as he traded glances between the unearthed box and his new girlfriend. One represented something from his past; the other a promise of a future he had yet to know.

He placed a shaking hand on the box. It was something he'd found against all odds; left to him by a mother he never really knew. He only had glimpses of memories, and he couldn't tell if they were real or remnants of dream.

But this was proof he lived a life before the orphanage. Before all the craziness.

And it was time to face his past.

CHAPTER 98

Pip took a deep breath, opened the box, and emptied its contents.

Lisa gasped, bringing her hands to her face. There were large stacks of cash, all bound tightly by rubber bands in equal amounts. Pip took a brick of bills and counted several thousand dollars, stopping about halfway.

"Looks like each of these are $10,000 stacks and there's ten or more."

"Wow!" Lisa exclaimed, jumping up and checking the front door to make sure it was locked.

But Pip suspended all emotion as he lifted up the rest of the bundles of cash and saw a letter in a plastic bag.

And it had his name on it.

My Dearest Pip,

If you're reading this, I'm dead and you may be a grown man. And if that's the case, it's been quite a while since I've hugged you, sang you a song, and told you how much I love you. These are things I do with you many times every day.

I hope you can remember that. God, I hope you do!

I guess it's been so long, so Pip... I love you. I love you so much! Please don't feel sad for me, because you saved me from a life where I would be dead anyway. I was so lucky to be your mom. You were my greatest gift.

I'm so happy that you unraveled the small, hidden clue in the letter I left on the kitchen table.

Now let me tell you a little more.

Today I walked you to kindergarten, something I look forward to every weekday. But instead of coming back and cleaning the kitchen and brewing coffee, I dug deep through your sand box and covered the hole with some of your toys.

In a couple of hours, I'll get some money and put it in a box along with this note and bury it. I've already gotten some new sand to place on top.

I've been involved with drugs for most of my life, Pip. But I have not taken any since your birth, you must know that. And things aren't exactly easy for an ex-user, single mother living on welfare. So, I've been doing some drops for a local dealer a few times a month.

I've always been diligent. Kept my head down and not made eye contact. They know who I am, and they know about you. I keep everything low key because I have so much to lose.

I overheard that a shipment was coming up from Miami and some major cash with it. Nicky—the main guy I deal with is a user himself and often dips into the product and skims off the top. He also talks a lot and I've heard some things about location and timing that no one knows.

Anyway, if you're reading this, I got caught, but you're also looking at one of those cash deposits, something like $130,000.

I'll never talk so this is off the radar. But if you read this, Nicky Dent was probably involved in my killing, as he's been with others.

But I don't want to talk about this dark part of the world.

It's been a minute, so I want to say I love you once more. I'll miss your big brown eyes. I can tell you're so smart and full of love.

You'll go far, my son. I'm sorry I can't be there to see it, but you have all my love, sweetheart.

I Love You, Pip!

Mom

The words transcended time. Pip felt his mother's presence as everything, including Lisa fell away.

And he was at peace.

CHAPTER 99

Pip read the letter again, this time more slowly. He became more emotional, deciphering the message, and paying closer attention to the hasty scribble and the worn edges of the paper. He noticed the words 'I love you' were written more deliberately than the other phrases. He discovered a couple smiley faces and hearts in the margins.

He handed it to Lisa with tears welling in his eyes.

Lisa read it eagerly, before placing it on the table, reaching for Pip and hugging him tightly. He sobbed softly, leaning into Lisa, who began rocking him. The calm he'd felt just moments ago dissipated.

"We could have had a life," he started. "But she got involved in a drug deal and stole money."

Lisa withdrew from Pip and touched his face, framing his reddened cheeks with her hands.

"Is that what you took away from this, Pip? That she was a thief?"

Pip stood, but the room started to spin, so he plopped back down on the couch, remaining silent.

"Because what I derived from it was that she had a horrible past and you were her greatest gift. You saved her and survived against all odds. Didn't you tell me you were born a preemie at just twenty-six weeks? Addicted to heroin and totally malnourished?"

It was a rhetorical question and Pip wasn't in the mood for talking.

"She was a single mother who wanted a better life for you. She saw an opportunity and took drug money hoping for the best. It didn't work out, but you can't blame her for wanting to provide for you."

Pip's eyes were concentrated on the floor.

"So, what are you gonna do?" she asked softly.

"I'm going to find this guy, Nicky and probably ask Seargant for some direction. I don't feel right keeping this money. It wouldn't be—"

"Pip, I would think hard about involving anyone other than us. No one could possibly know we have this, and there's no rush to do anything."

"But I work for the federal government and this is clearly drug money," Pip said, shaking his head.

"Yeah, you've also been seriously damaged by the whole thing. *This* money, while it killed your mother and forced you into an orphanage, could also be put to good use at *your* direction. You could do a lot of good and honor your mother and her sacrifice."

"You mean, like donate it to a few orphanages? Help out some of the kids who are like me?"

Lisa's face brightened and she nodded affirmatively. "That's perfect! And maybe even some local animal shelters! It's better than the money ending up in some evidence stockpile or the government seizing it to buy $900 mouse pads."

"Let's think some more. I still don't feel right about it."

Lisa kneeled next to Pip. "You mean, because you're a government employee and all, it would be against your protocols?"

"Exactly," Pip said.

"Then should I remind you that while you were a government employee, you were just forced into a case that gained worldwide exposure, and that you were on the run and shot in the head and almost died?"

"And your point is what?"

"Damn, Pip, you really are an amazing person, you know that? Stubborn, but your heart's in the right place!"

"What are you saying?" Pip asked.

"That you deserve the money after what you've been through! Give it to charity or use it for yourself, but don't feel bad about it!"

"I like the idea of the animal shelter and definitely the orphanage."

"Me too," Lisa said. Then she hugged him and stood. "I'll clean up this mess, lets hide the money somewhere, then go to an animal shelter to see who needs some love.

That afternoon, Pip and Lisa were saddened to see three rows of cages along a long wall, filled with dogs, none of which could tell their sad story. Their hearts broke as they peered into the vacant eyes of the shelter animals.

A clip board hung from each cage, containing handwritten notes, usually the name (if they had one), approximate age, and breed. Some described where the dog came from, and some detailed the animal's past and current medications.

Pip stopped at one cage.

His name was Chap and he was a five-year old mixed breed; something between a beagle and terrier. He was a rescue from a broken home. Beaten, starved, and neglected, he lived outside in a cage in every weather condition. He was only found when Family Services was called for a welfare check on the two children living there.

Pip liked how Chap was the same age as Pip when he was orphaned. Lisa was at the far end when she saw Pip place his hand inside the cage and lean in, talking. She couldn't hear the words but knew they were conciliatory, and that Pip was connecting with the lucky animal inside.

Lisa motioned to one of the administrators, who walked over and opened the cage.

The medium sized dog spun around enthusiastically. He licked Pip's face and an instant bond was made. Pip brought Chap close and hugged him, and the dog nuzzled his snout into the crux of his arm.

"This is the one. I love him already," Pip said.

"Chap's been here for a month, and I've never seen him so happy," the administrator said.

Smiles abounded and Lisa watched Pip jog away, with Chap following him, barking excitedly.

"They look like best friends already," the administrator said. "I'll get the paperwork started, but it'll take a few days before you can pick him up."

CHAPTER 100

Pip returned to the NSA in an elevated position in both rank and salary, but he retained his small office and the Key.

He immediately researched Nicky Dent and found that he'd been killed in a drug transaction within a few months of his mother's murder. That case was never solved, and after some deep thought and prayer, he turned his focus to things of national security.

Frog moved across the hall, and he and Pip were tasked with unraveling and leveraging the technology Robert Gangier had developed over the last several years.

And it was like nothing Pip had ever thought possible!

The young analysts were amazed as they dissected every one of Gangier's homemade programs. It reminded Pip of his initial interest in circuitry as a young boy, taking apart the old computer. But that was when he was eight years old, and what they were discovering now was seemingly impossible. Ingenious.

Gangier had not only been a computer engineer, but he'd also been a cutting-edge innovator. A virtuoso.

Pip uncovered how Gangier was able to trace his location so easily, and also how he'd successfully blocked himself from Pip's own tracing programs. They delved into the illegal surveillance technology Gangier had developed—including facial and voice recognition and disappearing DNA signatures—to find anyone on earth.

Gangier had prototyped invisible lasers that could extract DNA from a person, without them even knowing, just from contact with living tissue. And these lasers had been active for years in over a dozen airports and busy points of entry to the United States, fitting into small components that passed as security cameras.

Pip was amazed at the grander plan, to place the lasers on satellites high above the earth and use solar energy to fuel them. It was brilliant, really, using a localized renewable energy source to create the electricity from photovoltaic cells.

Pip had to hand it to Gangier. It was light years ahead of what anyone thought was possible. Despite what the man had done, he *was* a mastermind in software engineering, and Pip couldn't get enough, as he absorbed it all.

It took less than a week for Pip to annex Gangier's software into his own, making the Key the most capable system at the NSA.

Then, using the dead man's applications, it took less than an hour for Pip to find Falby several time zones away.

Falby crossed over to Guatemala from Belize, near Benque Viejo and Melchor, and stopped in Livingston for the day.

The weather was beautiful, with a high blue sky, low humidity, and temperatures in the 80's. He blended in easily with the locals, who paid him little attention, as they went about their simple lives.

Guatemala would be his short-term sanctuary and a welcome stop on his way to South America. It was a comfortable departure from the chaos of the greater world, and he was content in the slow-moving paradise.

Steve McCallister and Jack Seargant, both in baseball hats and sunglasses, ambled along Blanca Beach, edging the electric blue waters of the Gulf of Honduras. There were others in the background—there were always others—but they were invisible to the passerby and melted into the background.

The two federal agents from different agencies looked to each other and nodded in silence. Gone were any animosities of the past. The two men had spoken often since their interaction in West Virginia and realized they had more in common than not.

The Seargant's and McCallister's had gone out to dinner several times, and Susan and Dana talked and laughed nonstop. Likewise, Jack and Steve forged an easy and endearing friendship, and bonded even more in the meticulous planning of this joint exercise.

This was the end game.

The target was about a hundred yards away, sitting under a large palm tree. Seargant ambled up the shoreline, while McCallister maintained a deliberate, but casual walk up the beach.

It happened fast; exactly how they'd trained for it.

McCallister knew Falby more than anyone in the intel community and was all too willing to lead the mission. President Maclemore sanctioned it but also required 100% positive identification of the target. That meant human intelligence on the ground and McCallister was delighted at the prospect.

With Falby's obvious gift for disguise and his proficiency for escape, even in the most precarious of situations, they were ready for anything. McCallister recalled their confrontation in Chile and then fast-forwarded to being shot in the back at the Waldorf Astoria. It was a miracle he'd even survived!

McCallister walked right up to Falby and leveled his Beretta, as Seargant appeared from behind, doing the same.

"Hands!" McCallister yelled.

Falby sat unmoving, throwing off the command. He looked up through sunglasses, as a smile formed.

"Good afternoon, Steve," Falby said, calmly. "I was wondering when we'd meet again."

"Hands!" McCallister yelled again, and he was surprised when Falby complied and raised his arms high in the air.

McCallister inched closer to Falby. The Chameleon. The most wanted man in the world.

The mission was clear and wasting time with idle chatter was not part of it. So, McCallister simply raised his left arm high, and a single shot rang out from the tree line.

The sniper was waiting for visual confirmation.

Falby was staring straight into McCallister's eyes, seeing the man as a shadow against the screaming white sun. And McCallister held his glare, seeing the slightest pause in Falby's expression, before the top of the man's head exploded. Falby sunk into the chair, limp, and McCallister thought he saw whatever was left of the man's soul escape his body.

The Chameleon had changed his colors many times in his violent life, only to disappear into the cracks. But now the last color he saw was black, as he slumped forward, dead.

McCallister and Seargant lifted the lifeless body to the shoreline. Without pause, a fishing boat approached, and they carried the corpse aboard.

McCallister looked to Seargant, and the two men nodded affirmations. McCallister turned so his body cam could capture the entire scene. Knowing that President Maclemore and Pip were watching, he said "Target is down. Mission accomplished."

And they moved out to sea.

EPILOGUE

Greenbury Point Nature Center
Annapolis, Maryland

In May—one year after they'd met—Pip and Lisa drove to Greenbury Point, just across the mouth of the Severn River from historic Annapolis.

They passed the Naval Academy golf course and indoor sports complex and parked in the small lot. Pip turned off the ignition but made no attempt to exit the vehicle.

Instead, he took in a deep, satisfying breath and exhaled slowly. Lisa looked over, smiling, gingerly at the love of her life as Chap barked excitedly from the back seat of their new Chevy Traverse.

"I just love this new car smell," Pip said, breathing it in again. "I could live in this car."

"I love it too," Lisa said, reaching back and petting Chap.

"They should find a way to bottle this smell into a cologne," Pip said.

Lisa laughed. Pip had a way of making her smile. Even after a year, their relationship was fresh, and she'd fallen deeper in love with him.

He was methodical and immature simultaneously and embodied an upbeat sense of optimism that was electrifying.

She offered her own idea. "How about 'New Car Smell' Chapstick?"

Pip contemplated that, shaking his head. "What about Ben & Jerry's 'New Car Smell' ice cream, with a hint of leather?"

Chap barked and jumped into the front seat, landing on Pip's lap, and they exited the car.

The last several months had seen more positive change all around. Pip received yet another promotion at the NSA, though he continued to refuse the larger office the position allowed. Instead, he was content at his smaller workstation and the Key, with Frog and a small group of other analysts nearby.

Lisa finished her first semester in the nursing program at Towson University and was already enrolled for the fall. Her friend Amy was also interested in a nursing career and was planning a move to Annapolis over the summer.

Pip and Lisa donated to several animal shelters; and they were involved in a couple of orphanages in Baltimore, giving more money and their time. Pip started an ongoing clothing and donation drive at the NSA and became a Big Brother to a couple of teenage children in need.

Sam completed real estate classes and was working with the David Orso Group in Severna Park. He'd uncovered a hidden talent for numbers; and with his easy charm and broad natural market of twenty-something professionals, he'd exceeded all expectations. His success allowed him to move from Cornhill Street to his own place on Pinkney, and he was intent on buying and renting out two other nearby houses. He traded in his partying days for a strict schedule that began promptly at 6 a.m.

Pip and Lisa held hands as they started on the two-mile path that circled the three iconic radio towers. Chap stayed on his leash, as they treaded slowly, taking in the lush green landscape and wildlife.

A few times they left the trail to explore the water's edge. The Bay Bridge showed in the distance, with its two spans stretching proudly across the Chesapeake. There was no shortage of boats on the water, and their billowing sails expanded to the horizon in an uncontained parade of color.

Pip turned to see one of the three radio towers. He would never tell Lisa how integral they were in helping capture the Wolf Man and save her life. It would be too painful, and he vowed to never speak of his work.

Then he looked to Lisa and fell to one knee, holding a small box with an outstretched hand. She turned to him in a suspended moment of disbelief, suddenly realizing what was happening.

Pip spoke slowly in a confident tone. "Lisa, a year ago I convinced you to take a road trip, because I was an unfortunate part of a worldwide news story. I pulled a gun on some creeps in Florida, got shot by an international terrorist, and spent three months in a coma, almost dying. We found a dead body in Pennsylvania, buried treasure in Baltimore, and rescued Chap from an animal shelter in Annapolis.

"I love you more than anything, and while I hope the *rest* of our lives are more *uneventful*, I wouldn't want to spend it with anyone else.

"Will you marry me?"

Lisa closed the gap between them in a mad rush, falling on top of him in an embrace. Chap joined them, and they rolled in the pine needles on the forest floor, laughing.

"Pip, that's the sweetest proposal I've ever heard," Lisa said, giggling through tears. "Of course, I'll marry you!"

"Sometimes you have to get through the tears to find the laughter behind them," Pip said. "I think I finally understand what your grandmother meant by that."

Then they kissed passionately.

Several joggers ran by, but the happy couple was oblivious. Eventually Chap barked and jumped around them, eagerly, and Pip and Lisa stood and wiped off their clothes.

Both fell silent in contemplation.

Lisa put the engagement ring on her finger and raised her hand into the sunlight, studying it. Her new future.

Pip glanced back at the radio tower once more, before focusing on Lisa. He was done thinking of the past. His fiancé and their new world were the only path forward.

And he couldn't wait to face it all together.

Acknowledgements

Thank you to everyone who have been so supportive of this project over the last nine (wow) years!

This started with the American presidency, which I've always been fascinated by. I wanted to know more about the highest office, and writing a novel about it, forced me to do it. I've also been intrigued by the three radio towers at Greenbury Point in Annapolis, and upon researching them, I just *had* to tie them into the story. First as a way for Pip to find Lisa, and then on the very last page as a reflection point for him to *truly* let go of his past and finally embrace his open future. It was circuitous and I teared up as I typed the final words that moved Pip into a better place within his journey. Pip was the hardest character I've ever developed and one of my absolute favorites. We all need to be a little more like Pip!

Thank you to all of my manuscript readers! Your critiques were so helpful in honing my story. Thank you to Donald Hilliard, William Hooper, Steven Hilliard, Rob Gloekler, Linda Kreter, Stacie Zarriello, David Kushner, Dana Cate, Anne Callen, and Allen Warren. And another special thank you to my editor, Linda Kreter. She taught me that writing a novel and editing it are two completely separate things. The mistakes are all mine. Writing a novel is like making homemade gravy. There are always lumps, because it's just me, my imaginary friends, a keyboard, and a large black coffee, plotting away.

Thank you to the people who helped my research, many of whom have asked not to be named. Dr. Sean Duffy, Bret Salkeld, Trevor Simm, Stephen Barker, Mason Roberts, Ruth Quici, Dean Zarriello, Eddie Gilmore, Bill Lawrence, and Greg Wise.

Thank you to AuthorHouse. This is my third novel and fourth piece of work published, and your professionalism and dedication to quality are appreciated.

Finally, thank you to my home team: Kimberly, Chase, Summer, and Brady. You continue to inspire me every day!